THE SNAKE TASTED
THE AIR ONLY ONCE.

Shooting straight up out of the briefcase, it sank its pink fangs into the soft flesh of Eric Ivorsen's forearm. Hot cold pain shot up his shoulder.

Singh reached the top of the stairs and slammed and locked the door. Eric tore the snake from his arm and smashed it to death on the cold cement floor. But the lethal injection had been delivered. Poison began pumping through his veins.

Eric bolted for the top of the stairs. He threw himself against the door. The top hinge creaked away from the doorjamb. He rammed it again. It yielded even more. Panting, he dropped his head low, drew a deep breath, and threw his full weight at the door again. It crashed open. Parat Singh stood on the other side. *With one kick to Eric's head, he sent Eric tumbling back down onto the basement floor . . .*

Thrilling Fiction from SIGNET

THE VIKING CIPHER 2

ALL THAT GLITTERS

by
Rick Spencer

A SIGNET BOOK
NEW AMERICAN LIBRARY
TIMES MIRROR

PUBLISHER'S NOTE

This novel is a work of fiction. Names, characters, places, and incidents either are the product of the author's imagination or are used fictitiously, and any resemblance to actual persons, living or dead, events, or locales is entirely coincidental.

SIGNET TRADEMARK REG. U.S. PAT. OFF. AND FOREIGN COUNTRIES
REGISTERED TRADEMARK—MARCA REGISTRADA
HECHO EN CHICAGO, U.S.A.

SIGNET, SIGNET CLASSIC, MENTOR, PLUME, MERIDIAN AND NAL BOOKS are published by The New American Library, Inc., 1633 Broadway, New York, New York 10019

First Printing, November, 1983

1 2 3 4 5 6 7 8 9

PRINTED IN THE UNITED STATES OF AMERICA

CHAPTER 1

The night sea off Long Island was relatively calm. Long swells rolled slowly beachward—building to two-foot curls—ultimately tumbling onto the white sand shores. Shimmering on the cold dark waters off Westhampton Beach, the lights of luxurious Dune Road summer houses cast strings of dangling diamond sparkle across the black horizon.

On the oceanside decks of several of the expensive homes, wealthy weekenders stood talking, imbibing, and laughing. Night sounds in the cool air—the occasional screech of a sea bird, the intermittent bellow from the Moriches Inlet buoy horn, and the soothing rhythmic wash of waves splashing the shell-strewn sands—were usual. Nothing strange came from the shore. But on the ocean, an alien sound slashed the peace and tranquillity of the night—a faint slurping hiss sucked the air.

Slicing the black water, a glassy gray eye glided forward, followed by a thin spreading V of green phosphorescent glow. The eye turned left and saw the Dune Road lights, then right toward an empty horizon, then forward, scanning. Below, a pitch-black behemoth with long sinewy arms tucked tight against its body slid silently eastward toward its destination off Hampton Bays. Spotting nothing that would interfere with its purpose, the behemoth's eye sank slowly beneath the surface and the eerie sound ceased.

A small great white shark, prowling for a midnight meal, sensed the vibration of the ominous giant's approach, investigated, and then with powerful sweeps of its crescent tail cut quickly for safer waters.

"Fantastic night," Maggie McCabe whispered as she crossed the polished teak wheelhouse of the yacht *Lady Barbara.*

"As promised," Eric reminded her with a smile.

Standing at the helm of the elegant seventy-five-foot motor sailer, Eric Ivorsen felt and looked right at home. His thick dark hair and strong jaw gave the tall, broad-shouldered mathematician a distinctly Nordic appearance. He reached down, gently squeezed Maggie's shoulder, and returned his gaze to the distant green buoy light blinking on the horizon.

Maggie, with her long chestnut hair pulled back in a thick ponytail that spilled over a white nylon windbreaker, looked just as much at home standing next to him.

"How about that special midnight fondue you've been promising since we left Florida?" he suddenly remembered. "We bought everything you need in Hilton Head."

"Okay, you're right—tonight's the night," she admitted. "This cruise has been just about everything you promised."

"Just about?" he demanded, trying to sound hurt.

Maggie's smile widened, but she did not answer.

"I promised you two weeks of rest," he protested.

"Rest," she agreed.

"Relaxation," he added.

"Relaxation delivered as promised," she stated.

"And romance," he concluded.

"That's the part we're a little shy on—not enough romance yet."

"The two weeks," he pointed out, "are not over yet."

"Good," Maggie whispered, her right eyebrow raised seductively.

Eric smiled back. Maggie winked and turned to make her way down the companionway into the galley.

Although the clarity of the night made it unnecessary, Eric still took a quick reading on the yacht's compass before changing course slightly to a heading that would bring them closer to the shore. He turned the polished oak wheel and the long vessel eased to the port, its bow slicing effortlessly through the dark waves. Like most Hand motor sailers, the *Lady Barbara* responded best to slow sure commands.

Maggie returned carrying a tray with an iced bottle of Taittinger blanc de blanc '73 and two crystal champagne glasses. She set the tray on a small mahogany deck table, handed the bottle to Eric, and took over the wheel.

"Where are we headed?" she asked, peering into the darkness.

"Head for that inlet buoy," Eric stated, nodding toward the tiny pinpoint of green light just as it dimmed. At the same time, he peeled off the champagne bottle's lead foil and began untwisting the cork wire.

"Where?" Maggie squinted as Eric worked the cork.

"There," he said as the light glowed again. With a distinct pop, the champagne cork arced into the darkness precisely in the direction of the distant marker.

"Right," she laughed. "So where does that put us?"

"Shinnecock Inlet off Hampton Bays. We'll moor in the bay overnight and set out again at daybreak," Eric said as he poured.

As Maggie turned to accept the glass of sparkling wine, the steady rumble of the yacht's engine suddenly changed, a grinding screech rose from the engine compartment, and the entire vessel began to shudder. Eric immediately reached across Maggie, yanked back the throttle, and disengaged the gear. The *Lady Barbara* slowed in the water.

"What happened!?" Magie gasped, afraid she might have done something to cause the horrendous sound.

Suspecting propeller damage, Eric hurried out of the

wheelhouse and peered over the stern. But there was nothing to see except a swirling eddy of black seawater aglow with tiny whirlpools of dimming phosphorescence.

"Damn," he muttered.

"What is it?" Maggie asked.

"I think we've tangled a line or a net on the prop."

"What do we do?"

Eric looked into her eyes, took a sip of his champagne, and smiled. "Well, while I have a quick look below, why don't you go ahead and prepare the famous Maggie McCabe fondue. I'll be cold and hungry when I come up. And I'll probably need a backrub too—these underwater repairs can be very arduous."

"Not to worry—I'll warm you," Maggie reassured him, gently patting his thigh.

Disappearing below deck, Eric went quickly to a storage locker and returned carrying a face mask, scuba tank, and underwater lamp. He flipped the yacht's rope ladder over the starboard gunwale and screwed down the wing nut on the scuba tank's regulator. With assistance from Maggie, he stretched into the tank straps, pulled the regulator tube over his head, and tested the mouthpiece. Then, balancing himself on the gunwale, he winked once, adjusted the mask over his face, and tumbled backward into the sea, disappearing beneath a foamy splash.

Eric watched the sky go black, and for a moment he hung suspended in the cold dark. Sucking a gasp, he tasted stale metallic air from the tank, held it, and then exhaled slowly, listening to the thud of escaping bubbles. Staring upward, he could see the dark hull of the *Lady Barbara* just barely silhouetted against the night sky. A sudden chill ran through him. It had been a long time since he had been night diving, and while the claustrophobic watery darkness brought back memories of a rather scary first dive, it brought back none of the fear. His shiver was induced by temperature, not panic.

Smiling to himself, Eric pushed his thumb down on the lamp switch, and a shaft of light filtered upward through the green water. He traced the yacht's hull, gently kicking to propel himself toward the *Lady Barbara*'s stern. Then, gliding forward, Eric suddenly found what he was looking for. In the glowing green aura of light he saw a taut moss-covered line that rose from the murky depths to a thick bundle wrapped tight around the bronze propeller and its shaft. Tracing the grassy line down with the light, he could see only a few yards to where it disappeared into the black depths, apparently still securely attached to a lobster pot. Directing the light to the propeller, he inspected the knotted tangle closely, decided that it would have to be cut, and pushed himself away, swimming for the surface.

In the galley of the *Lady Barbara*, Maggie peeled the skin from a thick clove of garlic, sliced it in half, and coated the inside of a heavy copper saucepan with the pungent pulp. After squeezing lemon juice into a cup of Sauterne, she poured the mixture into the pan, and as it simmered, she sprinkled in handfuls of shredded Gruyère and natural Swiss cheese that quickly melted into a bubbling thick cream. As she dusted the surface with freshly ground nutmeg and black pepper, she heard a loud splash outside the open porthole to her right.

Peering out, she saw Eric treading water, his face mask propped on his head.

"Well, Jacques Cousteau, what is it?" she called.

"Lobster pot, probably."

"Can you fix it?"

"I need a knife. Keep cooking, it won't take long. And boil some water—the pot might be full. Lobster will go with your fondue, won't it?"

"Sure," she answered with a smile. "What kind of knife do you need?"

"There should be an old fishing knife in the locker by your feet."

Maggie looked down, nodded, and opened the locker door. After moving several coils of rope, she found a plastic tackle box that spilled open when she went to lift it. The rusty fillet knife clattered onto the galley floor amid a tangle of hooks, sinkers, and lures.

Maggie stood, holding the knife at a dangle between her forefinger and thumb, and asked with reservation, "This?"

"Drop it overboard . . . it'll float," Eric said.

As the wooden-handled knife splashed into the water next to him, Eric reached up, grabbed it, and then replaced his face mask. In an effortless somersault, he tumbled over, slid below the surface, and disappeared into a cloud of bubbles. Maggie watched the underwater glow of green light glide below the *Lady Barbara*. When the glow disappeared and the water darkened, she began setting the deck table for their midnight meal.

After balancing the underwater lamp between the bronze blades of the frozen prop, Eric went to work cutting away the tangled rope. It cut quickly. He had to slice back and forth only a few times before the tightly wound line began to part and separate. Within minutes, the propeller was free of the moss-covered bundle. As tattered shreds of nylon sank lazily into the darkness, Eric slipped the end of the line over the heavy propeller shaft and, holding himself away from the hull with his left arm, began hoisting with his right.

The weight came up easily. Too easily, he thought. Gaining yards with each hoist, he watched as a lobster trap emerged from the murky depths. Constructed of wooden slats lined with wire mesh, the trap looked fairly new. And even though it appeared weather-beaten from days drying in the blistering sun onshore and weeks of seawater saturation in the deep, it looked sturdy and firm on all sides. Unusually sturdy, Eric thought when he looked closer and inspected its detailed construction. Lined with bronze brackets, each corner and joint had been reinforced and screwed rather than nailed. Even the trap's door was secured with finely machined stainless-steel hinges and an intricate latch release.

The pot contained no lobster, and Eric was about to let its line go when something inside caught his eye. The pot, he discovered, wasn't completely empty either. After tying the line to the propeller shaft, he grabbed the lamp and directed its beam of light into the trap. Wired to the bottom was a plastic-covered object about a foot long and four inches in diameter.

Frowning, he peered through the trap's wooden slats. Whatever it was, he could see, it was meant to be there. Then three small objects floating at the top of the pot caught his eye. Drifting down through the wire cage, they sank slowly into the shafts of green light and appeared at first to be silvery fish. Minnows, he guessed. When the largest drifted to within inches of his face mask, Eric Ivorsen realized that he was staring at a freshly severed human finger.

In several quick chops of a razor-sharp carving knife, Maggie expertly cubed a loaf of crusty French bread, filling an ornate wicker breadbasket. Splashing a dash of hot cognac into the fondue, she swirled the bubbling mixture one last time and poured the whole creamy concoction into a makeshift chafing dish that she had fashioned out of a copper pot and the *Lady Barbara*'s portable Kenyon alcohol stove.

She lit a candle on the mahogany deck table, covered it with a crystal chimney from one of the wheelhouses's antique brass hurricane lamps, and then filled two fresh wineglasses with Mondavi Chardonnay. As she went about preparing the elegant little feast, Maggie thought about how delightful the last ten days had been. The weather had been perfect, the landside meals a gourmet's dream, and the lovemaking explosively satisfying.

She was sure that the photographs she had taken would please her editor at the *St. Petersburg Times* even if the bitch wouldn't admit it. So screw her, Maggie thought to herself. A photostory on East coast seaports and towns was a damn good idea, and those photographs would prove it.

Refusing to let herself think about how fast her time with Eric was coming to an end, she told herself that they'd find a way to be together. She could always fly up for weekends, she reasoned, or Eric could come down to Tampa.

Confident that their lives would now calm down to a normal pace, Maggie took a sip of wine, smiled, and began carving an apple into dunkable bite-size wedges.

Eric unhooked the clasp of the lobster trap, reached in, and untwisted the wires that held the mysterious prize. Extracting it, he found it heavier than it looked. The bleeding fingers floated out of the trap's open mouth and sank slowly into the blackness, instantly set upon by a school of small voracious blowfish. Suspended for a few moments by a frenzied feeding, the dismembered digits ultimately spiraled to the ocean's floor, stripped clean of all meat, muscle, and flesh.

Setting the lamp once more in a crotch of the prop, Eric began slowly peeling the carefully wrapped object. Wound tight in a bubble packaging, it tumbled in Eric's hand, growing heavier as he unrolled each buoyant protective plastic layer. The discarded material floated up and away as he pulled it off sheet by sheet. Finally, the last piece of packaging rose toward the surface and Eric found himself holding a purple velvet bag tied tight at one end with a gold cord. The knot yielded instantly to a quick stab of the rusty fishing knife and the thick wet velvet slid away with ease.

In the filtering shafts of eerie light, Eric was suddenly staring at something that stared right back.

* * *

Maggie stirred the fondue again. She took another sip of wine and strolled to the gunwale, peering overboard. When she saw the drifting line of floating plastic, she frowned for a moment and then with a quick little shrug returned to her deck chair to wait for Eric.

Staring out at the lights of Dune Road, Maggie wondered what the expensive contemporary homes were like inside. And what kind of people would spend the ten thousand dollars or more it cost to rent them for three months. Rich, she told herself.

Glancing over the side again and staring down at the flat black surface, Maggie began unconsciously drumming her fingers on the varnished oak gunwale. She refilled her wineglass, swirled the thickening fondue one more time, and sighed.

Painstakingly arranged on one of the *Lady Barbara*'s Dresden china serving plates, the carefully carved apple wedges began to brown.

Emerald eyes, set in solid gold, glistened in the underwater light. Shafts of dazzling yellow glitter pierced the underwater green aura as Eric turned the idol slowly in his hand. Stunned by both the discovery and its beauty, Eric held his last gulp of air and simply stared, mesmerized by the perfection.

Egyptian, he thought, like mummified funerary cats discovered in the Pyramids. Only this one was solid gold. The statuette's sculptor had captured perfectly the regal feline posture of an Abysinnian. Its huge emerald eyes seemed so lifelike that the slender figurine took on an eerie realness. Wait till Maggie sees this, Eric thought, and, exhaling finally, began to kick. A cloud of bubbles swirled from his regulator.

The first spear zipped by, missing the back of his head by less than two inches, embedding itself in the *Lady Barbara*'s hull. The dull thwack made Eric turn. He squinted at the deadly missile but didn't understand its purpose until too late.

Frowning in bewilderment, he turned slowly to the right, in the direction from which it must have come. A second spear hissed from the murk and smashed into the faceplate of his mask. Deflected slightly by the impact, the spear lodged itself halfway through the mask, its tip having sliced a razor-thin line across his right cheek. A blast of salt water and shattered glass punched against his face, and Eric began kicking furiously for the surface.

Now openly angry at this inconsiderate delay, Maggie stood leaning on the heels of her hands at the starboard gunwale of the *Lady Barbara*. Peering down at the flat black water, she began to rehearse what she would tell Eric when he finally did come up. She leaned farther over the side, hoping to see the glimmer of his underwater lamp, but she saw only the slow rise and fall of ocean swells washing along the yacht's waterline.

She was five feet away and staring right at him when Eric exploded from below, his face mask smashed and impaled with a two-foot spear. Maggie screamed, jumping back.

Dripping blood and water, Eric's mask was gone with one desperate swipe from his right hand. Scrambling up the rope ladder, he tossed the heavy statuette to Maggie, peeled off his scuba tank, and in a desperate dive for the wheelhouse, knocked over the mahogany deck table. When the *Lady Barbara*'s heavy GM 6-71 engine rumbled to life, Eric smashed the gear forward and shoved the throttle ahead full open.

It took a moment for the heavy vessel to respond, but she finally began to move just as two divers broke the surface, one still firing spears. Maggie hit the deck as a spear smacked against a halyard hoist on the mast. It ricocheted down and came to rest in a puddle of cheese, broken china, and spilled wine. At the port side of the deck, the Kenyon stove was on its side, its harmless blue flame growing quickly into an orange blaze as spilled alcohol fueled a fire rising on the teak planking.

With the *Lady Barbara* pulling slowly away from the murderous attackers, Eric scrambled to reach the wheelhouse fire extinguisher.

Maggie, openmouthed, looked up from the solid-gold cat in her hands and stammered, "What the hell is going on?!"

Eric, desperately spraying foam at the spreading blaze, did not answer until the last of the deadly flames had disappeared. A line of crimson covered his right cheek, and he was breathing fast.

Looking from Maggie's face to the golden cat to the upturned dinner table, Eric, still catching his breath, swallowed and said, "Must've interrupted some sort of smuggling operation. . . . Oh Jesus!"

"What?" Maggie gasped, wide-eyed.

Eric's attention was suddenly frozen on the wake of the *Lady Barbara*. Maggie snapped around in time to see a glassy eye rise in the foam. A hundred yards behind them, it was closing fast.

Had the motor sailer been under sail, outdistancing the underwater predator would have been an easy task. But propelled by just her one engine, the *Lady Barbara* moved through the waves too slowly.

"Sub," Eric whispered.

"What do we do?" Maggie shot back desperately.

"If it's armed . . ." Eric left the sentence unfinished.

Maggie bit her lip as the gray eye glided relentlessly closer. Eric bolted across the main deck to the portside davit hoist. Cranking down, he watched the *Lady Barbara*'s Asa Thomson yacht tender begin to lower.

"Eric!" Maggie called when she saw the periscope, no more than a hundred feet away, sink below the surface and disappear.

"I know . . . I saw it," Eric yelled back. He stopped

cranking when the small wooden skiff's stern touched the water, bouncing on the yacht's wake.

As he turned to grab life vests from the main deck lockers, a jolt shook the *Lady Barbara* from stem to stern and a dull underwater clang of metal on metal signaled the demise of the yacht's propeller. Sheared from its shaft, the bronze prop spun off into the black depths and the *Lady Barbara*'s runaway engine began to scream. With no time to raise canvas, the promise of flight faded to nothing. The elegant antique motor sailer slowed, powerless in the sea, now completely at the mercy of the predatory sub.

As Eric crossed to the wheelhouse, he realized what had happened. Yanking b᷍ k the throttle, he let the yacht's useless engine slow and die. An eerie quiet followed. The hiss of bubbles from below slowly dissipated and the only sound was water lapping at the still yacht's hull.

Scanning the horizon, Eric saw the periscope rise slowly in the water about a hundred yards to port. It turned, took bearing, and began to circle into position. As the eye carved a wide arc on the ocean surface, a faint slurping hiss sucked the night air.

"Now they're either going to fire," Eric said softly, "or ram."

Then the bulbous nose of the small submarine broke surface in front of the periscope tower and the ebony black vessel began to accelerate—on direct collision course.

In the cramped belly of the sub, a dripping wet Sonny Pike squinted into the eyepiece of the periscope.

Rising and falling on the gentle ocean swells, the long motor sailer was nothing more than a helpless seventy-five-foot target. Ramming the sub's throttle forward with his right hand, which was wrapped in a blood-soaked bandage, Pike watched the distant image grow.

A wave of white water washed over the sub's bulbous bow, spraying water on the glassy gray eye. The graceful lines of the *Lady Barbara* distorted for a moment, then cleared.

Pike growled at his two-man crew, "Hold on, boys . . . we're gonna sink this mother!"

Maggie's attention snapped from the approaching sub to the lights on Dune Road. She estimated the distance to shore to be at least a mile. Grabbing Eric's arm, she pleaded, "What are we going to do?"

"Escape," he declared and turned to finish lowering the yacht tender.

When the tiny boat hit the surface, Eric released its davit lines and pulled it close. Taking the golden cat from Maggie's grip, Eric steadied the bobbing skiff for her to climb aboard. He handed her the statuette and started down the ladder to join her. Peering one last time across the *Lady Barbara's* deck, he saw the black nose of the submarine protruding from the spreading spray fifty feet away and coming fast. Eric dropped into the wooden skiff, locked the leathered oars, and leaned forward, dropping the oar blades into the sea. Grunting from the depth of his soul, he ripped back with all his might.

At the same instant the skiff shot away from the *Lady Barbara's* port, the armor-plated bow of the sub smashed midship into her starboard. A crack of crunching hull split the air, and the yacht lurched sideways, raised from the sea. Her heavy oak timbers groaned and then gave way with a thunderous snap. Crashing back down, the long heavy hull smashed into the water, creating a billow that effortlessly pitched the tiny skiff leeward.

Trying desperately to hold the boat steady, Eric continued long hard pulls, each one putting more distance between them and the battered yacht.

The *Lady Barbara* came right, but listing decidedly to the starboard. Staring at the magnificent vessel, Eric watched the list grow worse until the *Lady Barbara* sat almost forty-five degrees to the sea. Gushing seawater poured through the gaping hole in her hull until her masts suddenly swung back perpendicular and she started to sink. It took only minutes for the elegant ship to founder and disappear beneath a foamy whirlpool of swirling water, splintered wood, and spilled fuel.

Eric and Maggie were half a mile from shore when the periscope rose again from the deep—dripping, scanning.

Rowing hard, Eric watched the periscope's head swing slowly, searching. It was having difficulty locating the tiny silhouette and soon began moving in a wide sweep that would ultimately bring it directly into their path of escape. Eric knew that their only hope was to reach shallow water, but his strength was giving out fast. Sucking for air, he bent forward and stopped rowing, unable to deny himself rest any longer.

"You want to trade?" Maggie asked.

Eric looked up into her green eyes and panted, "You row?"

"As well as you . . . if not better."

"In the future," he gasped as she climbed around him, "let's not keep these secrets from each other."

Maggie set the cat down in the skiff's built-in fishbox and began long steady pulls that brought the tender closer to the relative safety of waves breaking about a quarter mile from shore. Built by the powerful tides, the shallow bar offered the only protection available—dubious at best.

Then the periscope stopped scanning. It had locked in on its target.

"There they are, the sonsofbitches!" Pike snarled. "I told you I saw somebody climb off."

"Whaddya wanna do, Sonny?" one of his men asked.

"Get ready to release the fuckin' safety latches on the arms and make sure I've got pressure."

Checking a gauge on the hydraulic lines leading to the

controls by Pike's good hand, his man grunted, "Full power on the arms."

"Better take a look at that depth recorder," the other crewman cautioned.

Glancing down at the green readout on the sub's Inmar recorder, Pike spat, "Fuck it!"

"Like sex," Maggie explained as she continued long smooth strides, "the trick is not to use up all your strength in the first few minutes."

"Thanks for the tip," Eric replied, his head thrown back, his arms hanging on the skiff's gunwales. He turned sideways and saw the approaching glassy gray eye cradled in a V of spreading water. The sub was making its run. Snapping around, Eric gauged the sandbar breakers to be just a little bit too far away. Realizing that there was no time to switch places, he turned to Maggie and said with conviction, "Stroke, Irish, stroke!"

A wave of water swelled before the periscope as the sub started to close the gap. Eric and Maggie could hear the slurping hiss grow louder, but the rumble of curling waves also grew loud as they spurted closer and closer to the breaking surf. Eric looked back, then to the breakers. He knew they couldn't make it.

One hundred feet behind them, the sub's black bow rose like a serpent from the sea, water spraying out of its path. Then suddenly—like the limbs of a giant praying mantis—two black arms rose from its sides. Reaching up, their pincered tips opened like claws.

Groaning with each pull, Maggie continued her slow sure strokes, pushing the skiff to the edge of the curling waves.

Completely black, the dripping bow and mechanical claws glistened in the night air, relentlessly coming on faster and faster. Eric braced himself as the distance narrowed to thirty feet, then twenty, then ten. As the mechanical beast bore down, its long sinewy arms lowered, preparing to grab and crush the fragile little skiff.

Maggie gritted her teeth and gave one last rip at the oars as the sub smashed ahead. The tiny boat dropped over a wave just as the huge armor-plated bow struck. Propelled by the impact and caught in a breaking curl, the skiff split but shot forward out of the reach of the deadly claws.

One of the sinister pincers snapped closed, biting through the transom as the skiff fell away, but the black metal talon was left clutching nothing more than a wide chunk of splintered oak. Looming above Eric and Maggie, the dripping black bow and outstretched arms suddenly jolted to a bottom-scraping halt. The sub was aground.

Maggie tumbled off her seat and Eric fell forward as the skiff nosed under and cracked. The golden cat rolled forward, toward a yawning split in the cedar planking, but Eric lunged and managed a last-second grab that saved it. Then another wave broke, crashing down into the tiny craft, breaking it completely in two, spilling Eric and Maggie into the surf a quarter mile from shore.

Cold seawater filled her nostrils as Maggie, suddenly upside down underwater, panicked and gasped. Spluttering and coughing, she came up thrashing. Eric reached around her, and she calmed. It took a moment for her to catch her breath in the cold water, but Eric's firm grip and confident reassurances gave her the courage necessary to head for shore. Washed beachward by the breaking wave, they managed to swim away from the black submarine.

Eric turned only once, when he heard the sub's engines race. He saw the long arms fold into the sides of the black vessel, then the bow begin rocking back and forth. Slowly, the behemoth slid back into deeper water. Within minutes it was as if it had never existed; the rolling waves were empty and the starry horizon flat.

The same strong tide that had built the lifesaving sandbar now ripped viciously along the shore, turning the short swim into a deadly trial even for a fully rested swimmer.

Maggie, already drained from the rowing, could manage

only a few strokes before pausing to rest. Furiously treading water, she closed her eyes and took deep breaths. But numbed by the water's cold and disheartened by the ordeal of battling the relentless tide, Maggie's will began to waver.

Wave followed wave, pulling her down. Her wet clothing grew heavier. Her arms and legs refused command.

"Need help," she gasped.

Eric reached out for her hand. But staring at him through half-closed eyes, she slipped from his grip and went under. Still clutching the golden cat in his left hand, Eric dropped below the surface and grabbed her with his right.

Pulling her up, he shook the water from his face and demanded, "Where do you think you're going?"

"I can't," she gagged. "I can't make it."

Holding Maggie under her arms from behind, Eric whispered encouragement and began pulling her toward shore with long powerful kicks.

Forty-five minutes after being dumped into the sea, Maggie crawled from the surf and collapsed panting on the cold sand in front of the Westhampton Village beach. Eric stumbled out of the waves behind her, staggered to a lifeguard stand, and fell to his knees at the stand's whitewashed base. The salt water had stopped the bleeding on his face but left a swollen white gash. Pushing away mounds of fine dry sand, he reached a layer of wet grit and then excavated until he reached a depth of two feet. Pulling armfuls of sand back into the hole, he buried the golden cat and then fell flat on his back to rest.

After catching his breath, Eric sat up, took a deep breath, and stood. Then he walked over and helped an exhausted, shivering-cold Maggie to her feet. Together they stumbled down the beach to the nearest sign of life—an elaborate midnight cocktail party that was well underway on the oceanside deck of one of the houses. Climbing the wooden stairway, they came face to face with the party's already inebriated host standing next to a full wet bar built into the deck.

"Hey, hey . . . what can I getcha, pal?" the man slurred with a silly grin.

"The police," Eric answered.

CHAPTER 2

"You see, we made a little change in the plans. One of the pieces from the last shipment didn't quite make it to Paris. Been talkin' it over, Blinky an' me . . . and I'll come right to the point, Mr. Singh. We want another five thousand each."

The man to whom these word were spoken sat stonefaced across a thick wooden table in a crowded basement pub in the heart of Brussels' majestic Place du Grand Sablon. His almond-shaped eyes registered neither surprise nor anger. He did not blink. He did not nod. He simply stared into the speaker's face and remained silent.

A party of American tourists pushed open the door of the pub and noisily descended into the smoke-fogged room. Jonathan Peake, about to offer justification for his demand, looked nervously up at the boisterous group and instead of speaking, drained the last from his glass goblet of Grimbergen beer. Next to him, Blinky McCorkle, staring down at a plate of white cheese and radishes, shifted uncomfortably in his seat.

When the tourists passed, Peake wiped foam from his mustache with the back of his hand, cleared his throat, and continued, "Like I wuz sayin', me an' Blinky sees this as bonus for the work we done so far and it would sorta guarantee that your shipment gets delivered complete."

Parat Singh, a gaunt, dark, emaciated man, smiled slowly across the table at Peake. But the carefully controlled response was completely humorless. Singh's head remained still while his lethal stare slid snakelike to Blinky McCorkle.

Blinky, with his eyes darting nervously between Singh, Peake, and the floor, stammered, "Th-that's right."

"You have kept one piece?" Singh asked softly.

Trying desperately but without success to control his stutter, he explained, "Not that we'd be t-tryin' to hold you up or anything, you understand. Mr. P-Peake and I have come to the conclusion that this b-bonus is well deserved considerin' the extra risk we took."

"Yeah," Peake mumbled as if another endorsement would add credence to the blatant extortion.

Across the table, Parat Singh's smile grew into a hideous white grin as his sunken eyes closed. Crooked teeth jutted from his gums at all angles, giving his jack-o'-lantern smile a distinctly evil look. His dark skin, drawn tight over his flat features, remained satin-smooth. Slowly, his dark eyelids reopened, unveiling two jet-black orbs riveted in scleratic pools of bloodshot white.

Like most Indians, he spoke English in short precise sentences. He said softly, "I will see to it."

Peake shot a quick glance at McCorkle and then said to Singh, "Like Blinky says, you understand that we wouldn't be asking for this if we hadn't taken all that extra . . ."

By simply raising his bony brown hand, Parat Singh silenced the man. "No explanation, please. I understand. This will be taken care of."

A moment of uncomfortable silence followed before Peake finally grinned, "Okay. Then I guess that's it then, right?" He glanced again over at McCorkle, who, like himself, looked unsure of what should happen next.

Blinky leaned across the table and, with his own eyes

fluttering whenever he stumbled over a word, whispered, "When should we m-meet again, Mr. Singh?"

Singh did not answer. Instead, he cupped his hand over his untouched goblet of beer and pushed it away to clear a space. Then he lifted a black leather schoolbag briefcase onto the table and opened it only enough to extract a worn little book. He peeled open the book, read, and then placed it back in the bag. After setting the heavy-looking bag once again on the seat, he casually cupped his hand once more over his goblet of beer and drew it close. But he did not drink.

Blinky frowned at Peake, and Peake winked back.

Singh stood and turned, draping a dark-blue coat over his rapier-thin frame. Looking down at the two men, he said, "The shipments must all be complete by next Sunday. You can arrange to have the piece you are holding to me by then?"

"As soon as we're paid our bonus," Peake responded with newfound confidence.

Singh nodded, leaned down, and picked up the black leather bag.

"We'll b-be waiting to hear f-from you," Blinky added, staring at the mysterious accessory.

Singh said nothing more. He turned and walked up the stairs into the cool Belgian night. Once outside, he paused at one of the tiny windows of the pub and peered back through the thick leaded glass. When he saw Peake reach for his goblet, he smiled. Crossing the road to a nearby alley, he disappeared into the dark shadows of the Church of Notre Dame du Sablon, leaned against a cold granite wall, and began his wait.

"Well, that was easy," Peake said to Blinky, motioning a waitress to the table. Then, popping a radish into his mouth, he reached over and emptied Singh's beer goblet half into his own and half into McCorkles'.

"I don't know . . . the bloke gives me the heebie j-jeebies," Blinky responded, "I don't trust him."

"I told ya he'd go for the extra tap," Peake said smugly. "We got 'im by his Indian balls."

"He's got evil in his eyes," Blinky mumbled, taking a sip of beer.

"He's got money in his little black bag."

"You figure that's what he c-carries in there?" Blinky asked.

"He always pays me from that bag—always."

After drinking several more goblets of Grimbergen and devouring bowls of mussels and plates of french fries, they settled their bill and climbed back up into the winding streets of Brussels. Drunk and happy, they crossed the cobblestoned Place du Grand Sablon oblivious not only to the splendid gothic architecture of surrounding buildings, but also unaware that Parat Singh emerged from the shadows behind.

As they crossed the square circled by ancient homes, antique shops, and bookstores, Peake suddenly stopped, grabbed his partner's arm, and slurred, "How about we get a little bit before turnin' in, eh?"

"Not for me," Blinky replied, shaking his head. "But you have at it for both of us."

They parted company on the corner of Regentschapstraat and Rue de Namur when Peake whistled down a cab and ordered the driver to deliver him to Avenue du Boulevard Bolwerklaan near the train station, a block from Brussels' sleazy red-light district.

Blinky walked on to a dingy old hotel on the Boulevard de Waterloo. Slated for demolition as part of Brussels' ongoing renovation of its mass-transit system, the fifty-year-old Hotel Pishl offered cheap temporary lodging for the city's most undiscriminating transient clientele. Blinky McCorkle, feeling right at home, walked in and rode one of the derelict building's few modern conveniences to the fifth floor. When he went to unlock the door, he had difficulty inserting the key. His fingers tingled and his right arm felt numb. But after several attempts, he turned the lock and stepped into the grim little room. He began undressing without bothering to turn on the light.

Moments later, the tired elevator creaked into service again—carrying Parat Singh to the same destination.

The cabdriver turned right at the Place Rogier, continued past Brussels' north station, and stopped on a small side street lined with dimly lit storefront windows. The girls on display busied themselves as they waited patiently for admirers willing to rent time. Several read, one ate, others simply sat. A young-looking redhead caught Peake's eye as the Mercedes cab rolled to a stop; she sat perched on a tall stool with her squat legs crossed. Almost naked and looking completely bored, she stared down between the swell of her breasts at the knitting needles clicking in her hands.

She was illuminated only by a tube of red neon light at her feet, and the effect left her skin looking smooth and her face unlined. Her long hair cascaded over her bare shoulders and ended tickling two huge breasts that hung suspended in a lacy black brassiere.

When Peake saw another "window shopper" stroll toward the window, he quickly peeled off two hundred-franc notes, tossed them to the driver, and strode across the street. The other man, intimidated by Peake's purposeful gait, walked on to shop elsewhere. As Peake reached the window, the girl looked up. Her lips parted, the knitting needles stopped, and Jonathan Peake fell deeply in lust. He listened for a moment to the blood pounding through his ears, and then went inside.

Financial arrangements were concluded, the window drapes were drawn, and the redhead was sucking on Peake's penis all within three minutes. But the shriveled pink appendage did not respond. Instead, it simply hung limp. After five minutes of expert massage and coaxing, it was no bigger. Peake, with dismay and confusion locked on his face, stared down and mumbled, "Nothin' like this ever happened . . ."

The redhead shrugged, stood, and quickly tucked the money in a drawer, afraid that the unsatisfied customer might demand refund. But Jonathan Peake was too upset to negotiate. He stumbled back out onto the street, bumping into the doorway as he passed.

As he staggered toward a distant cab, the redhead opened the drapes, climbed back up on her stool, and continued knitting.

Blinky McCorkle fell twice as he undressed, slumping against the wall with his turtleneck pulled halfway over his head. Cursing to himself, he struggled out of the tight garment and fell sitting on his squeaky bed. He unscrewed the top of a flask of whiskey that he'd hidden beneath his pillow, sniffled once, and drank. Blinking in the darkness, he let out a wet belch, and fell back against a lumpy pillow stained brown from countless nights of his drunken drool. Within minutes, the room reverberated with a snore so loud that it could be heard in the hallway outside.

Smiling, Parat Singh tried the door and found that Blinky had either forgotten to lock it or had intentionally left it open for Peake. He stepped from the yellow light of the hall into the dark room silently, crossed to the sleeping McCorkle, and clicked open the gold latch of the black case. He then plucked a pair of plastic gloves from a fold in the lid and stretched them on his long slender fingers like a surgeon preparing to operate.

Carefully extracting a brown leather scabbard, Singh turned to the sleeping man. Glinting and gleaming in a shaft of blue light filtering through the room's grimy windows, the ornate instrument of death came unsheathed—an ancient kris with a long wavy blade that snaked down from a thick handle encrusted with jewels to a thin razor point.

Singh poised the blade's edge at Blinky McCorkle's throbbing jugular. Pressing a crease in Blinky's throat, he said softly, "Speak to me, Mr. McCorkle."

Blinky's eyes opened slowly, and even though paralyzed by the drug unwittingly consumed when he drank Singh's beer, he knew what was happening. "Anything," he stammered, unable to move.

"Where exactly have you placed my possession?"

Twenty minutes later, the elevator once again creaked to the fifth floor. Its doors parted and Jonathan Peake stumbled down the narrow hall.

"Hey, Blink!" he called as he fumbled at the door of the room. Numb and useless, his fingers wouldn't work the knob. Finally, after pressing both palms around the cracked ceramic handle, he managed to open the door. The room was dark and remained so even after several clicks at the switch.

"Hey, Blink, wake up. How you feelin'? Somethin's wrong, Blink. . . . I feel so damn weak. I can't even get it up—" Peake stopped suddenly when he saw the sparkling jeweled handle protruding from McCorkle's chest.

"Mr. McCorkle is dead," Singh said softly from the shadows.

"Wha?" Peake slurred, squinting into the dark corner.

"You will die too if you do not do exactly as I say."

The room was spinning and Peake was having difficulty comprehending. He stumbled forward, reaching out for Parat Singh, but fell. He hit face first and grunted a long painful groan. Rolling over, he found that he could not pick himself up. Splayed across the floor, he could now not even lift his head.

Singh dropped a pillow on the floor and lifted Peake's head onto it, into a position that would allow observation of what followed. With his limbs slowly degenerating into useless jelly, Jonathan Peake watched Parat Singh cross the room to Blinky's corpse. As Singh withdrew the dagger from Blinky's chest, Peake recognized it as the one that

Singh had commissioned him to steal from a dealer in Tangiers. A syrupy line of crimson dribbled from its point.

Kneeling, Singh picked up Peake's left arm and angled the stained wavy blade at a blue vein. Slowly, he dragged its razor edge across Peake's left wrist, and warm liquid oozed from the incision, across Peake's hand onto the floor.

"This is a slow death and one that can be reversed," Singh said softly. "I want to know which piece you have stolen and its exact location. If you lie, I will let you die."

"Don't," Peake slurred, his eyes wide.

Singh poised the dagger above the other wrist and looked into Peake's eyes.

"The necklace! We only meant to borrow it. Please, for God's sake, help me!"

"Where is it?" Singh asked in the same monotone.

"Call a doctor!"

"Where?" Singh repeated as he sliced through the soft flesh.

"In me pocket!" Peake cried.

"Which pocket?" Singh demanded.

"Me right pocket, in the handkerchief! Now call a doctor, for Christ's sake!"

Reaching his bony hand into the fabric of Peake's pants, Singh felt the ancient necklace and pulled it out. A smile came to his thin lips.

"Call the doctor, you bloody bastard!" Peake screamed, tears in his eyes.

Singh stood, holding the dagger in one hand and the carelessly wrapped necklace in the other. The job was done. Turning, he dropped the incriminating dagger at Peake's side, and it clattered to a rest against the dying man's hand.

"Forget about the extra money!" Peake cried in desperation.

Singh smiled. "Mr. Peake . . . I was going to kill you anyway."

Snatching up the pillow, Singh tossed it back onto the bed as Peake's head hit the floor with a sickening thud.

Dropping the precious necklace into the black bag, Singh headed for the door.

Staring wide-eyed straight down his legs, Peake watched as his murderer walked from the room. His last vision was a spindly silhouette framed in the yellow light of the doorway to the hall. The door closed, the room went black, and Jonathan Peake bled to death.

Returning to his shop, Objets d'Art Egyptien, in the Place du Grand Sablon, Singh unlocked the front door, crossed through the showroom, and went directly to the small office in back. Nine pairs of eyes followed his movement across the room.

Modest by Brussels standards, the little antique shop had only the one small showroom. Nevertheless, its showcases were filled with gold, jewelry, and art—the ill-gotten fortunes of the ancient world's dead and buried. Collected by graverobbers over three thousand years, the objects represented the desecrations, trespasses, and sacrilegious rape of countless tombs and graves left ransacked, pillaged, and destroyed. It was these things in which Parat Singh dealt, and it was these things with which he surrounded himself.

Seated comfortably at his exquisite antique Bureau du Roi desk, Singh methodically filled in all the information on the form necessary to file a report of stolen property with the Central Brussels Police. Turning to a file cabinet, he located a snapshot of the priceless kris now lying in a pool of blood on the fifth floor of the Hotel Pishl and attached it to the report. Then he picked up the phone and asked for an overseas operator. Within minutes, he was speaking to a recording device in the Objets d'Art Egyptien antique shop on Madison Avenue three blocks from New York's Metropolitan Museum of Art.

At the tone, he announced, "There has been a difficulty here. I have been forced to terminate the employ of local importers. Must see to delivery personally. Otherwise proceeding according to schedule."

Replacing the phone on its cradle, Parat Singh opened his leather case and extracted his worn little book. When he peeled it open, a tiny brown envelope fell onto the desk. Its contents having been consumed by Jonathan Peake and Blinky McCorkle, the envelope had served its purpose, and Singh set it aflame. Its yellow light brightened the dark little room for only a few moments and then went out.

Singh crushed the ashes into a small crystal vial that he kept in one of the carved desk's tiny drawers. Then he reached into the black bag and pulled from it Peake's dirty handkerchief. Unwrapping the stained square of fabric, he uncovered a dazzling gold-and-lapis-lazuli necklace that had been crafted by an Egyptian artist some thirteen centuries before Christ was born. Holding the treasure spread in his hands, Singh gazed at its perfect symmetry. Again his movements were closely watched. But this time by only one pair of eyes. Black unblinking eyes.

As Singh stood, the eyes rose. When he approached its terrarium, his deadly pet swayed back and met his stare. Other than tasting the air with short flicks of its forked black tongue, the three-foot krait remained motionless. Hungry for days, the snake was alert to any prospect of food. But Parat Singh only smiled. He offered no sustenance. Instead he reached over the glass cage and pulled a brochure from the shelf above. Turning, he returned to his desk and slowly paged through the expensive pamphlet. The krait's stare remained fixed on the back of Singh's lowered head.

Flipping through the full-page color photographs of ancient objects, Singh stopped when his gaze fell upon a photo of the necklace. Described as having been discovered in Thebes, the necklace was also listed as being on display in the Metropolitan Museum of Art. Holding the necklace next to its picture, Singh smiled and turned the page.

Jaded by a lifetime of collecting and trading stolen treasure, he should have had no reaction to the photo on the last page of the brochure. But of all the treasures listed, it was this that was the most beautiful—an ancient temple cat from Saqqara. Of all the objects described and shown, it was this regal statue of the goddess Bastet that would bring the highest bids. Fashioned out of solid gold, it stood twelve inches high and boasted huge emerald eyes.

CHAPTER 3

The late-afternoon sky over the Hamptons was crystal-clear and the sun still blindingly strong. Ben Chestle turned the unmarked Chrysler into the Municipal Building lot, parked in a reserved space, and after stretching the stiffness from his back, climbed the stairway to the back door. As he opened it, he peeled off his sunglasses and pinched at the two red marks they left on his nose. Deeply lined, Chestle's ruddy face was sunburned brown, giving the fifty-year-old policeman a healthy rugged look. Barrel-chested and fifteen pounds heavier than his ideal weight of 185, he lumbered more than walked and looked as if he could be serious trouble if angered.

Running his hand once over his bristly white crewcut, Chestle heaved a sigh and walked inside. Having wasted the better part of the day delivering a homicide suspect to the New York City police, he was in no mood to handle the previous night's arrests, reports, and complaints. He had no choice.

When he saw the well-dressed young couple sitting inside the door marked Chief of Police, Chestle tapped his young desk sergeant on the shoulder and grumbled through the side of his mouth, "Who's in my office?"

"Mr. Eric Ivorsen and a Miss McCabe," Sergeant Pete Halsey answered with a devilish smirk.

"What's their problem?"

"I'll let them explain it." Halsey grinned. "Wes Brocki responded to a call at a party down on the beach last night, took their statement, and told them to see you today. They've been here about an hour . . . came right here after the Coast Guard—"

"Coast Guard?" Chestle interrupted.

"Boating accident," Halsey said with a straight face. "They've been out all day on a search."

"If it's a boating accident, why are they here?" Chestle demanded in his unmistakable gravelly growl that subordinates, family, and friends had grown accustomed to, but that still struck fear in the hearts of strangers and enemies.

"It's all in the report," Halsey replied, handing over a freshly typed file folder.

Scowling, Chestle turned toward his office with his face buried in the report. Although he loved his work and admitted it, he did not like mysteries. He had enough of those without handling the Coast Guard's problems.

Eric, a white bandage stretched across his right cheek, sat with his arm around Maggie on a wooden bench at the side of the room. When Chestle walked in, he and Maggie introduced themselves, then sat quietly while the grizzled cop finished reading the report.

Snorting several times as he read, Chestle finally looked up and said, "You musta had quite a night."

Eric and Maggie carefully recounted every detail of the previous night's encounter. When it came to explaining the fate of the golden cat, however, Eric left the impression that the cat had been lost during their escape.

Chestle tried to look believing as he listened to the tale. He threw in an occasional question or grunt that made him sound as if he considered the whole episode possible, but he didn't really believe for a moment that it was, and even if he had, the Coast Guard report provided not one ounce of corroboration. Nevertheless, he remained polite.

"What do you do for a living, Mr. Ivorsen?" Chestle asked in a friendly inquisitive tone.

Eric smiled at Maggie. He'd always had difficulty explaining his occupation to people outside of the scientific community, and with recent events, it had become even more difficult to do so.

"Well, I am a mathematician basically. My office is at the Institute for Advanced Study in Princeton."

"Pay well?" Chestle asked offhandedly.

"Not really," Eric admitted.

"How can you afford a seventy-five-foot William Hand motor sailer?" Chestle asked with a disarming smile.

"The boat belongs to a friend."

"Friend? Coast Guard records show it registered to a C. Ivorsen, Monte Carlo."

"My uncle. He died recently and left it to his fiancée, Lady Barbara Falcounbridge. We were on our way to deliver it to her in Newport."

"I see," Chestle said as he walked around and sat himself on the edge of his oak desk. "You know how many submarine-attack reports we handle here every summer?"

Eric didn't bother to answer.

"The fact is, if we had just five more added to yours and counted in all the others we've had since I started as a summer traffic cop fifteen years ago, we'd have an even half-dozen."

"We're not lying," Maggie insisted, anger creeping into her voice.

"Were you two drinking last night?" Chestle asked.

Outside the office, a sudden burst of teletype rattled the otherwise quiet room.

"A little wine," Maggie admitted.

"Right. Maybe you—" The phone intercom buzzed, interrupting Chestle's suggestion. His rugged features crinkled into a squint as he listened. Then he glanced up at

Eric for a moment and barked into the phone, "Bring it in."

The desk sergeant appeared a minute later with a print-out in his hand. Without looking at Eric or Maggie, he set it in front of Chestle and departed, closing the door behind.

Chestle read from the sheet, looked up, and said finally, "Says here you're already pretty well known to the authorities."

Eric, seemingly unconcerned, shrugged. "I don't know what you're reading."

"FBI has a file on you, Princeton PD has a file on you, and you've even got a track record with Interpol. Young man like you doesn't supplement his income hauling illegal substances from one country to another, does he?"

Maggie's eyes widened in rage, but Eric laughed and replied, "If you take the time to investigate those files, you'll learn that my involvement with the authorities has been incidental, cooperative, and in the case of the FBI, invitational."

"We'll check it out."

"Do," Eric replied. "In the meantime, I'd like to take Miss McCabe to dinner. Any recommendations?"

"I'd hate to see you leave the area until I get these reports back."

"We wouldn't dream of it."

Chestle nodded, thinking to himself that this Ivorsen character was either damn cool for a liar and the girl unaware of her boyfriend's main source of income, or that, just possibly, they were telling the truth. "I'll have a car drop you off at the Marina at the end of Dune Road," he offered, and then added, "He'll wait for you, too."

"Thanks, but there's no need for such generosity," Eric replied. "I've rented a car. We'll try your recommendation, and I will give you a call tomorrow morning before we leave for Rhode Island. By then you'll have had a chance to run those checks."

Standing, Eric reached out and matched Chestle's bearlike

handshake. Then he led a still-fuming Maggie out to their rented car.

"How could you be so nice to him after he accused us of drug smuggling?" Maggie asked as Eric held open the door to a gleaming white X-J S.

"He didn't accuse," Eric said. "He just sort of wondered out loud."

As Eric walked around the sleek luxurious car, Ben Chestle leaned out the window of his office and called out, "You rented a brand-new Jag? I thought scientists and college professors were poorly paid."

Normally Eric would have explained, but he did not feel particularly inclined to do so and decided not to. He met Chestle's stare but said nothing.

Chestle's slow smile revealed a line of strong white teeth. He winked and said, "Don't forget to call."

Eric nodded in response, eased into the driver's seat, and wheeled out onto the road. A few moments later, a police car followed. Twenty minutes later, when Eric parked outside the Marina Restaurant, the police cruiser rolled slowly by, turned off Dune Road into the old lighthouse parking lot nearby, and stopped.

"Well, at least our car will be safe," Maggie quipped as they strolled into the dockside restaurant.

"Apparently," Eric agreed, waving to the driver. The policeman did not respond. Putting his arm around Maggie, Eric said, "Now how about that lobster dinner I promised you?"

"Listen, if you can't come up with one this time, you needn't go through such a big production again—I'll just have a burger and fries."

Eric's expression eased into a smile and then a wide grin. They walked into the dockside dining room and were seated at a table overlooking the fishing boats below. After they had sipped away two incredibly delicious icy Stolichnaya martinis, Eric ordered clam chowder, a dozen oysters, and one three-pound lobster.

"A bit hungry?" Maggie asked.

"Losing priceless yachts gives me an appetite."

"C'mon in . . . leave 'em alone," Ben Chestle barked into the police radio microphone.

In the cruiser parked at the end of Dune Road, the young officer responded, "Roger, terminating surveillance at five forty-five . . . over."

"Out," Chestle sighed and clicked off the mike.

"What gives, chief?" Patrolman Wes Brocki asked.

"The guy you brought in last night."

"The submarine guy with the good-looking girl?"

"Yeah. I thought they might be involved with trafficking."

"And?"

"Clean as a whistle," Chestle replied, dropping an FBI printout on the desk. "He's some sorta mathematical genius or something. Apparently had a little run-in with the Russians once—some guy got shot in his apartment. Anyway, the Bureau says he's got a top security clearance."

"What about his submarine story?"

"I'll check it out again before they leave. Where they stayin'?"

"The Dunes. He told me they plan to stay the night and leave for Newport tomorrow."

"Yeah, that's right—somethin' about some old dame named Lady Barbara," Chestle grumbled. Pacing back and forth in the small office, he began mumbling to himself.

"Something else bothering you, chief?"

Rubbing his face with his hand, Chestle squinted at the young patrolman and blurted, "You remember that time the missus and I drove up to Buffalo for the bowling convention, and some sonofabitch ripped off my old blue Impala?"

"Yeah."

"My wallet was in my jacket in the trunk with a brand-new Ebonite Blue that I got especially for the tournament. All we had with us was what Doris had in her pocketbook and what I had in my pocket—twelve bucks or so. Anyway, it took three friggin' days to get our bank to wire money to a bank in Buffalo. We lived on saltines and cheese and kept tellin' the motel guy to be patient."

Nodding, Brocki replied, "Yeah, so what's the point?"

"So how come this Ivorsen character comes ashore with only his dick in his hand and a coupla hours later he's slidin' around town in a brand-new Jag, wearin' a whole new wardrobe, and livin' on the beach like a goddam millionaire?"

Brocki thought for a moment, shrugged, and suggested, "Ask him."

"Yeah," Ben Chestle muttered, "I think I will."

The waitress cleared away the plate of empty oyster shells and placed a steaming red lobster in front of Eric. He began expertly cracking its shell, spilling huge white chunks of sweet meat onto Maggie's plate.

Maggie emptied the icy bottle of Liebfraumilch into their wineglasses and watched him. His usual smile was missing, his manner uncharacteristically quiet—limited to one-word responses to her attempts at conversation.

Finally, she set down her glass, reached over, and, gently touching his arm, asked, "Hey, where's my devil-may-care-it's-all-in-the-game hero type?"

Eric looked up, smiled into her eyes, and replied, "About two miles offshore."

"Why?"

"I keep thinking about that sub. Very strange."

"Strange because it was there or strange because it attacked?"

"Strange because it was designed as an armor-plated undersea exploration craft with a retractable periscope and robotic arms, painted black with no markings or brightwork, and from what I could see when it ran aground, had no tower or topside hatch."

"So what does all that mean?" Maggie asked.

"It means whoever goes aboard, does so underwater. And that means that it has to have an airlock, which means that that was no inexpensive piece of hardware," he concluded.

"What do you think it was doing out there?"

"I have to believe that it was a smuggling operation. What I cannot figure is why someone would go to all that expense to move something as small as that golden cat unless . . ."

"Unless?"

"Unless that was just one tiny piece. That exploration sub was equipped for heavy-duty deep-sea salvage. I wonder what else they were loading or unloading down there."

"The police and the Coast Guard will investigate."

Eric shook his head, "I don't think the Coast Guard or Chief Chestle really believed a word of what we said, do you?"

"Maybe we should show them the cat."

Eric shook his head. "Can't do it. It's our only bargaining chip. Claude will know what to do. He and my uncle used to dabble in these things."

"Who's Claude?"

"Ah, Claude . . . Claude Bocuse is a distinguished Frenchman, a world-class chef, and the oldest permanent crewmember of the yacht *Lady Barbara*. Close to seventy now, he has cooked onboard for nearly forty-five years. He'll be distressed to learn of her loss but will discreetly say nothing. The fact that she went down with a fondue on the deck and an open bottle of wine in the galley will bring some measure of comfort, I'm sure."

"If he's the only permanent crewmember, how is that we had the yacht all to ourselves?"

"He takes care of Lady Barbara. If she leaves the yacht, he leaves the yacht. He's in Newport tending to her needs."

"Her needs," Maggie repeated, picturing a wrinkled hand tinkling a little bell and someone dashing out with a hot-water bottle.

"Speaking of which reminds me, when we get back to the hotel, I want to call and thank the Senator for helping us with ours."

When they finished the meal, Eric called the waitress, asked for the bill, and immediately peeled off four twenties from a thick stack of cash—cash that had been made available at the Westhampton Beach branch of Long Island Trust as a result of one quick phone call from retired Senator Lester Walters, Charles Ivorsen's former lawyer and business partner.

When the young girl returned with Eric's change, she was followed by an eager busboy who went to work clearing the table. And when Eric stood to leave, the young man stepped back gazing up at the towering Eric, stared for a moment at the long white dressing on his cheek, and joked, "Geez, mister, I'd hate to see the other guy."

"You'd know him in a second—he's only got seven fingers," Eric quipped offhandedly, not expecting a reaction from anyone but Maggie.

The busboy blinked and squinted slowly up at Eric. Without saying a word, he grabbed up his tray of dishes and walked quickly toward the kitchen, turning twice to look back at Eric.

"Funny reaction," Maggie observed.

"He just didn't understand," Eric decided.

By the time Eric and Maggie strolled hand in hand from the restaurant, the sun had set, but the horizon still glowed a golden blue. As they walked to the car, they saw the young busboy hurry out of the restaurant's kitchen door and disappear down onto the docks.

Sprinting along the bulkhead, the busboy stopped suddenly when he reached a battered stern-rigged fishing boat whose transom bore the name *Sea Puss*. Jumping onboard, he made his way around a large canvas-covered crate and knocked hard on the cabin door.

Another young man, brawny and deeply tanned, answered the knock. Long dirty-blond hair spilled out from under his black wool cap. Dressed in blue jeans and a plaid shirt over a thin black turtleneck, Digger Murdock looked like every other young commercial fisherman on the docks.

He was not alone in the cramped cabin. Behind him there was another man, slightly older, who looked somehow out of place. Murdock claimed to his friends on the docks that the man had been hired as a mate, but whenever they were seen on deck—which was seldom—it was the older man who gave the orders and Murdock who carried them out.

Dressed in a greasy gray armless sweatshirt and faded jeans, Sonny Pike looked hard and mean, his eyes cold and cruel. The purple tattoo stained into the flesh of his left forearm was incongruous—a small bird standing on an anchor, above the name *Whimbrel*. He favored his right arm, holding it slightly elevated to relieve the pain. His right hand was wrapped in fresh bandaging from which only a pinky and thumb protruded.

Murdock and Pike listened to the tale the busboy told, and then Pike grabbed Murdock, pulled him out of the way, and turned to dig through his seabag. "Lemme get my gun," he spat.

"No, no," Murdock shot back, "I got one in the truck . . . let's go before we lose 'em!"

"I think we've lost our escort," Maggie said as she settled in the Jaguar's red leather seat. "I don't see the police escort."

"The FBI report must've come back," Eric surmised and gunned the engine.

As they pulled out onto Dune Road, Eric noticed headlights appear in the rearview mirror. "We may have spoken too fast," he commented.

Maggie turned, saw the lights of an approaching vehicle, and sank back down in the seat. "That car is following us?"

"Doesn't look like a police car," Eric commented, squinting into the mirror. "Too high off the ground."

The lights came up quickly, and Eric could see clearly that they belonged not to a car but to a truck. He slowed, turned to take a look, and then returned his stare to the road ahead. Jacked up three feet and riding on balloon tires, the vehicle appeared to be a Chevy 4 + 4 pickup that had undergone extensive and expensive customizing and was prepared to ride anywhere onroad or off. The big truck thundered along on the Jaguar's tail. A loaded shotgun rack filled its rear window.

"That's no cop," Eric said and eased off the gas to see if the truck would pass.

The Jag slowed to a crawl. The truck did the same.

"I think he's on us," Eric said and lowered his foot on the gas. Accelerating, they sped along Dune Road toward Westhampton Beach. The truck paced them. Glancing repeatedly in the mirror as they drove, Eric felt too much like the rodent in a game of cat and mouse—the truck would fall behind whenever he accelerated but never far enough to lose sight.

When he reached the turnoff for the Quogue bridge, Eric slowed, watching the truck lights grow. He waited until the last possible second and then wrenched the Jag's wheel to the right. Screaming, the car's tires left black streaks on the pavement as the Jaguar slid sideways up onto the bridge ramp.

Shifting down, Eric slammed down on the accelerator and shot across the bridge into the quiet streets of Quogue. Braking and downshifting, he slowed enough to rip around a small traffic circle, but then, turning right, Eric accelerated again. After several fast turns and maneuvers, he slowed and once again checked the mirror. He saw only streetlights and darkness.

"Well, if it was following us," Eric said, "it's not now."

After winding through the back streets, Eric found himself back at the traffic circle and realized that he had trapped himself in a box canyon of streets. The only way out was the only way in—back over the bridge to Dune Road. But the truck was nowhere in sight.

Eric drove slowly over the bridge and turned right toward Westhampton Beach. Several cars approached from behind and passed, but still there was no evidence of pursuit. Nevertheless, he kept a close eye on the mirror.

"Getting a little paranoid, aren't we?" Maggie smiled.

"Yes, you're right," he said with a hint of sarcasm in his voice. "Perhaps I'm a tad tense, but it happens whenever somebody shoots me in the face with a spear gun—it always takes a couple of days for me to get back to mellow."

"I have a sure cure for tension." Maggie smiled, reaching over and stroking the inside of his thigh. "And when we get back to the hotel, I'll show it to you."

From the dark cab of the truck, Digger Murdock and Sonny Pike watched the white Jag roll over the bridge and turn right on Dune Road. With the truck lights off, Murdock pulled out of the bullrushes and paced along about a quarter of a mile behind. When the car turned left into the Dunes Hotel parking lot, he pulled off to the side of the road and watched Eric get out. He turned to Pike and said, "Well, whaddya think?"

Pike, resting his bandaged right hand on the truck's dashboard, answered, "You turn around and keep the truck runnin'. I'll have a look. If it's the fucker from that yacht, I'll ask him if he's got our merchandise and then I'll pay him back for takin' off my fingers."

Pulling onto a dirt path that led down to a construction site on the bay, Murdock turned the truck and stopped in a thicket of bullrushes, ten yards from Dune Road. Then he reached into the glove compartment, pulled out a cheap .22 pistol, and handed it to Pike.

Staring at the Saturday-night special, Pike looked up and snarled, "What am I supposed do with this piece of shit?"

"It works good," Murdock blurted, a little hurt by the rebuff.

"You asshole." Pike scowled and bolted from the truck.

Crossing the dunes onto the beach, he ran along the shore until he reached the Dunes Hotel and then, crouching, sprinted across the beach to the side of the hotel. Crawling along the building, Pike cautiously peered in windows and sliding glass doors, hoping to locate the recent arrivals.

He froze when he saw a streak of yellow light fall suddenly on the sand near the front of the building. Inching along under the building's windows, he crawled spiderlike to the source of the light, rose slightly to look into the suite, and saw the big man dialing the phone.

Then he eased himself up onto the deck and crawled to the bedroom's sliding glass door. Pushing gently, he found it unlocked, and the door cracked open. The room was dark except for moonlight spilling through the wide windows and sliding glass doors. Inside, the door to the bathroom was closed and lined in light. Pike guessed correctly that it was occupied by the girl.

He slid the glass doors open wider, and through the opening could hear one end of the phone conversation. As he listened, he raised Murdock's pistol and held it tightly in his left hand.

"Hello, Senator, this is Eric. I just wanted to call and thank you again for your kind assistance with the local bank." Eric paused and then answered, "No . . . no problem at all. As soon as they received your call it was taken care of . . . Right. . . . No, no luck with the yacht. . . . I'm afraid she's lost. . . . Thanks again."

Pike's thin lips pulled back in a snarl. He had the right man, and in a moment he would have either the stolen merchandise or the satisfaction of revenge or both.

Pike watched Eric hang up the phone, snap off the living-room light, and cross to the bedroom. Moving silently to the side of the sliding glass doors, Pike could see the entire room reflected in the mirror over the dresser. He waited, hoping to glean more information before confronting Eric. Then Maggie stepped from the bathroom wrapped only in a towel. Pike's eyes widened.

Eric walked into the bathroom and closed the door. Alone in the bedroom, Maggie let the towel fall, and Pike watched her lean to a drawer in the dresser. She pulled out a brand-new pair of panties, a V-neck cashmere sweater, and a pair of jeans. Standing and stretching, she paused for a moment to admire herself in the mirror. Pike did the same. Staring at her pert breasts and round little bottom, he licked his lips.

Maggie turned right and left, wondering if she should surprise Eric and wait to dress or go ahead and get ready for the walk they had planned. She decided to dress. Stepping into the white cotton panties, she unknowingly gave Sonny Pike one last intimate view. Then she wriggled into the tight-fitting jeans.

Eric, carrying a small canvas duffel, stepped from the bathroom wearing khaki shorts and a crewneck sweater. Maggie, still naked from the waist up, crossed the room and planted a quick teasing kiss on his neck. As he reached up to grab her, she squirmed out of his powerful grip and quickly pulled her sweater over her head.

"After we dig up the little treasure cat," she said.

"As soon as we dig up the little treasure cat," Eric shot back, a smoky lust burning in his eyes. He threw the empty bag's strap over his shoulder and held out his hand to Maggie.

As soon as he heard the words "treasure cat," Pike froze. He saw Eric and Maggie approach the glass doors and backed silently away—off the edge of the wooden deck. Sliding down onto the cold sand, he flattened himself and slid into the space between the deck and the ground. Stiff blades of beach grass pricked into the skin of his back, but he remained motionless, listening to the footsteps above. He emerged to stalk only after he was sure that they wouldn't turn and see him.

Eric and Maggie strolled down to the lapping waves and turned toward the Westhampton Village beach. Except for two young girls jogging in the other direction, the beach was deserted. The rising moon, growing small and white, shimmered silver moonglades across the rolling sea.

Paralleling his prey's progress along the shore, Sonny Pike remained close to the houses near the dunes, maintaining a safe distance. The little journey had lasted about ten minutes when Eric and Maggie stopped walking directly in front of the Westhampton Village beach. Pike could see Eric climb up an incline carved by tidal erosion, and then, squinting hard, watched him fall to his knees at the life-guard stand.

Digging handfuls of sand, Eric slowly uncovered the golden cat that he had buried the night before. As he stood, he brushed circles of sand from his knees and then straightened, holding the golden masterpiece up in the light of the moon. Bathed in blue, the cat's emerald eyes seemed to glow.

"It's fantastic," Maggie whispered.

"I think it's solid gold," Eric mused, bouncing the heavy treasure in his hands. Even though regally thin, it was still surprisingly heavy.

"I wonder who it belongs to," she breathed.

Eric blinked at Maggie and said, "It belongs to us."

"We can't keep it," she replied.

"Oh no?" Eric laughed. But then headlights suddenly swept the beach. Eric turned away from the glare, dropping the cat quickly into the duffel bag. Approaching fast, the lights nodded as the truck they were mounted on bounced across the sand.

"Uh oh," Eric muttered and stepped in front of Maggie.

The blinding lights passed by as the truck slowed and stopped several yards away. With the glare out of their eyes, Eric and Maggie could see the police insignia painted on the side of a four-wheel-drive Blazer.

"Hiya, Mr. Ivorsen," Patrolman Wes Brocki called out. "Give ya a ride?"

Eric turned to Maggie, shrugged, and replied, "Sure."

Maggie climbed in the front seat, Eric climbed in the back, zipping the canvas bag at the same time. In the dunes near the bathhouse, Sonny Pike blew a thick glob of spit at the ground and growled, "Fucker!"

Brocki dropped Eric and Maggie off at the Dunes Hotel, waved, and pulled away. As he drove out onto Dune Road, he grabbed the radio microphone and reported the delivery to his superior.

Once inside the suite, Eric tossed the duffel bag onto a chair, excused himself, and stepped into the shower. He emerged a few minutes later wearing a towel and nothing more. He crossed the dark room to Maggie, grabbed her, and spun her around. He wanted her more than ever, and for the first time in their relationship, he simply took her.

There were no gentle kisses this time. No handholding whispers. He pulled her sweater away, and she offered no protest. Pushing her back on the bed, he ripped off her jeans and panties. Supporting herself with her left arm straight, she lay curled naked on her side in the moonlight. Looking over her shoulder at Eric, she licked her lips lightly and watched him rip away the thick white towel.

Already breathing fast, she was all too well aware that this would be one of their last nights together. Her hunger burned with a deep hot urgency. She knew he had sensed that the moment he looked in her eyes, but she didn't expect him to take such sudden advantage of it. Now his unbridled lust excited her even more. Naked, Eric gazed down at Maggie but did not move.

For a brief moment, nothing happened. Sexual electricity tingled in the room. They both felt it. They both savored it. Then together they yielded to it and the floodgates of passion burst wide open. Maggie flew into his arms and the same instant Eric came down on her. His lips crushed against hers, and Maggie responded instantly. Bruised by the passionate impact, his lower lip split slightly, and the taste of Maggie's stabbing tongue and his salty blood excited them both.

Her silky legs spread open and curved around him. Raking her nails down his back, she clawed at his muscular buttocks and pulled him tight. Hard and huge, he slid slowly up into her. Wet and eager, she offered no resistance. Shifting to accommodate him, Maggie rocked back and locked her legs around his back. Eric filled her completely.

When he felt Maggie's warmth surround him, he pushed deep, and a stifled female animal sound escaped from the back of her throat. They fell into rhythm, and the excitement started to grow. As she thrashed and arched under him, Eric, gritting a smile of pleasure, slowly opened his eyes and became distracted by the movement of a strange shadow on the wall. The expression on his face faded from ecstasy to confusion. It took a few moments for him to realize that someone was watching from the sliding glass door.

His mind racing, Eric stared down at Maggie and frowned. She immediately sensed the change in his concentration and blinked up wide-eyed. "Hey, what's the mat—"

Clamping his hand over her mouth, Eric quickened his thrusts and pushed her toward the edge of the bed. Maggie grunted in pain with each powerful lunge. They tumbled clumsily onto the floor, with Eric trying to soften the fall with his arm. Coupled, they landed on his right elbow and Eric cried a guttural grunt of pain as the joint cracked.

Sonny Pike grinned at the animal sounds and peered into the room, but they were down behind the bed, out of his sight. Staring impatiently into the darkness, his lust quickly turned to suspicion and his fingers began working the grip of the cheap gun. Sliding the door open, he pointed the gun at the empty bed and stepped into the dark room.

"Okay, loverboy, you and me got a little business to discuss," he called out menacingly.

Eric released his hand from Maggie's mouth, held a finger to his lips, and whispered, "Get under the bed and don't come out until I tell you to."

She could tell from his tone that there was no room for debate. Then three things happened at once. Maggie rolled under the bed, Eric dove over it toward Pike, and there was a loud knock on the hotel-room door.

Eric caught Pike in the jaw with a powerful left hook, and the hard-muscled Pike reeled back, smashing into the metal frame of the open sliding glass door. The knock at the hotel-room door turned to pounding. Pike sprang back, raising the gun in his left hand. Eric threw a right, but it was an inch too short and a second too late. Pike sneered and squeezed off a round point-blank at Eric's gut.

An explosion filled the room, Maggie screamed, and the frame of the hotel-room door splintered as Ben Chestle kicked it in.

For a split second, the dark room was deathly quiet and nobody moved. Then Pike, his left hand bleeding, spun and dove out the open sliding glass door. Chestle pointed his service revolver but did not fire. Eric, white as a ghost and stark naked, flipped on the light. On the floor at his feet was Murdock's gun, grotesquely twisted and dripping blood. Blown apart by the misfire, the gun's barrel and chamber leaked a curl of blue smoke.

"Your lucky day," Chestle observed as he bolted past Eric. He ran to the broken glass door and took off in pursuit of Pike.

Maggie crawled out from under the bed, trembling. She fell into Eric's arms, and he kissed her lightly, then held her a few inches away, and whispered, "So, how was it for you?"

By the time Ben Chestle again knocked on the splintered frame of the hotel-room door, Maggie was dressed and patrolman Wes Brocki had come and gone, taking with him the twisted gun.

Eric sat on the edge of the bed while Maggie finished packing the few new clothes they had purchased. The golden cat was at the bottom of the bag.

"Did you get him?" Eric asked when Chestle walked into the room.

"Nope," the old cop replied in his gravelly voice. "But I know who it was, or at least who he's with—recognized his truck as he pulled away. Name's Digger Murdock . . . local fisherman who hauls in more cocaine than bluefish."

"Did you happen to notice his hand?"

"Can't say as I did. Imagine its pretty sore, though," Chestle answered, glancing down at the trail of blood on the floor.

"No, not his gun hand. His right hand was bandaged. Looked like he might have lost some fingers."

"That right?"

Eric nodded.

"So I'll look a little more carefully into your story."

"I'd appreciate it."

Rubbing the stubble on his chin, Ben Chestle squinted at Eric. He shook his head slightly and said, "You lead a pretty exciting life."

Eric's expression remained blank.

He walked over, laid his big hand on Eric's shoulder, and said, "Do me a favor and lead it someplace else."

CHAPTER 4

"It is not normal for a man to keep such things."

The postman's French was thick with a native Belgian accent. He didn't like delivering mail to Parat Singh's little antique shop, and he showed no reluctance in conveying this displeasure to Singh whenever possible.

Singh stared into his eyes, but said nothing in reply.

"You should buy alarm systems like everyone else," the postman declared as he passed the showcase and nine stares meet his gaze. Dropping Singh's mail on the counter, he departed without further comment.

As always, Singh ignored the advice, picked up the mail, and locked the shop's front door. Returning to his dark windowless office, he lit the candle on his desk, set out the small ceramic dish and next to it, the antique crystal vial. With the desk drawer open, Singh quickly rifled through the various pieces of correspondence and extracted only one—a bone-white envelope that bore a postmark cancellation from Abu Dhabi, United Arab Emirates.

The rest he dropped in the drawer and pushed away to be read at some more convenient time.

Hunched over the desk, he jabbed his right thumbnail under the flap of the envelope and ran his thumb along its length. Splitting open, it yielded a square engraved card, which Singh looked at through half-closed, satisfied eyes. Pushing the card back, he began absentmindedly tapping it against his fingetips as he gazed into the air. This last one, like the six that came before it, was the response to an invitation sent one month earlier. And like the others, it was an acceptance. Seven invitations—seven acceptances. Singh smiled.

He reached down, opened his black bag, and extracted his worn little book. Peeling through it, he stopped at a page with a column of names. Lifting an antique quill pen, he carefully and slowly bisected the last with a thin black line of ink. The seven crossed-off names were a list of clients, known to unethical art dealers and antiquity brokers in major cities everywhere as the world's wealthiest and most ruthless collectors of stolen art. Bound by one common interest, all seven were also known to share a relentless obsession to own Egyptian antiquities. Especially gold.

Each of the seven had received a copy of the color brochure. And each knew it to be much more than simply a photographic collection of the rarest pieces from the finest museum collections. Some of the invited had been waiting ten years for this auction, and receipt of the brochure signaled its long-awaited scheduling.

Singh squinted across the room, but his gaze remained unfocused. Once again he reviewed each and every preparatory step. Once again he reviewed each and every concluding step. Nothing was to be left to chance. The fates would play no part. Like the ancient priests, architects, and engineers buried alive with their pharaoh's mummy, no tongues would be left to wag—no trails left to follow.

To be held in Paris in exactly nine days, the auction itself would be the culmination of thirty years of planning, plotting, and work. Like most auctions, this gathering would offer the potential bidders an opportunity to inspect the offered merchandise. This was courtesy on the part of Singh and his employer. But it was a courtesy that was actually a self-serving formality—If the bidders could not determine authenticity, then there would be no auction.

Each piece would be bid individually, and increases were to be in multiples of ten thousand dollars with payment due at the auction's close. New American currency was specified. At first, Singh's employer had insisted on negotiable bonds as payment. But his silent partner, confident that the collectors would never risk being traced by the mistake of paying with marked or sequential bills, convinced him that thousand-dollar bills would be the easiest to handle and transport. Since he was the one financing the operation, there was no argument.

Singh looked down one last time at the envelope from Abu Dhabi, picked it up, and touched its edge to the candle's flame. Curling into itself as it burned, the envelope ultimately fell from his fingers a twisted black crisp. It landed squarely in the center of the ceramic dish, and Singh crushed it into powder with his fingertip. Then he spilled the tiny pile into the crystal vial that stood next to the dish.

He stood, turned, and walked to the glass-enclosed window showcase in the front of his shop. Filled with rare Egyptian statuettes, canopic jars, and temple jewelry, the glass case displayed each object on a bed of black velvet. But the eerie environment of the display case was by no means static. Tongues flicked. Heads flattened and swayed.

Singh smiled, thinking how quickly the temptation of shoppers to reach in and touch the antiquities disappeared upon discovery of any one of the nine deadly cobras that were now sunning themselves in the warm afternoon light.

Several were content to lie curled around the rare objects. One had draped itself over a small wooded ibis, and another had wrapped itself around the forehead of a gilded gesso-and-bronze bust. The rest lay stretched across the soft ebony velour, basking in the intense light. Like the long-deceased manufacturers of the treasures they guarded, the snakes considered the sun to be at the center of their existence. To the Egyptians, the worship was religious conviction. To the snakes, biological necessity.

Deadly and quick, they filled two important functions for Parat Singh—the lesser of which was dissuasion for would-be thieves. Their primary function was about to be demonstrated.

When Singh moved, all nine pairs of eyes followed. As he approached their showcase, several of the small cobras backed down, several slithered behind the ancient funerary objects in the case, and two froze, occasionally tasting the air with their shiny forked tongues. It was one of these that Singh captured with a quick swoop of a tiny leather noose. Twisting and writhing, the snake undulated in the air as Singh closed the showcase lid.

Then he returned to his desk in the back. Gripping the reptile's head, he draped its fangs over the lip of the small glass vial and pressed his thumbs into the soft glands behind its jaw. A chalky venom dripped from the cobra's pinkish-white fangs down the side of the vial, seeping down and soaking into the homemade desiccant of powdered ash. Dried and stored, the venom would retain its lethal toxicity for twenty years or more. Singh grinned, thinking that it would help to replace some of the venom powder expended on McCorkle and Peake.

Once the small cobra had been milked, Singh carried it back to the small terrarium behind his desk, lifted the cover, and dropped it in. It was in this case that Singh placed his most valued possessions, and the most valued of all guarded the others. In the corner of the long glass cage, his pet krait retracted, slowly coiling.

The small cobra hit the sand-covered floor and sensed danger instantly. Slithering to an ornate alabaster canopic jar set in the middle of the terrarium, the cobra found itself trapped, and turned. Desperate and fast, it climbed to find shelter. The priceless funerary jar, designed to hold the mummified organs of the royal dead, was Twelfth Dynasty el Lisht. It contained the dried heart of an Egyptian princess, protecting it for nearly twenty-seven hundred years. But it offered no protection to the terrified cobra. There was simply no escape.

The coiled krait licked the air once and then its tongue slid slowly back into its permanent scaly smile. With its black eyes fixed, the krait's head rose an inch. The cobra dropped and began a desperate run toward the princess's open jewelry box, but it was a futile and pathetic attempt. Singh's krait shot across the showcase with lightning speed and sank its fangs into the cobra's back. The cobra snapped over, flailing at the merciless attacker. But the deadly krait had done its damage and was gone—recoiling almost as quickly as it had struck.

Working its mouth open and shut to replace its fangs in their soft sheaths, the banded krait watched impassively as the cobra squirmed in the throes of a gruesome dance of death. Singh observed it all with a wide grin stretched across his face.

The cobra was dead within three minutes and the krait slithering into position to begin feeding within four. Singh chuckled softly as his pet's mouth yawned open, its jaw unhinged, and it began ingesting the cobra's corpse. Slowly gagging forward, the krait worked itself around the cobra's lifeless head. Inching on in slow gulping spasms, it engorged itself until the cobra's head bulged in its gullet.

After several minutes, the tip of the cobra's tail, protruding like a thick grotesque tongue, slid slowly into the krait's mouth. Sated and full, the deadly snake turned to Singh and met his smiling stare.

"You are satisfied, Sheeli?" he whispered. "It is always worth the wait, yes?"

Singh went back and carefully cleared the desk, packing away all of the papers. Then he lifted the phone from its cradle and placed a call to Objets d'Art Egyptien, New York. It rang four times before it was answered not by a tape machine but by Singh's employer.

"Yes?"

"Can you talk?" Singh asked softly.

"Just briefly."

"Shall I call back?"

"No, go ahead."

"You have received my message?" Singh inquired.

"Yes. What happened?"

"The local importers withheld delivery on the necklace you sent."

"They wished to impose a surcharge?"

"Ten thousand dollars," Singh replied.

"They are foolish men. It is worth thirty times that."

"Is is recovered."

"And the importers?"

"I have terminated their employ."

"Very good."

"I will now need assistance in the moving," Singh said.

"Fascione's man will be aboard the *Whimbrel* when it docks in Le Havre. He is strong. But we have other problems."

"Explain, please," Singh requested.

"In the last transfer . . . an accident. One of the pieces has been lost."

Singh digested this information for a minute, then asked, "Lost or stolen?"

"Lost."

"Which piece?" he asked.

"The cat, of all things . . . the cat."

"This is not good," Singh responded.

The comment was reflexive and needed no response. A brief silence followed, and it was Singh who broke it. "It could be duplicated again," he said.

"A most dangerous suggestion."

"The mold still exists?" Singh asked.

"Yes, but I feel it is too dangerous. What would happen if it were discovered? It could not be subjected to inspection."

"That can be arranged," Singh promised. "That one piece will be unveiled only at bidding. Perhaps convinced of the authenticity of every other piece, no one will question the cat."

Singh's employer considered this all for a moment and then made a decision. "No. We cannot offer a counterfeit. It is simply too dangerous."

"Very well," Singh acquiesced.

"The invitations . . ."

"All have accepted."

"Good . . . very good!"

"The exporter there . . . has been properly rewarded?" Singh inquired.

"Tomorrow at sea."

"And the others?" Singh asked.

"You should handle the local manufacturers when you arrive here. That leaves only Mr. Pike and the rest of Fascione's people. And they'll all be safe aboard the trawler *Whimbrel* when it arrives in Le Havre at the end of the week. I want loose ends cleaned up here first."

"I will be there tomorrow morning. My flight leaves in an hour," said Singh. "Is there anything I should bring?"

"I needn't mention that you should bring your black case."

"That is correct," Singh said softly. "You need not mention it."

CHAPTER 5

"C'mon, Pops . . . move it!" the dock tender yelled, and an old man in a spotless white Nova pulled his car slowly onto the ferry ramp. Bumping up onto the ferry's main deck, the meticulously cared-for car glided across the parking bay until the driver stopped a foot short of the ferry's dented steel bulkheading. Eric followed without being told to do so. He pulled in tight behind the little white Nova and killed the Jaguar's engine.

A few minutes later, a young attendant wedged chocks under the sports car's wheels, took a two-passenger ticket from Eric, and went about her business.

Eric and Maggie got out and climbed a spiral staircase to the forward deck of the ferry. At precisely 7:30, the huge motor vessel thundered out of Orient harbor for the one-hour cruise to New London.

Leaning on the foredeck guard railing with containers of hot coffee steaming in their hands, Eric and Maggie watched morning sunlight sparkling on the waters of Long Island Sound.

"We should probably stop and get something to take," she declared.

"Like what?"

"Something for lunch," Maggie answered.

"If you think so," Eric agreed.

"I feel sorta sorry for her." Maggie sighed. "Lady Barbara, I mean."

"You do, huh? Why?"

"You said she was devoted to Charles, and now that he's gone all she has is their yacht. What's she going to do? Where's she going to live?"

Eric frowned, turned to Maggie, and replied, "Well, I know she's scraped enough together to rent a cottage for the summer . . . at least until we were to deliver the yacht. Then she was going to move aboard. I guess she'll have to make other arrangements."

"That's the point," Maggie insisted. "We lost her yacht, and what if she can't find someplace to live? Did your uncle leave her any money?"

"No," Eric admitted. "Just the yacht."

"The poor thing . . . what is she going to do?"

"Okay." Eric nodded sternly. "I'll see if she needs a few bucks to tide her over."

Ben Chestle wandered along the marina fishing docks, past racks of drying net, to Digger Murdock's slip, and found that it was still empty. It came as no surprise, of course. The dock was the first place Chestle had looked the night before, so this visit was more reconnaissance than raid. While he didn't expect to find the *Sea Puss* or its owner, he did hope to dig up some background on both.

Morning activity on the docks was as usual—charter boats were already out to sea, the night's catch was being unloaded, and daily equipment repair was well under way. Hovering just feet above an old man cleaning fish, squawking seagulls dropped to the ground, fought for discarded entrails, and then flew away to feast on the spoils. A pungent blend of fish guts, brine, and diesel fuel hung heavy in the still morning air.

Two dockhands, hauling boxes of bluefish from the deck

of the nearest boat to a truck on the dock, went about their work without acknowledging the presence of the easily recognizable chief of police. Dressed in a blue windbreaker, gray sweatshirt, and chinos, Chestle looked more like a weekend fisherman than a cop. Nevertheless, everyone on the docks knew he was and reacted accordingly.

He wandered over to the empty slip and gazed down at a spreading rainbow of fuel slick floating on the flat water between two thick pilings. The bow lines of the *Sea Puss* dangled limp in the brackish green soup, drooping down from ringbolts that had been hammered through the seagull-stained piling poles.

He strolled to the nearby boat, watched the two workers for a minute, then asked, "You guys work here all the time?"

"Yep," the taller of the two answered without looking up.

"You know Digger Murdock?"

"Yep."

"Know where he is?"

"Nope."

"Seen him lately?"

"Nope."

Chestle nodded, walked over to the truck that they had loaded, and said, "This your truck?"

"Yep."

"Needs inspectin'."

The tall dockhand straightened up and answered, "Yeah, I meant to get to that—"

"Too late," Chestle cut him off. "You run a big risk takin' this rig out on the road. Why, a cop could stop you, impound the truck, and leave it sittin' out in the hot sun all day while he runs the ID number through those slow DMV computers. Rotten fish are hard to sell."

"Look," the man said. "Murdock and his boys hauled outta here last night around eight. We don't know why and don't much care."

"Okay. Fair enough." Chestle smiled. "Anything un-usual going on around the docks the last few days?"

The tall man lowered his head, shooting a sideways glance at his partner. The shorter man piped up, "Look, we don't get no healthier on these docks stickin' our noses in other people's business. We don't ask questions . . . we catch fish."

Chestle's friendly smile disappeared, and he glared at the short man. With his jaw muscles tightening, he leaned forward as if he were about to come aboard swinging. It was a ploy that had worked with others, and it worked now. The small man took a half-step back.

"Okay, look," the other blurted. "Only thing unusual around here is that Murdock's customized his rigging."

"Yeah, so?"

"I mean, heavy-duty stuff . . . too heavy for fishin'. Like he was plannin' to haul somethin' pretty heavy . . . maybe salvage. Had some big piece of equipment under tarp on the stern of his rig."

"What kind of equipment?"

"Don't know. We don't ask what other people catch."

Squinting up into the sun, Chestle asked, "What kind of rigging?"

"Industrial winches—reinforced gallows hoist—and he ain't brought in a box of fish in three weeks."

"He ever use diving equipment?"

The two men looked again at each other before the short man answered, "They all dive. The whole crew."

"How many?"

"Sometimes three . . . sometimes four."

"You know 'em?"

"Nope. Not one. All new faces on the dock a coupla weeks ago."

"They with him now?"

"One is. Lately this one guy is always with him."

Chestle nodded and then, a little embarrassed, asked, "You, uh, seen anything of a black submarine?"

Laughing, both men shook their heads.

"Okay, thanks for the help," Chestle said. When the laughing lasted a little too long, he turned and added, "Be sure an' get that truck inspected."

The laughter stopped.

The short voyage to New London was pleasant. The sun was strong, the breeze salty, and the seas calm. The ferry completed the trip in just under an hour and fifteen minutes. The hour drive to Newport proved to be uneventful. Nevertheless, Eric kept a constant watch in the rearview mirror. He saw nothing unusual and decided that there was no reason to believe that they were still being followed.

"I want to stop and call to get directions to the cottage," he announced as they turned onto Newport's America's Cup Avenue. Winding through street after street of beautifully restored colonial homes, buildings, and shops, they finally found a parking place near Bannister's Wharf, and Eric headed off for a phone. Maggie found a gourmet delicatessen and ordered cold meats, cheeses, and fruit.

Sliding into the Jaguar next to Eric, she held up the brown bag of groceries and declared, "This should do it. I bought enough ham to last a few days."

Smiling, Eric turned his head away and checked oncoming traffic before pulling onto the busy street. Five minutes later, he turned onto Ocean Avenue, and they rolled past sprawling seaside estates protected from view by high stone walls, iron fences, and tall shrubs. Halfway down the street, Eric turned into an opening between two beautifully sculpted privet hedges.

Whitewashed gate pillars stood on the sides of the drive, ornate gas lamps perched on top of each. A small brass plate, imbedded in the brick of the pillar on the right, bore the name of the estate, Windswept. A gray stone castle sat at the end of the drive, with the Atlantic shimmering behind.

The Jaguar's tires crunched across the crushed-stone

path that wound across the meticulously manicured grounds to the mansion's front steps.

Like so many of Newport's "summer cottages," Windswept was at the same time ostentatious and breathtaking. Situated high on a bluff overlooking the ocean, the twenty-five-room stone mansion enjoyed a sweeping panoramic view of shoreline, sea, and sky.

"What's this?" Maggie said as Eric braked to a stop.

"Lady Barbara's cottage," he answered, fighting back a smile.

Openmouthed, Maggie climbed out of the car and gazed up at the carved-stone facade. Eric walked casually up the marble steps and lifted the oak door's heavy brass knocker and tapped twice. A young French girl answered the door and said, *"Bonjour, Monsieur.* I will tell Mademoiselle you are here."

"Merci," he replied, and then turned to Maggie and asked, "Coming?"

She followed him into a vast center hall that was lined with polished walnut wainscoting, stained-glass windows, and priceless antiques. At a loss for words, Maggie simply did a slow pirouette, gazing at the decor. She froze when she saw the vision at the top of the stairs.

Lady Barbara Falcounbridge, a stunningly beautiful woman with golden hair and brown eyes, was dressed in a white summer dress that did nothing to hide her exquisite body. She swept down the stairs right into Eric's arms. Maggie, clutching the brown paper bag, turned beet-red.

"Eric, my love," Lady Barbara whispered in an elegant English accent as she hugged him tightly. "How good it is to see you."

Maggie, sensing more than a casual relationship, felt a sudden stabbing pang of jealousy. Lady Barbara stepped back, still gazing into Eric's eyes.

"I'd like you to meet Maggie McCabe," Eric said, and more slowly than he should have, released Lady Barbara's delicate shoulders.

She turned, taking Maggie's hand between her own, smiled warmly, and said, "Eric's told me all about you, and I must admit that I'm more than a little jealous."

Flustered, Maggie stammered, "Yes, well, I am most pleased to meet your acquaint . . . to meet you."

Lady Barbara smiled even more deeply, turned, and said, "Excuse me for one minute—Claude is preparing brunch. I'll tell him that you're here."

With that, she turned and disappeared into an arched doorway below the stone stairs.

Furious, Maggie turned to Eric and planted the point of her shoe in his ankle.

Wincing, Eric leaned down and whispered, "Do you think I should slip her a twenty as Claude serves lunch or just leave it on the guestroom fireplace mantel?"

"You think that's funny?" she seethed. "How could you do this to me?"

"Do what?" he asked innocently. "I think it's a nice gesture on your part."

"I feel like a fool—standing here holding a bag of meat."

"What ever made you think Lady Barbara was some doddering old lady with no money?" He grinned.

"You said your Uncle Charles lived right on the edge all the time."

"Uncle Charles, yes. But Lady Barbara's family has more money than God. Probably the only reason she didn't buy this museum is that it's too much like the family castle in Scotland . . . only smaller."

"And just how long did she live with dear old Uncle Charles?" Maggie demanded.

"About twenty years."

"So how old was she when they met—nine?"

"She was twenty at the time . . . that makes her forty now. Looks pretty good, doesn't she?"

"I hope to look that good when I'm thirty!"

"I'm sure you will," Eric replied with a wink.

"And what should I do with this?" Maggie said through

clenched teeth, holding up the brown paper bag. When she heard Lady Barbara returning, Maggie snapped the sack of groceries around and held it behind her back. Wiping his hands on his apron, a white-haired gentleman followed Lady Barbara and lit up when he saw Eric.

"Ah, Eric, it is wonderful to see you," he said in a French accent.

"Claude Bocuse, I'd like you to meet Miss Maggie McCabe."

"A pleasure, mademoiselle," he said, bowing slightly.

Reaching down behind Maggie, Eric pulled the bag from her hands and explained, "I stopped in town to purchase a midnight snack. Would you be so kind?" He handed the groceries to Claude, who nodded and carried them away to the kitchen.

Lady Barbara curled her arm in Eric's and, pulling him toward the patio doors, said, "Now come with me and tell me all about how you managed to sink my boat."

Eric shot a glance back at Maggie and frowned. He hadn't mentioned the loss of the yacht when he'd called from town for directions, and he couldn't figure out how Lady Barbara could know.

Maggie glared back at him and shrugged. Eric offered her his left arm, but Maggie was truly angry with him and not at all comfortable in the presence of the ravishing Lady Barbara. She chose to follow as they strolled out into the flower garden. Beds of mums formed formal patterns along a winding path of brick that widened into a huge patio. Walled in on two sides by six-foot trellises covered with thick lush ivy, the patio enjoyed an uninterrupted view of the sea, but remained unaffected by even strong breezes. A glass table with a setting for three was in the middle of the brick. Cushioned white wicker chairs completed the elegant setting, and Maggie felt as if she were on a movie set.

As Claude poured five glasses of champagne, the young girl who had met Eric at the door set a bouquet of freshly picked wild roses in the middle of the table.

"To old friends and new loves," Lady Barbara said, lifting her long-stemmed champagne glass to Eric and then Maggie. Maggie smiled for the first time, but it was forced. Claude joined in the toast but not in the meal. Instead he cooked and the young girl, Petra, served.

Eric recounted the mysterious midnight encounter over strawberry crêpes and cheese soufflé. As they ate, he described the bizarre submarine and its long mechanical arms. Maggie remained mostly silent and seemed not to enjoy either the excellent Fumé-Blanc wine or the fine food. Eric finished the story by reaching into the duffel bag and producing the golden cat. Plopped in the middle of the table, the regal feline gleamed brilliantly in the strong midday sun, its emerald eyes bright and sparkling.

Petra stood transfixed by its beauty. Lady Barbara too was impressed. Claude, in the process of preparing cappuccino chocolat, simply looked once and declared, "I am no expert, of course, but this is most definitely Egyptian in origin. Fourth or fifth century B.C., perhaps."

"That's what I thought," Eric responded.

"It looks like something out of King Tut's tomb," Maggie said and immediately felt foolish for making the comment.

Because it was the first time Maggie had joined the conversation, her statement received undivided attention, and that made Maggie even more self-conscious.

"Oh, have you seen the Tut exhibit?" Lady Barbara asked, trying to break the ice with Maggie.

"No," Maggie admitted and felt even more foolish.

Claude broke the discomforting silence that followed. "Your uncle and I knew a man at the Louvre in Paris, Jean Paul LeBrun, on whom we relied to authenticate several objects that came into our possession. I mention this because I've just read in the *Times* that he is in New York at the Metropolitan—director or curator of something or other."

"Perhaps if you were to show the cat to him . . ." Lady Barbara suggested.

"Not show," Claude warned. "Describe."

"I understand," Eric nodded.

"If I can locate him, I will ask that he meet with you," Claude offered, and upon returning to the kitchen, he began rifling through a stack of *New York Times* issues bundled for the trash until he found the edition he was looking for. After carefully cutting out the column, he prepared desserts of poached pears, toasted almonds, and Stilton beignets.

When he returned to the patio, he served the three delicacies and then showed the clipping to Eric. The article described a tour of funerary objects on loan from the London Museum. The show was scheduled to be in New York for two years at the Metropolitan, and the opening was to coincide with a lecture series conducted by Sir Thatcher Smythe. Jean Paul LeBrun was mentioned as having recently been appointed Assistant Curator of Egyptian Antiquities and being the man responsible for the show.

"This LeBrun," Eric asked after scanning the article, "is a friend?"

"Acquaintance," Claude corrected. "We never really got to know him. We asked his opinion on a piece that Charles had acquired. He was considered the leading expert on the subject. I cannot honestly say that a friendship developed, but I must say that we respected his opinion and found him to be an honest and serious man."

"If it can be arranged, I would like very much to speak to Mr. LeBrun," Eric announced.

Claude nodded and went right to the phone. Eric turned to Lady Barbara and finally asked the question that had been bothering him since they'd arrived. "How did you know that the yacht was lost?"

"A Constable Chestle rang me up this morning."

"Of course . . . the thorough chief of police," Eric said.

"He was somewhat puzzled by your ability to acquire

new clothes, a car, and oceanfront accommodations within such a short period. I assume that you sought and received assistance from the retired Senator whose law firm represented Charles in his litigation against the government of Bermuda."

Eric nodded and sipped from his cup of cappuccino.

"Your uncle sued Bermuda?" Maggie asked.

"Rather successfully," Eric answered. "Had to do with salvage rights on a wreck we explored."

"He sued to keep sunken treasure?"

"Well, sort of. Uncle Charles made several dives on a wreck he discovered. I was fifteen at the time. My job, as I recall, was to keep watch topside in the *Lady Barbara*. Immediately after the third dive, he called his old friend in New York, Senator Lester Walters, and with the aid of Walter's old law firm, instituted a widely publicized suit that, if successful, would've allowed Uncle Charles to keep all the gold and half the gems, but would have mandated that he return all the recovered art and sculpture."

"It must have been quite a find," Maggie commented.

Claude, setting out dishes of mint candies, chuckled and Lady Barbara smiled as Eric explained, "In a way. The government prepared an equally impressive case in an attempt to keep the traditional fifty-fifty split on everything."

"But Uncle Charles won his case?"

"Not quite. Halfway through the case, he became so exasperated that he sold his salvage rights to a group of Argentinian speculators and paid off the legal fees, and we all left for Capri."

"He didn't get any of the gold?" Maggie asked.

"In a way he did. He sold his rights for one hundred and fifty thousand dollars. The legal fees were fifty thousand, so he netted a clean one hundred thousand."

"But how much gold did the Argentinians bring up?"

"None."

"No gold?"

"There was no gold, there were no gems, and the only art to be found was in the audacity of Uncle Charles's presentation. When pressed, he simply pointed out that he had never claimed there had been any treasure. A check of the court records proved that to be true."

"The whole thing was a con?" Maggie asked.

"I miss him so," Lady Barbara sighed.

"FBI on five seven," Pete Halsey called into the chief's office.

"Chestle here," Ben Chestle grumbled, grabbing up the phone.

"This is Special Agent MacDowell," the man on the phone replied, "I was the agent who authorized the Ivorsen data that was sent. You called again?"

"Yeah. I was wondering if you could give me a little more background. Are you familiar with this guy?"

"Just what's in his file," MacDowell answered.

"What is this Institute for Advanced Study?"

"It's a private think tank in Princeton."

"And what exactly is Ivorsen's connection?"

"He's got a fellowship there just as his father did. But now he's reportedly working on a project that involves computer forecasting—something his old man pioneered back in the fifties. According to a National Security Agency archives file, Ivorsen's father and a whole cast of heavyweights, including Albert Einstein, worked on a secret program called the Viking Cipher. Our guess is that Eric Ivorsen is in the process of resurrecting it."

"Your guess?" Chestle scoffed.

"Private funding, private institution, private citizen . . ."

"Yeah, yeah, I gotcha," Chestle said. "The thing that's bothering me is his background. He's awfully young to have found his way into so many files, unless of course he's dirty."

"No, no," MacDowell was emphatic. "His recent troubles were a result of his father's work. Apparently he was to receive notes that his old man had saved for him. Someone else wanted them, took a shot, and missed. We don't know for sure, but we believe Ivorsen did indeed get those notes and plans to work with them at the Institute."

Chestle listened closely and then related Eric and Maggie's submarine story.

After a moment of silence, MacDowell asked, "You believe him?"

"I didn't until he was attacked by a local drug runner, and now I'm wondering if there's any possibility that he was involved in a drug deal that went sour."

"Like I said, we don't show any illegal activity in his background. Send up a report on this submarine thing, though. The list of Ivorsen's potential enemies could easily include people with those kinds of resources."

"You got it. Thanks for the help," Chestle replied and then dropped the receiver on its cradle. Stretching his legs up on the edge of his desk, he sat back and wondered to himself why a punk like Digger Murdock would want to kill Eric Ivorsen.

Only two reasons, he told himself—revenge or money.

Claude Bocuse and Petra finished clearing the patio table and went to work straightening the kitchen.

"Pardon, Papa, s'il vous plaît—"

"Uh, uh, uh," he scolded, "You are here to learn English—so you will speak English."

"I'm sorry, Papa," she said.

"Now what is it you want to know?"

"How long have you known Monsieur Ivorsen? He is very good-looking."

"I have been preparing his meals since he was your age. His parents were killed in a climbing accident, so he came to live with his uncle and Mademoiselle Falcounbridge."

"Why did you live with them, Papa?"

Claude turned to his small granddaughter, petted her

hair, and replied, "Because I loved them ... and they loved me."

"Like a family?"

"*Oui*, just like family."

"Why did Monsieur Ivorsen's uncle die? Was he sick?"

"He was murdered. These things are not for little girls to wonder about. Go out and play. Bring back fresh flowers for the kitchen."

While Petra gathered flowers, Claude began tracking down Jean Paul LeBrun by first calling the Metropolitan Museum. It took several phone calls but he reached him at last. LeBrun agreed to meet with Eric the next day.

Petra pranced across the green lawn, pausing to watch a butterfly. When she reached the wildflower gardens, she kneeled to pluck fresh blossoms, but froze when she found herself staring at a pair of shoes. She looked up slowly into the pale-pink face of a very old man. Gouged deep with wrinkles and spotted by age, his face crinkled when he put on a smile. Dressed in baggy brown trousers, a garish green plaid sports coat, and a wrinkled white shirt buttoned to the top collar but with no tie, he did not look like any of the men who came to visit Lady Barbara. Petra frowned.

The old man looked down, winked, and said, "Hiya, little girl. Whatcha pickin'?"

"*Pardon?*" she squeaked.

"Never mind, kid. Tell me, do you know who those people are?" He pointed a trembling finger across the estate at Eric and Maggie walking toward the bluffs.

"*Oui.* Monsieur Ivorsen and Mademoiselle McCabe."

"That's what I thought. They stayin' here?"

"They stay only tonight."

"Right. Hey, do me a favor, will you? If I give you this, don't mention I asked you anything, awright?" He held out a shiny new penny in his palsied right hand.

Unsure of herself and becoming frightened, Petra simply

nodded and then ran back to the house without accepting the prize.

The old man walked from the hedgerow, fished in his pocket for keys, and then unlocked the door of his spotless white Nova.

CHAPTER 6

"C'mon, c'mon," Sonny Pike growled at the empty sea.

Standing on the prow of the *Sea Puss* with his bandaged hands folded, he swayed slowly with the rhythm of the waves.

The heavily rigged fishing boat rose and fell on the long swells, her diesels bubbling at idle speed. Swinging in the breeze, four loosened cables drooping from the hoists smacked against rusted supports, filling the air with constant metallic tapping.

Thirty miles off Montauk, Digger Murdock was holding her position steady. There was only one other vessel in sight, and it sat on the horizon at least eight miles away. It did not seem to be coming directly closer but it also did not seem to be pulling away.

Worried that the Coast Guard would be searching for Murdock's boat, Pike was relieved when the distant craft got within binocular range, close enough to categorize. It looked to be nothing more than a big pleasure cruiser. An Egg Harbor, he guessed from her lines.

In an ugly mood since the night before, when he and Murdock had fled the marina, Pike hadn't spoken to Murdock all day except to berate him for owning a worthless gun, and occasionally to bark some command.

Scowling down at the brown-stained gauze wad that he wore like a boxing glove on his right hand, Pike suddenly turned and yelled, "Anything on that goddam receiver?"

"Nope," Murdock called back from the wheelhouse.

"Shit," Pike spat.

He dropped his right hand and stared down at his left. Also wrapped in bandaging, it was painfully sore but whole. The prospect of submerging the open wounds in salt water made Pike even crankier.

An aircraft appeared from the western horizon, and Pike snapped to. "What the fuck is that?" he growled at Murdock.

Scanning with Pike's binoculars, Murdock yelled back, "Small plane . . . no problem."

Distrusting, Pike glared at it until it grew small and disappeared.

Then the small Pearce-Simpson transceiver in the wheelhouse began to beep. Pike scrambled to the stern and pulled away the tattered tarp covering the large packing crate on the deck. The size of a coffin, the wooden box had been sprayed with a blueish plastic coating that made it waterproof but difficult to handle when wet.

Pike climbed to the rigging, checked the position of the winch controls on the gallows hoist, and then, working as fast as he could with mounds of gauze in the way, began attaching the hoist cable snap shackles to ringbolts on the corners of the crate. Once the lines were secure, Pike checked each with a hard yank, wincing whenever he put too much pressure on his hands.

Murdock watched from the wheelhouse, waiting for a command. But none came. Pike seemed to want to run the show alone.

He jammed back a lever on the winch and the heavy mechanism began to whir. The stainless-steel cables came taut and the box began to rise. Creaking and groaning as they took the load, the hoist's supports began to shiver. When the box swayed free in the air, Pike pushed the lever into lock, the winch ground to a halt, and the cargo stopped rising. Then he turned and stared out at the open sea. Anticipating what would come next, a cruel smile came to his lips.

This rendezvous had been hastily arranged by radio when he and Murdock reached the *Sea Puss* the night before. Informing the *Whimbrel* that local authorities were close behind, they put out to sea and hid all night in a fleet of fishing boats working Cox's Ledge off Montauk. At eleven, they broke from the pack and headed at full speed to the coordinates agreed upon. Once there, they switched on undersea transponders and began the tedious and dangerous wait. The receiver, now beeping loudly in the wheelhouse, signaled that the wait was finally over.

Pike's fears of discovery vanished when the sun caught a glint in the waves about a thousand yards away. The periscope rose and the submarine began closing fast. The familiar hiss made Pike smile. Lowering the gallows boom, he swung the crated treasure over the stern.

Inside the ebony submarine, two of the three-man crew rubbed spit and seawater onto the glass of their face masks, preparing to enter the sub's small underwater hatch.

When it was a hundred yards away, the sub's dented black bow broke surface and the vessel slowed in the waves. Powering slowly closer to the *Sea Puss*, it blew ballast and started to rise. Its powerful hydraulic arms extended from its sides and rotated down into the water. Then, as the pincered talons rose up out of the waves, the explorer sub took on the appearance of a giant sea creature begging for food.

Powering closer, it drifted to a stop, its arms extended below the swaying crate and the pincered tips opened.

"Comin' down," Pike yelled.

Watching the whole operation with mild interest, Digger Murdock began spending the twenty-five grand he was about to receive. He would buy a shipment of coke wholesale, he decided, cut it a little, and sell it in Southampton through the winter. Small market, he told himself, but a hungry one. Turn a 500 percent profit, he figured.

Sinking into the mechanical creature's grip, the crate came to a rest cradled in the hydraulic arms. The sinister limbs closed, locking themselves around the precious cargo.

Inside the sub, the two divers slipped down the hatch into the sea, surfaced immediately, and went right to work unhooking the cables. As soon as they finished, they tumbled over, submerged, and did not reappear. Digger Murdock was slightly confused by this. He thought that they were supposed to accompany him. He spun around to ask Pike, but Pike was at the *Sea Puss*'s engine-compartment hatch for some reason.

"Whaddya doin'?" Murdock demanded.

"I thought I heard her grind," Pike lied. "Don't worry . . . she's okay. Just a wrench clanging against the tanks."

When he stood, Pike walked to the transom, stepped up, and dropped overboard himself, swimming for the sub.

"Hey, what's going on?" Murdock yelled. "What about my final payment?"

Pike turned in the water and yelled back, "Just keep your pants on. Stay onboard. I have to get it from the explorer." When he reached the black hull, he sucked a deep breath and tumbled into a dive.

Salt water, soaking into the gauze, washed into his wounds, and Pike stifled a cry. Grimacing in pain as he swam deeper, he told himself that it would all be worth it. Blinking in the green water, he looked up and saw the open hatchway gleaming like a silver disc in the black underbelly of the sub. Kicking forward, he rose to it and broke surface inside the cramped vessel.

Pulling Pike aboard, the other two men dropped the hatch cover and locked it down.

"Let's get outta here," Pike gasped, his long wet hair dripping down his face.

The man at the sub's helm eased her into reverse, and the ebony vessel slid back from the *Sea Puss*.

Murdock, waiting patiently on the stern of his boat, realized what was happening and screamed, "Hey, hold it, you sonofabitch! Where's my money?"

Backing steadily away and bubbling furiously as it took on ballast, the ebony sub began to sink slowly into the sea. The black arms gripping the blue crate disappeared beneath a swell of green water. Then the sub's gray periscope dropped from sight as well.

"You lying bastards!" Murdock screamed.

He turned, gunned the *Sea Puss*'s engine, and started to make a last-ditch run to damage the sub. But it was too late . . . the sub and her cargo had sounded.

Below, Pike looked at the Rolex diving watch on his wrist, watched the sweep hand click down to ten seconds.

On the deck of the *Sea Puss*, an infuriated Digger Murdock was on the verge of tears. He paced back and forth desperately trying to figure out what to do. He pounded his fist against the cabin door and looked again at the empty sea.

The sweep hand clicked down to five seconds.

"You sonsofbitches!" Murdock screamed out.

Three seconds.

"I'll never work for you again!"

Two.

"I'm gonna go to the police!"

One.

Digger Murdock was standing above the engine compartment when the limpet mine detonated. He felt the explosion but never heard it—the tympanic membrane of his eardrums imploded with the blast. He spun like a toy in the air above his boat; his last vision was a wall of orange flame that enveloped and consumed him almost instantly.

Placed strategically on the tanks, the device sprayed diesel fuel and ignited it at the same time. Murdock's seared body smashed back down and snagged in the cables of the gallows hoist. The inferno raged, and within minutes, the *Sea Puss*'s cabin and deck were engulfed in flames that billowed black smoke into the clear afternoon sky.

In the belly of the sub, the crew felt a mild jolt and then Sonny Pike grabbed the periscope. As the watery image cleared, he watched through the sub's gray eye as the *Sea Puss* took on water. Digger Murdock's charred corpse, suspended in the flames above the blazing tanks, twisted slowly as it burned.

"Home to mother," Pike commanded with a smile.

Tracking a transponder beacon, the battered black exploration sub slid eastward on a direct course to the source of the signal, the salvage trawler *Whimbrel*. Of all the salvage operators in the world, the man whose organization owned the *Whimbrel*, Anil Fascione, was by far the most mercenary.

Although the innocent-looking trawler most often carried highly profitable contraband—everything from guns to heroin—it and its crew were also available for salvage work anywhere at any time. For the right money. Or the right cut. In this case the cut was fifty-fifty.

Commissioned by Parat Singh in Le Havre, the trawler *Whimbrel*, with her black exploration sub tucked safely on deck, would soon be en route to home port with a manifest complete except for one item of merchandise . . . the Sacred Cat of Bastet.

CHAPTER 7

"I have spoken with Monsieur LeBrun and he's agreed to meet with you tomorrow at the Metropolitan," Claude reported, proud to have so quickly arranged the meeting.

"That's terrific," Eric replied. "Did he sound as though he recognized the statuette?"

"He said it sounds like one they have on display. He will show it to you."

"Thank you, Claude," Eric replied and was about to turn to join Maggie near the bluff.

"One moment, Eric," Claude whispered. "I want you to be careful in this matter. If this cat is a true antiquity, then you may have stumbled upon a black-market trade . . . and this is an aspect of antiquity brokerage that attracts all sorts. LeBrun will have no knowlege of such things. We found him to be a very, very serious man. Your uncle and I had only one occasion to deal with him. A gambling debt owed Charles was settled with an ornate faience griffin, purportedly Egyptian from the second century A.D. We had no way to determine its value, and we were told to visit LeBrun at the Louvre. He authenticated it and the debt was considered paid. He had no idea how we came to possess such a treasure and asked if we planned to give it to the museum's collection."

"And did you?"

Claude replied with a smile tugging at the corners of his mouth. "You remember that brothel in Pigalle that your uncle owned until he gave it to the girls as a token of appreciation?"

"That was before my time," Eric reminded him.

"*Oui,* of course. Anyway, he traded the griffin for the business and then gave a party that lasted several weeks. When we left for the South Seas, Charles turned the business over to the girls who ran it . . . with the understanding that he could return anytime to live out his retirement in the best room in the house."

"Monsieur LeBrun was never told, obviously."

"Never. It is wise not to tell serious people too much . . . it is best to keep a few secrets in such matters."

"Yes, you've taught me that before." Eric nodded and took the advice to heart, because he knew that Claude Bocuse would pass along a warning only if he felt it to be absolutely necessary.

"Keep it in mind, please. He may be of help, he may be of no help, but he may also inadvertently be introducing you to a world where there are no set rules and integrity is a commodity, not a virtue. The code of ethics is rewritten with every new acquisition."

Eric nodded, and then joined Maggie, taking her hand. Together they started down a winding little path that led down to the shore. He had his smile back, and she wondered if the change in attitude was due to the pleasant surroundings or rather to being reunited with the all too attractive Lady Barbara.

"You seem in better spirits," Maggie said, staring down at the rocky path.

"Well, it's a relief to have explained the loss of the yacht, and I like the idea of talking to this Jean Paul LeBrun."

"Seeing old friends didn't hurt either," she replied without looking up.

"You're right," Eric answered, missing her jealous tone.

Deciding not to press the issue, Maggie asked, "What's Claude's story?"

"Claude Bocuse . . . was something of a mystery to my parents and me. He has been with my uncle for as long as I can remember . . . long before Charles met Lady Barbara. When I was a child and they'd come to visit, I would always ask how they had become friends. Uncle Charles would always answer the question, and the answer would vary depending on how much brandy had been consumed. Never the same twice, the stories were always funny . . . but never true. One year my mother and Claude were preparing dinner in the kitchen of our house in Princeton. She asked, he told her, and then she told us. The subject was never discussed again."

"Sounds mysterious," Maggie commented.

"Not so mysterious as it is painful. . . . They met in Salerno in 1941. Claude is Jewish. He was one of Paris's rising young chefs whose career ended when the Nazi's goose-stepped down the Champs Élysées. The Gestapo was evil but not stupid. They allowed Claude to live because he had a talent they could not duplicate. He was taken to Italy to cook for a high-ranking SS officer who'd developed a taste for *haute cuisine*. The officer had commandeered a brand-new sailing yacht that had been built in America for an Italian industrialist, and was using it as a private floating seaside retreat. He had christened it *Herrenklub*. Claude and his family were shipped off to serve.

"Upon arrival, Claude's pretty young wife was promptly raped by the officer and his three Lieutenants. When it became apparent that was to be a regular thing, she committed suicide, leaving behind a heartbroken husband and their only child, a two-year-old girl. Female and Jewish were not healthy things to be in Nazi territory, 1941. Claude went numbly into servitude, living only for the purpose of protecting his daughter.

"One night some weeks later in a dockside café, the SS

officer is celebrating the recent success of Rommel's Africa campaign, drinking with his men, and taking on all comers in a spirited game of backgammon. Uncle Charles, passing through on one of his adventures, challenged. The stakes were high and Uncle Charles lost almost four thousand dollars. But Claude Bocuse came to him after the game and offered to steal the money back if he would take the little girl to safety. That too was suicide, but Uncle Charles claimed to have a better idea.

"The next night, he demanded a chance to win back his money. The SS officer was happy to oblige. The stakes were unlimited. Charles Ivorsen, like his brother Kyler, my father, was very good with numbers. The games proceeded at an unremarkable rate until Uncle Charles saw his chance. Then the doubling cube rolled almost as fast as the dice. When he reached fifty thousand dollars that the SS officer could not match, he suggested the yacht, the chef, and the little girl. The dice rolled and Uncle Charles won. The three drunk lieutenants found this all too amusing and began raucously berating their superior.

"Apparently the SS officer was a cranky loser. He stood and drew his Luger. Having bragged to his three men how stupid he was making the American look, he became somewhat piqued upon discovery that it was he who had been played for the sucker. Mumbling something about showing the American why Germany would rule the world, he leveled the gun at Uncle Charles. Charles, sitting calmly at the table, smiled and then unloaded half the clip of a stolen MP40 that he'd hidden beneath the table earlier that day. That action resulted in four instant ex-Nazis, one café full of nervous Italians, and Claude, his daughter, and one crazy American on the lam in the Hand motor sailer, renamed the *Lady Barbara* some twenty years later."

"My God," Maggie whispered.

"You are all too well aware of the fate of the motor sailer. You may be interested to know that the little girl grew up to be a lovely woman, now married and living in

Lyons. She gave birth to a lovely daughter of her own, and that little girl picked the flowers on today's lunch table. Except for occasional visits to his happy family, Claude Bocuse never left my uncle's side. His loyalty is now to Lady Barbara.''

Puffing, Ben Chestle jogged across the Shinnecock Coast Guard Station parking lot to the dock, where a Coast Guard Groverbuilt 24 sat idling with a full crew.

"Come aboard, chief," the operations officer called out, beckoning him with an urgent wave.

As Chestle's feet hit the deck, two crewmen, one in the stern and one on the bow, cast off the lines and pushed away from the dock. Squinting out at the horizon, Chestle could see the Coast Guard's forty-four-foot motor lifeboat already under way, powering full-speed toward Shinnecock Inlet. The Groverbuilt's bow rose in the water as the helmsman opened her up. It took only a few minutes to overtake and pass the bigger vessel crossing the bay.

"How do you know it's the *Sea Puss* out there?" Chestle yelled over the roar of engines.

"We got a chopper over her . . . name's still legible on the transom. Charred but legible.''

Racing through the narrow Shinnecock Inlet with blue lights flashing, the Groverbuilt smashed through the three-foot waves, bouncing hard each time. Chestle and the operations officer, standing on the bridge deck, braced themselves and held on. Breaking into open sea, the boat pitched through raging surf toward a distant black smudge of smoke on the horizon.

The salty spray of smashed waves caught wind and showered the bridge. Dripping seawater, Chestle quickly accepted an invitation to borrow foul-weather gear. Stretching into a waterproof windbreaker, he spread his feet and held on.

The wet voyage lasted almost forty minutes before Chestle

could see clearly the source of the pollution. Charred and sitting low in the water, the *Sea Puss*'s hull still smoldered.

Standing on the bridge deck with binoculars raised, the operations officer panned until he had the wreck in sight. Focusing, he whispered, "Jesus Christ."

"What?" Chestle demanded.

"Here, take a look," the officer replied, handing over the glasses.

Chestle squinted and blinked. Dangling upside down in the rigging was Digger Murdock's charred skeleton.

"Holy shit," Chestle muttered.

Powering through a haze of fumes and smoke, the Groverbuilt eased alongside the *Sea Puss*. The stench of cooked flesh filled Chestle's nostrils, and he had to fight to keep lunch in his stomach.

Twenty minutes later, only the one body bag came off the *Sea Puss*. The rescue team completed their search and returned aboard the Groverbuilt. The motor lifeboat arrived on the scene, and her crew immediately began setting line to tow the wreck in.

"Hey, wait a minute," Chestle yelled. "That's it?"

"Yessir," a young crewman answered.

"One body?"

"Yessir."

"There were one or two other men on board."

"No sir. No one else. If there had been anybody else aboard, we'd have found them or their bodies. I think we found everything there is to find."

"No you didn't," Chestle insisted. "I have witnesses who claim there were other men on board."

"Well sir, then they must've been picked up by another vessel."

"Did your chopper spot any other vessels out here?"

"Only the Egg Harbor that reported the fire, and they sure didn't pick anyone up."

"Doesn't make sense unless . . ."

"Sir?"

"Any diving equipment on board this wreck?"

"As a matter of fact there is. Pretty badly damaged. One tank, or rather what's left of it after exploding, and one melted suit."

"How'd the fire start?"

"That'll have to wait for the inquiry, but off the record . . . there's an odd hole below the waterline near the fuel tanks. He might've forgotten to vent the bilge before starting up the engines."

"Or maybe something vented it for him."

"Sir?"

Chestle just shook his head and braced himself for the long haul in.

At midnight, Eric found that he could not sleep. Next to him, Maggie was breathing in long restful sighs. He walked down to the dark kitchen, snapped on a small light over the huge Garland stove, and opened the refrigerator. Pouring himself a large glass of milk, he sat on a stool at the kitchen's butcher-block table and began going over in his mind the opening statement he would present to the selected members of the Viking Cipher Project.

He was surprised to hear someone coming down the back stairs, and looked up to see Lady Barbara. Wearing a plunging red satin nightgown that just barely concealed her full breasts, she was breathtakingly attractive. Clinging to her legs and flat tummy, the shiny fabric fit like a second skin. The split at the side revealed an enticing tan thigh.

"Hi," Eric said with a devilish smile.

"Oh, hello. I didn't expect anyone to be up."

"Midnight snack."

"Yes." She smiled. "Me too."

Pouring herself a glass of sherry, she slid onto the stool across the small table and smiled. "Maggie McCabe is a lovely young girl."

"Yes, she is."

"You have fallen in love with her."

Eric looked up and asked, "Why do you say that?"

"I see it in your eyes when you look at her. You used to look at me that way."

"I still do and probably always will."

"Ah." She laughed. "You inherited your father's good looks and your uncle's charm." She stared across the table for a moment and then took his hand. Eric looked into her eyes.

"I've inherited more than that," he said as his smile disappeared.

"The Viking Cipher is troubling you, isn't it?"

Surprised that she would know, Eric looked up with an expression of inquiry on his face.

Lady Barbara explained, "Charles knew from the time of your parents' death that you would one day come into possession of your father's work. Everything he did for you—all the adventures, the international schooling, the trips to all countries—all of it was in preparation for that day."

"I never knew that," Eric said softly.

"You were not to know. He wanted you to enjoy as much carefree living as possible, for he knew that your life would change when you discovered the nature of the Viking papers."

"Do you know what the papers contain?"

"No, and I don't believe that Charles knew exactly either. He listened to and trusted your father more than I can describe. Your father came to see us in Zurich the year before he and your mother were killed. I remember thinking that your father knew he was in great danger. He asked that if anything should happen, Charles take you to safety immediately. Before that meeting was over, they discussed the best way to provide an education that would expose you to as many different philosophies, cultures, and religions as possible."

Eric nodded, realizing for the first time that a master plan had guided his life.

"And while I know you had wonderful times, it was always with that purpose in mind. You have the most comprehensive background of experience that a person can have. You, better than anyone, are now in a position to complete your father's work."

"The Viking Cipher," he stated, "is incomplete. The notes that I received are only a partial blueprint for its recreation. In fact, the last section is in a code which I still haven't completely deciphered."

"But you know what must be done to make the completion?"

"Yes, and this week, I assemble the first group of scientists to begin."

"It is dangerous and very important, isn't it?" she asked.

"Yes."

"Then you must put out of your mind this unfortunate incident with the yacht. We had wonderful times on it, and I shall always treasure those. But now there are new worlds to conquer and more important goals to achieve."

Eric nodded. He knew she was right.

Lady Barbara slid off the stool and opened the refrigerator door. The light inside filled the dark room and cast her silhouette through the flimsy veil of a nightgown. Naked in silhouette, she was even more stunning.

"Ahem!"

Eric and Lady Barbara turned. Maggie, wearing Eric's huge sweater as a nightgown, looked as if she were dressed in a sack. Standing with her hands on her hips in the doorway, she said sternly, "Well, this is cozy."

"I didn't know you were awake," Eric replied.

"Apparently not."

"Would you like a glass of milk?" he asked.

"I won't stay long . . . three's a crowd and all that," Maggie shot back.

Slightly stunned by the sarcastic remark, Eric could not find an appropriate reply.

"Well, if you two will excuse me," Lady Barbara said, raising her eyebrows at Eric, "I'll leave you alone."

"Don't let *me* ruin your little midnight rendezvous," Maggie snapped.

Lady Barbara leveled a brief laser stare into Maggie's eyes and then continued up the stairs.

When she was out of earshot, Eric turned to Maggie and demanded, "What's the matter with you?"

"What's the matter with me?" Maggie gasped. "We were almost killed by a submarine, shot by a Peeping Tom, and now I find you whispering sweet nothings to Lady Godiva here and you ask me what's the matter? I want to go home, that's what's the matter."

"Listen, Maggie, I've known Lady Barbara for fifteen years and you for five months. Friendships don't evaporate because you're the center of attention."

"Friendship?" Maggie laughed. "Did you see that night-gown your friend was almost wearing? For whose benefit was that? Not mine."

Eric started to smile, and that infuriated Maggie.

"You're jealous!" he said with surprise.

"Jealous? What's to be jealous? Just because she's beautiful, rich, and cultured and she has memories with you that I can never share, and she probably speaks as many languages as you, and she's traveled all over the world with you? Of course I'm jealous. Put yourself in my shoes . . . wouldn't you be?"

"No," he answered honestly.

Maggie's mouth fell open, and she shook her head.

"Listen," he said. "You'll feel better after a good night's sleep. We'll talk about it tomorrow after we meet LeBrun—"

"And that's another thing," Maggie blurted. "You never asked me if I wanted to go along with you to visit this LeBrun guy. You didn't even ask my opinion. You just went ahead and made plans without consulting me."

"I naturally assumed that you were interested in finding out a little more about who tried to kill us."

"Well, you naturally assumed wrong. What I'm interested in is leading a normal life. I have a job to get back to in Tampa. And a helluva lot of explaining to do when I tell my boss why I don't have any of the photographs I promised the paper. Give me a call when you're ready to go out for a pizza and a movie. I've had it with this James Bond stuff."

Now Eric was becoming annoyed. "You had a life full of pizzas and movies with Carl Millbank and look at how well that worked out!"

Openmouthed and furious at the mention of her ex-fiancé, Maggie demanded, "Just who do you think you are?" Her Irish temper rose quickly to a full head of steam and she answered her own question: "Prince Charming who swept me off my feet to carry me off on a white charger?"

"Yes," Eric answered seriously, "now that you mention it."

"Of all the nerve!" Maggie cried.

"As I recall, the original Prince Charming also fell in love and did just that."

Maggie was about to retort when the word "love" stopped her. It was the first time Eric had ever used it, and the effect stole her thunder.

"Huh?" she mumbled.

"It's the living-happily-ever-after part we've got to work on now, princess," he said softly, reaching out for her.

"You love me?" Maggie's face softened and she looked like a little girl.

"Anyone who would bring a ham sandwich to a million-airess is hard to resist," he said with a smile. "And besides, you're such a snappy dresser."

Maggie looked down at the sweater hanging like a sack down her sides and the last of her anger disappeared.

CHAPTER 8

Stretching and blinking the sleep from her eyes, Maggie wandered to the bedroom window, pulled the Irish-lace curtains to one side, and gazed out at the horizon. The morning sun was blocked by a leaden overcast that left the ocean gray and forbidding. Behind her, Eric rolled in the big brass bed and sat up, yawning.

"Good morning," he said in a deep sleepy voice.

"I'm sorry about last night," Maggie said without looking at him.

"Forgotten," was his reply.

Maggie turned and smiled, but it was a smile betrayed by sadness in her eyes. Having felt like a fool since she arrived, Maggie now had to face Lady Barbara after embarrassing herself the night before by that damnable display of jealousy. Nothing Eric said managed to ease the anxiety.

But at breakfast, Lady Barbara was as gracious as she had been the moment Eric and Maggie arrived. The uncomfortable midnight meeting was not mentioned. Lady Barbara joked and laughed easily while Claude and Petra served a gourmet morning feast. For the first time, Maggie enjoyed his cooking. But then Eric excused himself and disappeared upstairs to collect their belongings. And Petra accompanied Claude into the kitchen. Maggie and Lady Barbara were left sitting alone across from each other at the dining-room table.

Except for the chink of china on china as Lady Barbara set her coffee cup on its plate, the elegant room was distressingly silent. Maggie stared down at the croissant flakes on her plate, vigorously stirring her tea with a silver spoon. The distant rattle of plates in the kitchen gave Maggie the escape she was hoping for. Mumbling something about giving Claude a hand, she rose to carry her empty dish to the kitchen.

"Petra will be hurt if you take those plates to the kitchen," Lady Barbara pointed out. "She prides herself on her proper table service."

Maggie sat back down without saying a word. Glancing up, she took a deep breath and thought to herself, Here it comes.

Then Lady Barbara spoke. "I'm very fond of Eric . . ."

Sitting up straight and leaning slightly back, Maggie stared across the table into her soft brown eyes.

". . . and of you."

Flustered by the unexpected compliment, Maggie did not know how to respond and so said nothing.

"And it is because of that fondness that I would never compete with you for Eric's affections. Never. You've apparently made him very happy, and I thank you for that. Eric, like my Charles, learned early to live in the present and put past unpleasantries to rest. This is not always an easy task. I see in Eric now a contentment and happiness that I have not seen for many years. I know in my heart that you are the source of this glow. Please know that you are always welcome in my house and that I consider you to be a friend. I will hope that as you come to know me, you will feel the same toward me."

Before Maggie could reply, Lady Barbara stood, picked up her empty cup and saucer, and carried them with a smile to the kitchen.

Ten minutes later, goodbyes were said. An hour later, Eric and Maggie were hurtling along Interstate 95 headed for New York. Somewhere near Bridgeport, Maggie blurted out, "You know, that Lady Barbara is okay."

Frowning, Eric turned, stared at her, and then shook his head. They continued on. The ride went quickly, and it seemed to Maggie to take as long to find a parking place near the Metropolitan Museum of Art in New York City as it did to complete the journey. After locking the duffel bag in the trunk, they headed off for their appointment with Jean Paul LeBrun.

Entering the museum, Eric and Maggie strolled across the huge concourse to the information desk in the center.

"Excuse me," Eric said. "I'm looking for Jean Paul LeBrun of your Egyptology department."

The receptionist looked down at a clipboard on her desk and asked, "Mr. Ivorsen?"

"Yes."

"How many in your party?"

"Two."

She handed up two guest pass badges, which Eric and Maggie clipped to the breast pockets of their shirts.

Spreading open a brochure of the museum, she made an X at their location on the floor plan of the main floor, and as she lined a route for them to follow, said, "Please walk through the Wallace Galleries, bear to the left, and go directly to the entrance of Sackler Hall. There you will see doors roped off and a sign that indicates the area is being prepared for the new exhibit. Show your badges to the security guard and he will take you to Mr. LeBrun."

Eric thanked her, and they began the short walk. But Maggie stopped when they reached the Mastaba of Pernebi, a limestone mortuary chapel reconstructed in the Egyptian wing on the main floor.

Eric, suddenly aware of her wonderment, asked, "Have you ever been here before?"

"No. I've only been to New York City twice in my life,"

Maggie admitted. "Once as a little girl and once for the paper to photograph Rockefeller Center at Christmastime."

"This is one of the three or four finest collections of Egyptian art in the world. Cairo, Paris, London, and here," he informed her.

"This building looks like something from *Raiders of the Lost Ark*," Maggie whispered and wandered into the stone passageway and chambers etched with hieroglyphics. Eric followed.

He walked to the glass-protected walls and, tracing his finger along a line of figures, mumbled as he read, "Mmmm . . . uh huh . . . of course."

Maggie stood back and watched with judging eyes. Finally she said with a tinge of sarcasm in her voice, "Don't tell me, let me guess . . . Uncle Charles taught you to read hieroglyphics."

Eric ignored her and continued reading, mumbling as he followed the figures along the wall of the narrow stone passageway.

"Okay . . . so what does it say?" Maggie sighed.

Eric turned with a slight look of disdain on his face and condescendingly sighed as if exasperated. Walking back to the beginning of the passage, he placed his index finger on the first figure, and began, "It says quite clearly: 'For a good time, call Nefertiti at Pyramid seven three three nine eight.' Then it says something about her being a great piece of asp . . . or something to that effect."

Maggie laughed and confirmed, "You can't really read hieroglyphics, can you?"

"No," he admitted. "But that's what I'd have written."

Continuing through the galleries filled with antiquities, mummy cases, and papyri, they finally came to the huge Sackler Hall. Three stories high with one sloping full-length wall of glass, the auditorium-size room was extremely bright and a little too warm. A moat of blue water stretched across the room, surrounding a gray granite setting from which the Temple of Dendur rose. Rescued from the rising waters of the Nile River near the Aswan Dam, the structure had been disassembled stone by stone, numbered, and transported from Nubia to New York. Rebuilt and protected, it represented archaeological preservation at its most ambitious. To Maggie, the two ornate massive columns standing at the temple's entrance made the ancient building seem mystical.

"I wonder if it carries a curse," she said with a smile.

"Yes. Whoever gazes at the Temple of Dendur must make love to Nubian-size lovers," Eric answered seriously, brushing off his shoulders as if readying himself.

"Eeeewww, that is a curse," she shot back, crinkling her nose. "I wonder where I'm going to find those in Florida."

"It's a pretty specific curse—they have to be Princeton Nubian-size lovers. I think I can help you out. We'll discuss it later."

As they walked the perimeter of the shallow moat, Maggie marveled at the cultural achievement of preserving an ancient treasure that was about to be sacrificed to accommodate the need to cultivate more land. Circling all the way around the room, they came back to the area being readied for the new, much anticipated Egyptian exhibit.

Eric showed his badge to a guard, who nodded and then opened two solid gray doors that had been locked and plastered with a red-lettered sign that forbade entrance to anyone other than museum personnel.

They stepped into cool, almost total darkness. The contrast with the bright sunlight of the glass-paneled hall left them blinded. In a small circle of light near the middle of the vast new hall, Jean Paul LeBrun sat with his glasses perched on the tip of his nose. Looking up from a sketch pad in his hands, he called, "Over here! Mr. Ivorsen?"

The guard nodded and departed, pulling closed and locking the solid doors. Maggie and Eric crossed the vast, seemingly limitless room, their footsteps echoing off the dark glass cases that lined the walls.

A Frenchman who spoke with little accent, Jean Paul

LeBrun was just as Claude had described, extremely serious about his work and also quite proud of his position at the museum. Wearing a light-gray lab coat, dark slacks, and museum identification badge, he looked right at home, and he was.

"I'd like to thank you for taking the time to meet with us," Eric said. "I know that you're on a very tight schedule."

"Nonsense," LeBrun answered. "Always willing to take the time to discuss Egypt. When Monsieur Bocuse called, I was delighted. I met him with your father once—did he tell you?"

"Yes," Eric said.

After minutes of polite conversation, LeBrun explained, "I took the liberty of mentioning the story Bocuse told me about your discovery to Sir Thatcher Smythe, an old colleague of mine from my days as curator at the Foundation Egyptologique Reine Elisabeth . . . he was with the London Museum at the time. He is with us to present a lecture when this show opens next month, and he's also agreed to meet with you. I think it might be of interest, because it was he who discovered the Sacred Cat of Bastet. It is here, did you know?"

"Claude mentioned it, and we are very anxious to see it," Eric replied.

LeBrun broke into a wide smile. "Of course you are anxious to see it. That is why I keep you here making the small talk. Anxiety breeds appreciation. We have waited long enough, no?"

Looking past Eric, Maggie squinted at the forms in the darkness beyond LeBrun's little worklight. She could make out only the vague silhouettes of people-shaped objects. For an eerie moment, she thought she saw one move in the shadows. Stepping closer to Eric, she returned her attention to LeBrun.

"You will excuse the theatrics," he apologized, "but it is only once in a while that I get to surprise someone. In one week, the public will just wander in through the big open doors of Sackler Hall. Some of the mystery will be lost. But now it is just us . . . standing in the darkness as these objects did for three, some four, millennia."

Eric tilted his head and frowned, wondering what all this was leading to.

LeBrun slid off his stool, and vanishing into the darkness himself, walked to a corner of the dark hall.

His proud voice echoing, he said, "Imagine, if you will, that these figures and works of art stood a silent vigil in darkness like this for a thousand years before Abraham walked on the earth. Another thousand years before Mary gave birth to Jesus Christ. And yet a thousand more before the Norsemen ruled and the Dark Ages began . . . and that that took place over a thousand years ago. Imagine all of that time and realize that during those thousands and thousands of years, this beauty was locked in total isolation . . . in total darkness for no one to appreciate but the sightless dead."

Clicking switches, Lebrun illuminated bank after bank of spotlights recessed in the ceilings of the display cases. Shafts of white light flooded down, bathing each showcase in columns of bright white light. Suddenly the entire room glittered with gold and treasures and sculpture and art. Case after case of alabaster, bronze, black granite, silver, and gold. Walls of ancient jewelry, gems, and precious stones. The busts and statues of gilded gods, goddesses, and minor deities surrounded them. Silver and gems sparkled light in all directions. Maggie gasped and Eric's mouth fell slightly open. A glance in any direction brought more breathtaking beauty. Each case was more spectacular than the last.

"Something to see, yes?" LeBrun was bursting with pride.

Eric's gazed across the treasure-filled room until his eyes fell on the centerpiece at the middle of the hall. Standing in the center of the room in a thick glass case was the cat Eric had buried under a lifeguard stand in Westhampton Beach and that was now locked in the trunk of a 1983 Jaguar X-J S parked on 84th Street.

Perched on a mound of black velvet, the Sacred Cat of Bastet glinted in shafts of white light. Solid gold with emerald eyes, it was the exact same cat. Maggie saw it at the same instant and, blinking, shook her head to clear her vision. She grabbed Eric by the arm and looked up into his eyes.

"The Sacred Cat of Bastet lay entombed for nearly twenty-five hundred years." The voice was not LeBrun's. It came from behind them . . . from the same spot where Maggie had seen a shadow move. "You are too much a showman, Jean Paul," Sir Thatcher Smythe scolded, stepping forward into the hall from a doorway marked private.

LeBrun laughed and nodded. "Please, please, come meet Eric Ivorsen and Maggie McCabe."

"A pleasure," Thatcher Smythe replied.

With his proper British accent and drooping white mustache, he was the picture of what Maggie thought a Thatcher Smythe should look like. And even though it was the end of summer and the days were still relatively warm, he was dressed in a heavy gray wool suit. Average in height, he had remained slim, and the only concession to his sixty-five years was a slight stoop when he walked. This might be attributed to too many days in the desert on his hands and knees. His hair was white and scarce, and he smiled almost constantly. Yet, in his eyes, there was a vague expression of constant concentration, as if he were working to look relaxed. Somewhat frail and a little stiff, Smythe seemed to consider every move carefully before executing it. Perhaps due to his training as an archeologist, mused Eric.

"Do you know Egyptology?" he asked.

"Not enough," Eric replied.

"Then I will give you a quick education."

Smythe led them through the exhibit, explaining funerary technique, customs, and traditions. An uncommonly eloquent speaker, he mesmerized Maggie with his descriptions of the archaeological sites and tales of the trials and tribulations of a person dedicated to uncovering the past.

LeBrun wandered along for the first hour, but then excused himself to get back to work. He said he hoped he had been of assistance and that Thatcher Smythe could probably tell them more than they really wanted to know. Certainly he knew more about the Sacred Cat of Bastet than anyone.

When the tour was near an end, Smythe declared, "I would like you to join me for an early dinner."

"We wouldn't impose . . ."

"No imposition. I insist, and I've already rung them up to change the reservation to four."

"Four? Will Mr. LeBrun be joining us?" Maggie asked.

"No, no. I am to meet another colleague."

"We don't want to intrude."

"I insist. This is no intrusion. Please, I will feel insulted now if you refuse."

Perplexed by the insistence, Eric shrugged and agreed.

They walked to the museum entrance, dropped off the visitor badges, and descended the steps to a cab waiting at the curb on Fifth Avenue.

"Excuse me, sir," Thatcher Smythe said to the driver. "Would you be so kind as to deliver us to the Triveni Restaurant on 51st Street?"

The cabbie, rolling a toothpick in the corner of his mouth, didn't bother to answer. Sitting with his wrist draped over the wheel, he simply reached over and snapped down the meter flag.

Maggie and Eric climbed in the backseat and Smythe in the front.

Maggie, interested in returning to Smythe's stories, reminded him, "You were saying about the mummies . . ."

Turning halfway to answer, Smythe again seemed stiff, unable to turn completely around. As a result, whenever he spoke, he simply leaned back against the seat, tilting his head.

"Did you know, for instance, that it is estimated that there are some seven hundred million mummies? And in the nineteenth century, the British and the Americans dug up and imported mummies by the tens of thousands. We used the linen wrappings to make paper and powdered the bodies for headache remedies and fertilizer. Quite simply, we ate the Egyptian dead."

The cabbie braked for a light on 78th, turned to the distinguished scholar, and said, "Hey, pal, you wanna gimme a break, here? I'm gonna toss my waffles you keep talking like that."

Thatcher Smythe frowned at the incomprehensible reference, the traffic light turned green, and the cabbie stepped on the gas.

When they reached 59th, traffic had ground to a halt in front of the Plaza. Horns honked and crowds of pedestrians wormed through the gridlocked cars. The cab driver sat gazing out the window looking bored, tired and unhappy.

"I only get to New York once a year and it never ceases to amaze me," Smythe commented.

"In what way?" Eric asked.

"The pace, the excitement, the electricity. After spending forty years in quiet deserts, one grows accustomed to solitude and inactivity. Are you a New Yorker, Maggie?"

"No," she answered, "Floridian . . . I live in Tampa."

"You both live in Tampa?" Sir Thatcher asked with genuine curiosity.

"I live in Princeton," Eric replied. "Maggie and I met while traveling in Europe earlier this year. When we returned, I persuaded her to join me on a short cruise that unfortunately has ended in disaster. The yacht we were sailing sank."

"Yes, oh yes, LeBrun mentioned something about that. You must tell me over dinner."

The little restaurant had cloth walls and ceilings that drooped down over the candlelit tables, giving the room the appearance of a large tribal tent. An aromatic blend of curry and spice filled the air. Strains of sitar music wafted through the room, lending the whole dark atmosphere an alien feeling of another world.

"You must tell me about this cat you've discovered," Smythe declared. "But first I will tell you about the real one. . . ."

Eric smiled. Smythe was obviously more interested in reminiscing about his glory days in the desert than hearing about some boating accident. And, Eric admitted, he was damn good at it. Maggie listened wide-eyed to each description and anecdote.

Smythe turned to a waiter and said, "I am expecting another party. In the meantime, please bring us an order of *pratha* and *panir pakora*." Turning back to Maggie and Eric, he explained, "Something to nibble on. Do you know Indian cuisine?"

Eric nodded. Maggie shook her head.

"The best food in the world," Smythe declared. "Well, you'll see."

"You were saying about the dig that produced the Cat of Bastet," she said.

Thatcher Smythe nodded. "The dig that produced the Cat of Bastet was my first . . . a beginner's luck, if you will. And I remember that day in 1937 as if it were yesterday."

A darkness came to his face, and Maggie felt a sudden tinge of *faux pas* . . . that she'd asked him to do something unpleasant. He cleared his throat, took a sip of water, and then his eyes brightened as he spoke. The bizarre atmosphere of the restaurant, the strange music, and Smythe's uncanny narrative combined to make Maggie feel that if she were to close her eyes, she would be in the desert with a twenty-year-old Thatcher Smythe.

"Late in the afternoon . . . dusk . . . I wandered home, which was at the time a small frame bungalow erected near the site. The setting sun sat baking the desert sands, burning its way into the horizon, melting as it sank. A sea of violet inched across the valley floor as purple shadows rose on the plateaus. The cloudless sky grew black, its canopy of twinkling stars grew bright. Pausing in my climb to the bungalow, I observed the children and oxen on the ridge. Clouds of choking dust hung in their wakes, settling slowly in the motionless air. I was tired and sore and depressed.

"As a rule, I never drank, but on that particular day, I broke my rule and poured three fingers. I remember that a swirl of dust floating in my drink did not trouble so much that I did not drain the tumbler in one or two healthy gulps. My knees ached from a day of fruitless digging. And then I heard it. My chief reis, Tewfik, shouted for me to come . . . to come right hasty, as he put it. I taught him his English . . . admittedly a rather poor job.

"Across the wadi I found a knot of my men pointing and gawking like children at a side tunnel that we'd abandoned months earlier. Pulling them aside, I saw it . . . a perfect crack in the ground where no crack should have been. I knew at once what it meant. It was in exactly the wrong location to have been part of the tomb that had once covered it and had long ago been plundered. This was a passage to an older tomb . . . I could feel that in my soul."

Smythe's rising enthusiasm was infectious, and Maggie was enthralled. The waiter brought out a platter of steaming *pratha* pancakes and bowls of orange onion. Next to that he set down *panir pakir*, cheese fritters.

Smythe popped one of the delicacies in his mouth, chewed slowly until it was gone, and continued, "We worked by twinkling blue starlight all night long. When the charcoal sky began to turn blue, I was already exhausted but in no way ready or willing to rest. We worked on. As the sun broke over the plateaus at dawn, that mysterious crack widened and stone yielded to our crowbars. The reis chattered like chickens behind me as I strained to lift that weight. Finally, mercifully, it rose. First a millimeter, then a centimeter, then ten. More bars were inserted and more men pushed. Groaning in protest, that blasted slab abandoned its twenty-five-century defense.

"We had indeed found a new tunnel. A tunnel filled with choking dust, sand, rubble, and rock. By nine, the blistering heat of the desert cooked us out of the ground. I stood guard, sleeping against a hastily manufactured gate, under a tent all afternoon. And we resumed digging at five. For six hours, we cleared rock and rubble from that corridor. Ten meters, then twenty, then it broke open and I could see clear passage for another fifty. Crawling, I carried a torch to two wooden doors that stood sealed for nearly two thousand, five hundred years.

"My photographer took photographs . . . hundreds. We labeled everything, catalogued everything, numbered and registered everything. Then at precisely midnight on March 15, 1937, we broke open those doors. I became paralyzed . . . unable to draw breath. I felt strange standing there. I saw what you saw earlier. More gold than I could imagine. More wealth than I could conceive. I found it. I uncovered it. And yet I could not comprehend it. As it has turned out, I discovered that I could not possess it either. The London Museum got half, Cairo got half, and I got the pictures." Thatcher Smythe grinned and shook his white head.

Maggie laughed at the humorous anticlimax, but Eric detected something more in Smythe's tone, a bitterness that was not completely camouflaged by the easy chuckles.

"Now tell me all about how you discovered your cat," Smythe said with a twinkle in his eye. But before Eric could begin, Smythe's attention went to the restaurant door. "Please wait a moment," he said. "I see my associate has finally arrived."

Smythe stood, as did Eric, and waved. His associate nodded and crossed the room.

"I am pleased to introduce Mr. Eric Ivorsen and Miss Maggie . . ." Smythe stumbled, apparently forgetting Maggie's last name.

"McCabe," she finished for him and held out her hand.

Smythe's associate reached across the table, wrapped his bony cold fingers around Maggie's, and shook once. Then, turning to look up into Eric's face, he smiled and bowed slightly.

Sir Thatcher Smythe said with pride, "Eric, Maggie, please meet my closest friend and associate, Mr. Parat Singh."

CHAPTER 9

After parking his white Nova in a municipal lot, the old man ambled into the Princeton Public Library, asked for a local phone directory, and looked up Eric Ivorsen's address. According to a neighborhood map, locating the apartment was simply a matter of walking two blocks and crossing Palmer Square. He wrote all this down and set off at a slow but purposeful gait, pausing to catch his breath when he reached a bench in the heart of the handsomely land-scaped square. Oblivious to his surroundings—some of Princeton's finest shops, restaurants, and apartments—he squinted to make out the address on the stone and brick buildings. Then he saw the building he wanted.

Approaching it, he came to a young woman, approximately eighteen he guessed. With her arms wrapped around a huge cardboard carton of clothes, she was backed up to the doorway, having difficulty negotiating the door and balancing her load at the same time.

Nice tits, the old man thought to himself, but a fat ass. "Give you a hand?" he said, opening the building's door.

"Oh, thank you," she replied, with a girlish giggle in her voice.

"You live in this building?" he asked as they climbed the stairs.

"Just moving in. I start at the university this semester and I'm trying to get settled." She set down the box and held out her hand. "My name's Susie."

"I'm Ed," the old man replied, still breathing a little heavily from the one-story climb.

"Are we neighbors?" she asked.

"I been thinking about renting an apartment here. Wanna be close to my grandson. He's going to Princeton too."

"Oh, really?" Susie's eyes lit up. "What's his major?"

Ed's mind raced for a moment. Then he mumbled, "Uh, law."

Confusion swept Susie's face. "You mean prelaw?"

"Yeah, that's it . . . prelaw. You know the young fella lives in this apartment?" he asked, pointing at Eric Ivorsen's door.

"That's my apartment now. I sublet it from Mr. Ivorsen this summer. He isn't your grandson, by any chance?"

"No, no," he replied. "A friend of my grandson's."

"Well, he's moved to a house out on Mercer Street."

"I see."

"I haven't seen him in several weeks . . . since I rented the place." Then, leaning over to whisper, "They say a Russian spy was once killed in this apartment trying to steal a secret formula."

"You don't say."

"At first it gave me the creeps, but now I think it's kind of romantic. Anyway, all my friends think it's awesome."

"You wouldn't happen to have Eric Ivorsen's new address . . . what was it, Mercy Street?"

"Mercer Street. I sure do. C'mon in."

Susie wrote out the address and handed it over. "You want me to tell him you stopped by if I see him?" she asked.

"Oh no. It was going to be a surprise. I'll catch up to him."

"Okay," she bubbled. "By the way, what's your grandson's name, in case I run into him on campus?"

"Huh? Oh, uh, Tom," Ed stammered, trying to think of a name.

"Tom what?"

"Tom Palmer."

"Right." Susie smiled. "I'll look for him."

Don't hold your breath, Ed thought to himself as he ambled down the stairs onto the street. He returned to his car and drove out along Mercer Street until he came to the address on the slip of paper. Crawling at a snail's pace and reading house numbers as he drove along, he managed to back up a line of ten cars on the busy thoroughfare. Horns blared and headlights flashed, but Ed was unconcerned. Finally he saw the number he was looking for and pulled off onto a side street across the road.

A hundred-year-old Victorian, white with black shutters and big front porch, the house was in impeccable condition, and looked as if it had been plucked from a Norman Rockwell painting. A gardener was trimming the small shrubs that lined the fieldstone walk leading to the front door.

Ed turned to the back seat of the Nova and began rumaging through his brand-new camera case. He extracted a new Canon F-1 camera and wandered across the street. After taking several pictures of the house, he walked up to the gardener and said, "This sure is an old beauty. You live here?"

"No sir," the man answered. "Just work here."

"I'm in the real estate business and I been looking for a place for my son and daughter-in-law to buy. Whaddya figure a place like this would go for?"

"Can't rightly say. Two hundred thousand, I bet."

"Whew!" Ed whistled, truly amazed.

"Most houses in this neighborhood bring the big bucks," the gardener added.

"Whoever lives here now must be pretty rich," Ed said.

"Mr. Ivorsen lives here now," the man replied.

"Not Eric Ivorsen?" Ed succeeded in his attempt to sound surprised.

"Yeah, you know him?"

"Young fella. Big tall drink of water."

"Yeah, that's Mr. Ivorsen."

"Howdya figure a young guy like that can afford a place like this?"

"That ain't so hard to figure. Belonged to his family. He inherited it. Didn't live here, though. Rented it out to university faculty up until just a while ago."

"That right?"

"Yeah, but he's movin' back in now. We been fixin' it up for about a month now gettin' it ready. New paint inside and out. They been deliverin' new furniture, computers, all sorts of good stuff."

"Computers?"

"Yeah, he's some kind of scientist. Most the people around here are connected with the university or the Institute."

"Sure looks good," Ed said, staring up at the stately old home.

"Thanks."

Small talk and smoking out rats made Ed feel good. And now he felt terrific. He went back to the library before it closed and photocopied all the local articles about the shooting in Palmer Square. Then he dropped by the Princeton Borough Police station, claimed to the officers on duty that he was a retired cop, and learned even more. Finally he stopped by the offices of the *Princeton Packet* newspaper, said that he was a retired newspaperman writing an article about Eric Ivorsen, and finished his day with a complete dossier on the young mathematician.

Returning to his room at a dingy little run-down motel out on Route 1, he settled down to a box of Kentucky-fried chicken and two bottles of beer, and was sound asleep by 7:30.

*   *   *

"Well, that was strange," Eric commented as the cab pulled away from the curb in front of the Triveni Restaurant. On the sidewalk outside, Thatcher Smythe waved one last time and then turned to talk with Parat Singh.

"What a strange duo," Maggie said as the cab sped them back to the parking garage where they had left the Jaguar.

"An odd conversation about Tampa," Eric mused.

"Did Mr. Smythe say he knew Tampa, or did I imagine that?" she asked.

"No. He clearly stated that he knew Tampa, and then . . ."

"And then when I described where I live, he didn't know anything about it at all."

"Very strange," Eric concluded. "And Singh claimed to know Princeton but then seemed unfamiliar with the layout of the university. I don't understand it."

"At least we found out that our cat is a fake."

"Unless there are two solid-gold sacred Cats of Bastet."

"Which Thatcher Smythe claims is impossible."

"So we have an exquisite copy. Still, I think I might just take up Singh on his offer to check it for gold content."

"It sounded as though he wanted you to do that today," she said.

"We can't. You've got a plane to catch, and I've got to get ready for tomorrow's meeting."

"Speaking of which, I'm going to get on that plane, and there's a question I'd like to ask before I do.

"And that is?"

"What's the next chapter in our fairy tale?"

Eric smiled. "I introduce the Viking Cipher tomorrow, to the colleagues I need to continue the work. In one week, I'll have their answers. If they refuse to take part in the project, I'll be down to getcha in a taxi, honey. And we'll take a real vacation. If, as I suspect will happen, they agree to participate, I'll have to leave to begin reassembling some aspects of the project that are scattered around the world.

I'm hoping you'd like to come along on some of those little sojourns."

"Nowhere in there did I hear pizzas and movies."

"No pizzas, no movies," Eric confirmed, "Oh, wait . . . there is a movie house in Kathmandu. Seats fifteen thousand."

"Bowling alley?" she asked with a grin.

"Calcutta Lanes," Eric replied.

"It's a date."

"The gods are with us, Parat, the gods are with us," Thatcher Smythe commented as he watched the yellow cab carry Eric and Maggie into the Manhattan traffic. Then he turned to Parat Singh, who smiled a hideous grin. Together, they turned to stroll up Fifth Avenue.

"They have the cat. A most fortunate turn of events."

"We must make a decision," Smythe declared.

"Yes," Singh agreed.

"Do you remember everything she said about her home?" Smythe asked. "I don't think she poses a danger, but still, if we must . . ."

"But she has seen the cat."

"She's going back to Florida. Their relationship seems superficial. And with her away, she'll be in no position to harm us."

"But if she tells someone . . ."

"By the time she gets someone to believe her, the auction will be over and we'll be gone. They'd never trace us."

"And him?"

"Yes, him . . . he's the problem. We should get him and the cat to Paris, if possible. Kill him if it makes it easier."

"Tonight?"

"No, we can't kill him tonight. Suspicion might fall on my meeting him. No, it must be more subtle. I would have preferred to lure him to Paris with the promise of a great reward if he produces the cat. But as you heard at dinner, he is reluctant. I think we must take him and see if we can't locate the cat ourselves, or hope that it does not surface before the auction. Do you agree?"

"Yes. It is the only way left open to us."

"Then we must arrange a trip for Mr. Ivorsen. He's quite large . . . bigger than you alone can handle."

"You still have two employees here in the city?"

"Bruno and his brother. They will demand more money for something like this, but it will be worth it."

"Perhaps I should have insisted . . ." Singh began, thinking that he might have been able to go with Eric to Princeton.

"No, you were wise not to push him too hard. If he does not call you tomorrow, go see him on Tuesday," Smythe said.

"And if he does not come to me?"

"Then we will go to him, and you will need Bruno. I was hoping to clean up the loose ends here in New York, but we may find their presence necessary for this one last job."

"If force is necessary, we create more loose ends . . . ends that then must be taken care of themselves."

"You are quite capable."

Bowing slightly, Singh replied, "Thank you."

"Peake and McCorkle are dead?" Smythe confirmed.

"Yes. An obvious murder and a suicide."

"That's official?"

"Yes."

"Very good," Smythe said without smiling. "And I received radio communication today from the *Whimbrel*. Mr. Murdock had a very unfortunate boating accident at sea."

Singh nodded.

"The *Whimbrel* docks in Le Havre in three days . . . just long enough for Pike to unload our shipment," Smythe pointed out.

"He will go directly to the warehouse in Paris?"

"That is what Fascione and I have agreed upon."

"We will be there to meet him," Singh concluded.

"Yes, and we shall have taken care of Ivorsen by then."

They walked along in silence for almost ten minutes, each reviewing the last-minute details of the auction.

Finally his mind came back to the potential problem that Maggie McCabe presented and Singh asked, "What about the girl?"

"Forget her for now," Smythe decided.

"Then I can think of only two major concerns," Singh declared, "The transportation of the outer coffin, and the disposal of Mr. Ivorsen."

"I agree, Ivorsen and the coffin."

"We could combine the two tasks," Singh suggested.

"Eric Ivorsen and the queen's coffin?"

"A perfect vessel in which to transport the remains of Mr. Ivorsen."

Sir Thatcher Smythe grinned. "Of course! You are a gifted man, Parat . . . a gifted man."

CHAPTER 10

Maggie's flight to Tampa was scheduled to depart on time. Eric kissed her, promised to call to make sure she arrived safely, and then kissed her again. Once the plane left the gate, he returned to the rented Jaguar and drove it to a rental return counter at Newark's North Terminal. He settled the bill with cash.

The attractive young woman at Specialty Car Rentals took the keys to the sports car and smiled up at Eric. He asked where he could catch a ride to Princeton, and she told him that she got off at nine and would be glad to drive him wherever he wanted to go. Eric laughed, asked for a raincheck, and then had to wait fifteen minutes for a limousine shuttle bus.

An hour later, the limo bus dropped him off at its last stop in Palmer Square. Stepping out with the duffel bag under his arm, he paused for a moment, staring up at his old apartment across the street. He could see Susie Trescott balanced precariously on a chair in the window. She was hanging frilly curtains where he'd had shades, and Eric wondered what other feminine touches had been added to brighten the place. He considered stopping in to see how she was getting along but then thought better of it and continued home. Smiling as he strolled past the university, he found the walk to the house on Mercer Street to be exceptionally pleasant. Activity around and on campus was increasing with the arrival of new students, and vans were being unloaded everywhere.

Even though it was evening and the streets were dark, he could see all the landscaping that had been done in the front yard. The old homestead looked as it had when he was fourteen, before he went to live with his uncle. Unlocking the front door, Eric stepped inside, and the sudden stark absence of hominess erased his smile. Unpacked boxes lined the walls. The draperies, curtains, and rugs were still at the cleaner. Some furniture had been moved in, but mostly the high-ceilinged rooms were barren. His footsteps echoed as he crossed the wide center hall.

A smell of fresh paint filled his nostrils, not the curiously comfortable blend of his mother's cooking and his father's pipe that used to greet him as he walked through the door . . . too many years ago. He crossed to the parlor and looked around. No books. No pictures. All those things had yet to be unpacked. Even the silly pencil lines on the doorjamb into the dining room—readings of his rapid annual growth, taken each of thirteen birthdays by his mother and duly recorded with pencil and ruler—had been stroked away by the painter's brush. Nothing familiar remained except the shape and shell of a home that had disappeared almost twenty years ago. Eric felt alone. He glanced around one last time and then began moving boxes out of the parlor and dining room, making room for tomorrow's guests.

He waited two hours before dialing Maggie's number and was just about to hang up on the tenth ring when an out-of-breath Maggie picked up.

"Hello," she gasped.

"You made it."

"I was just coming in and it took a second to get the door open."

"Well, I miss you already."

"Me too. I would've stayed if you'd asked."

Eric laughed. "And listen to a bunch of mathematicians sitting around taking life too seriously?"

"Is that what you're going to be doing?"

"No question."

"Well then, I wish you were here."

"I will be soon. I just wanted to make sure you got home all right."

"I really do miss you, Prince Charming."

"Listen, everything will settle down and be back to normal now," he promised.

After several more goodnights, Eric finally set the phone on the cradle and climbed the stairs to his bedroom. He stripped, took a quick hot shower, and fell into bed. With his hands behind his head, he tried to organize in his mind the next day's presentation. But his thoughts kept drifting back to Maggie. Sighing as he fell asleep, he told himself, "Ah well, this will all work out. After tomorrow, things will settle down."

Across the room, the gold cat stared down from its perch on his dresser, a knowing smile on its ancient lips.

Monday morning brought two things to Mercer Street, rushing traffic and a spotless white Nova. Parked on the side street across the road, Ed sat in his car, watching. Armed with a full day's supply of coffee, sandwiches, and film, he sat back and waited. When nothing much happened, he twisted a brand-new FD 300mm telephoto lens onto the camera and aimed it at Eric's house.

The top half of the front door filled the viewfinder, and Ed smiled, confident that he would get good, if not great, photographs. Then he opened the owner's manual and read how to work the new attachment.

By 9:30, not much had happened. Ed noted it in a small red diary.

By 10:30, the mailman was the only interesting subject

to wander into view, and Ed snapped off three shots. Time noted and recorded.

At 11:00, Eric walked outside to meet Davidson's delivery truck. He took three bags of groceries, paid cash, and went back inside.

Ed took seven shots, jotted it down, and ate a sandwich.

Then at shortly after one, the cars started to arrive.

When the first pulled up, Ed clicked off two shots of the black man who got out, noted the time, and wrote down the car's license plate.

Each arrival got the same treatment. At least two photos, time, and plate. When the oriental woman arrived, Ed licked his lips and ran off five close-ups.

Eric welcomed each of his colleagues into his home, trying his best to make each comfortable in spite of the condition of the house. Helmut Brandt, from Berlin, took cognac, as did Richard Lowndes, who had flown in from New Zealand. Ling Chu, as usual, drank nothing. Nigel L. Wyndham sipped a glass of sherry, and Ariel Goldman asked for a Coke. For Chu the trip was convenient. She was in the United States anyway, coordinating an experiment at Brookhaven National Lab. Goldman had stopped in London to confer with Wyndham, and they had completed the journey together. Brandt complained about the whole affair from the first phone call, but he showed up anyway, just as Eric had suspected he would. Once the invitation list was revealed, Brandt wouldn't have missed it for the world.

A handsome black man with strong features and an easy smile, Richard Lowndes had been the first to arrive and was the only man in the group with whom Eric felt he had a sincere friendship. The others, Wyndham, Brandt, and Goldman, were of such different backgrounds and interests that relationships other than professional never had had a chance to develop. Of the three, Ariel Goldman was the one Eric hoped to know better.

Sometimes abrasive, but never obnoxious, Goldman was

a decision-maker and far-thinking. Eric considered him, like Lowndes, vital to the project. Wyndham was something of a mystery. Eric was reserving judgment until he saw how Wyndham reacted to the proposal.

Brandt was Brandt. There was nothing that could be done about that. He was a royal pain in the ass, but as sharp as Eric in almost every aspect of logic and mathematics.

Ling Chu had been born in Hong Kong and educated at Oxford and in Zurich. Eric felt she would be an anchor for the group, and although he didn't feel her participation to be absolutely essential, he knew in his heart that it would make life a lot easier if she accepted. Soft-spoken and calm, she brought a sense of balance to the gathering. Not because she was a woman, although she displayed a keen femininity, but because she was kind and considerate . . . in making her own opinions known, in listening to the arguments of the others, and in her tactful ability to summarize discussion.

Including Eric Ivorsen, the group represented the finest mathematical genius in the world . . . outside the iron curtain. After everyone was seated, Eric explained the rather unusual reason for the gathering.

"I'd like to thank you for taking the time to attend. I'll come right to the point and open this meeting to discussion. Several months ago, I came into the possession of a computer model which was theorized and created in 1950 by a team much like ourselves. My estimates are that it also includes the work of the top thirty or forty scientists alive at the time. My father worked on this project, as did Albert Einstein, Hans Schmidhuber, and several others you will read about when I distribute my notes. The program, coded 'The Viking Cipher' encompasses two phases. Phase One was a computer forecast model with projections to the year 2000. Completed in 1958, the forecast has thus far been accurate to within 2.3 percent."

Brandt snorted in disbelief. Wyndham raised his eyebrows. Goldman frowned at Lowndes. Chu remained expressionless.

"Why have we not heard of this Viking Cipher before?" Brandt demanded.

"Its creators wished it kept secret until another time."

"I remember your father's early work in computer theory. Is this the same?" Lowndes asked.

"The Forecast Phase, yes. Phase Two has never been published," Eric answered.

"Thirty top scientists worked on a project and never published?" Goldman asked with a definite note of disbelief in his voice.

"Hard to imagine, but true," Eric continued. "If we were to reprogram the projection model using updated social, economic, political, religious, and scientific factors, the margin of inaccuracy could be reduced to .13 percent."

Brandt guffawed. "I'll be interested in the logical progression that proves that!"

"All in good time," Eric replied. "There was purpose behind the creation of the forecast. Our predecessors weren't interested in simply peeking into the future. . . . Phase Two of the Viking Cipher includes the unfinished work of the other scientists. Work that was begun before the war and work that was far more powerful than the technology produced during and after the war. These things are described in the briefs at the end of my notes and are copied directly from the originals. Note, please, as you read, the different handwritings on each of these documents. You will no doubt recognize many of them."

"So what was the purpose?" Brandt demanded.

"You will realize when you see the nature of each man's work why each kept secret his progress. For example, Ivorsen, Einstein, and Schmidhuber worked on nuclear fission and made only a very small part of that technology available to the military. I need not detail where that leaves us today."

"If they had not," Ling Chu said softly, "it might well have left us unable to work."

"I agree," Eric said, holding up a defensive hand. "I am

not here to debate the advantages and disadvantages of unleashing nuclear technology. It is now fact and must be viewed as unalterable. However, when you see what they held back, you will understand why we are meeting."

Passing out thick looseleaf books to each, Eric announced, "I will prepare a lunch while you read. This meeting is open to discussion."

Chu settled in to read on the couch. Lowndes and Brandt wandered off into the small garden behind the house, reading excerpts to each other. Wyndham followed Eric into the kitchen, asking questions as he scanned through the text. Goldman skipped the Forecast Phase and sat alone at the dining-room table, hunched over the private notes of Phase Two. He looked up only once, as Eric set food on the table, and whispered, "This is all quite incredible."

"I know."

"I had no idea that Einstein had progressed this far with the unified field theory."

"Nor did I. Certainly no one at the Institute knew."

Wyndham walked in with his book open, his finger in place at the middle of a page. "Do you realize the impact of this immunology research?" he asked, his voice rising.

Eric looked up and nodded. Wyndham shook his head and turned to continue reading.

Lowndes, fascinated by a proposed food-production experiment, could barely take himself away from reading long enough to eat the food Eric laid out.

Ling Chu finished reading first and opened a bottle of Jardot Beaujolais as Eric finished setting out glasses, plates, and silverware.

"These notes are just introductions," she pointed out.

"I know," Eric replied.

"The works themselves?"

"Some available. Some not so available . . . lost in countries inaccessible to us through normal channels."

One by one the group wandered to the table. Eating and

reading, they cleaned the plates, and characteristically argued among themselves for almost three hours.

"What do you propose?" Lowndes asked Eric finally.

"I propose we set this work back into progress. As scientists, we have no choice. The development, execution, and application of this project will raise the standard of living worldwide. Although partial, the notes on nuclear fusion alone suggest the possibility of an inexhaustible and inexpensive global energy source within two decades. The same level of achievement is possible in the areas of food production, medicine, and cultural communication. I believe this project will work, and I believe that we are the people to make it do so."

"How would you accomplish it?" Wyndham asked.

"With your commitment, support, and cooperation, I can gather the missing pieces and rebuild the Viking Cipher. Using the forecast as a guideline, we will be able to judge the optimum timing for release of new technology."

"The political ramifications of what you propose are, at the very least, explosive," Goldman declared.

"A poor choice of words, Ariel," observed Lowndes.

"But accurate, I fear," Eric sighed.

"Eric is right," Ling pointed out. "The forecast program alone is too powerful to be handed over to powers of narrow vision. Imagine the result if we succeeded in recreating and developing Phase Two. It would have to be secret, and already there is no secret . . . six of us know."

"I would propose that each of you think about what you've heard and read today. In one week, I will contact each of you and I will expect a decision to either participate or withdraw. It is in the best interests of all of us that you keep your decisions to yourselves. If you withdraw, you will do so without further concern about the rest. If you participate, you will be sworn to a secrecy that if violated, may tip power into very undeserving hands."

"And who will decree which hands are deserving and which are not?" Brandt insisted.

"We are all logicians here. We will decide together," Eric explained.

"Naive," Brandt shot back. "Rule by committee never succeeds."

"It must. This work is too valuable to lose."

A new round of debate ensued. Finally Eric said, "Please feel free to stay as long as you wish reviewing the material, but please leave all papers when you leave. You should have enough information to make a decision by the week's end."

Another hour passed before the guests began to depart. When she reached the door, Ling Chu looked up and said, "You know my answer. I hope the others go along with us." She turned and walked out to her car.

Across the street, Ed snapped her picture.

"Ariel," Eric said as he walked the stocky Israeli to the door, "I'll call you in a week for your answer."

"Don't bother," Goldman replied. "I'm in."

Ed clicked off three more shots.

Lowndes took Eric aside in the kitchen while Brandt and Wyndham argued loudly in the parlor about a theoretical mathematical assumption in the text.

"Eric, you know that I've been offered a fellowship in London."

Eric nodded.

"You know that I've wanted this more than anything else."

Eric nodded again, looking into his deep black eyes.

"But I fear this might be more important."

"Perhaps you can do both," Eric suggested. "This is going to be a program of communication as well as collaboration. Possibly we can be every bit as effective spread out. I'm willing to try it on that basis. After all, we used to play chess long-distance when you were in Sydney and I was here in Princeton."

"We had NASA communication satellites available to us for that."

Eric answered seriously, "We're going to need that and more for this project. We'll have to tap into every possible source of information and communication."

Lowndes raised his eyebrows and asked softly, "Will these sources be aware that they are supplying us with such sophisticated technology?"

"Perhaps not always," Eric admitted to his friend.

Lowndes thought about the consequences of such an arrangement, grinned, and replied, "Then I am honored to be a part of the Viking Cipher."

Eric walked him to the door and down the fieldstone path.

Ed took one shot of both and then sank into his seat to hide.

Wyndham and Brandt were still arguing when Eric walked back into the house. Wyndham refused to concede that the whole affair was dangerous, and Brandt continued to berate his position. Finally Wyndham declared that he would make his decision privately and stood to leave. Eric walked him to the door.

Ed caught both of them in full-face close-ups.

Brandt, of course, was the last to leave. It was Brandt who raised the most bothersome questions, and it was always Brandt who was worried about what the government's position would be.

"The government," Eric said finally, "is not to know."

"You are a crazy man," Brandt declared.

"Perhaps."

"We could be arrested!" he cried out.

"It's a private project."

"That's just an excuse, and you know it!"

"Yes, but a good one."

Brandt scowled in disgust.

"Give it some thought," Eric said calmly and left him alone in the parlor. After washing off the dishes and pouring himself a brandy, he wandered back in and found Brandt engrossed in the papers of Phase Two.

"You would be invaluable," Eric said.

"Of course I would, but . . . I don't know," Brandt said, shaking his head. "So much power not evenly distributed. Very unstable. Very unsafe."

"Does that mean no?" Eric asked.

"I don't know. I'll have to give it thought. This is a very serious question. We must not treat it like some game."

"I'll call you on Friday."

"Perhaps I'll have reached a decision by then."

"Perhaps," Eric said with a forced smile.

Brandt hurried down the fieldstone path staring at the ground, shaking his head, frowning with worry.

Across the street, Ed took one last shot and ran out of film.

Eric packed away the dishes, gathered all the looseleaf notebooks, and wandered upstairs. When he saw the cat, he remembered Parat Singh. He glanced at the clock, decided it was now too late to call, and instead dialed Maggie's number.

"How'd it go?" she asked eagerly.

"I hope you like crowded theaters," he replied.

Maggie laughed and asked, "When will I see you?"

"As I said, everything will be getting back to normal now. If everyone agrees to participate, I'll spend next Saturday finishing preliminary structuring of the Viking Cipher team and I'll fly down on Sunday and we can make some more definite plans for the future."

It was a poor choice of words. There was a stony silence at the other end of the line.

"By that I mean . . ." Eric began.

"I know what you meant," she assured him. "Neither of us is ready for long-range definite plans. You were talking short-range to slightly less than intermediate but certainly not more than mildly longer than short-range definite plans . . . right?"

"Exactly. Sunday through the end of the year," he suggested.

"I'd love to spend Sunday through the end of the year with you."

"Then it's a date," he said.

"Great." Maggie giggled.

"How's it going at work?" he asked.

"Miss Burke is on an assignment up in Tallahassee. She won't be in until tomorrow . . . maybe the next day. I'll tell her then that I lost the pictures."

"Tell her we can make the run again," Eric said. "I'll rent an Island Trader and—"

"Forget it, Horatio," Maggie interrupted. "I've had enough salt water to last me a lifetime."

Eric laughed and said, "Okay, I'll let you get to bed."

"I'm already in bed."

"I wish I were there," he whispered.

"Me too. I'm naked."

Eric was silent for a moment. Then he asked in a tight voice, "You don't have anything on?"

"You got me out of the tub."

"I see . . . or rather, I'd like to."

Maggie's voice was suddenly deep and sexy. "I'm just lying here all alone, stretched out across this big lonely bed, with little drops of water clinging to me in the most interesting places."

"Stop," he whispered as if in pain.

"I just wish my nipples weren't so hard . . . and my breasts didn't need a good toweling off . . ."

"Don't do this to me, cruel siren."

". . . but my thighs are still a little warm, especially where you were kissing me the other night, and . . ."

"Maggie," Eric said, "this is wholly unfair and I insist that you stop."

"Okay," she whispered, "if you insist."

"Just finish the part about the thighs first. . . ."

CHAPTER 11

Eric was on his knees, unpacking books, when the doorbell rang at 10:00 the next morning. Standing, he walked to the long windows that looked out on the porch and was astounded to see Parat Singh standing at the door. Holding a black schoolbag briefcase, Singh looked like an old-fashioned family doctor . . . only sinister. Dr. Jekyll makes a house call, Eric thought and smiled. He opened the door and welcomed him in. "This is a surprise."

"I am intrigued by your story of the Bastet copy," Singh replied.

"I meant to call yesterday. . . ."

Singh closed his eyes and said, "There is no need to explain. We are both busy men. That is why I took the liberty of arriving unannounced."

"No problem."

"Is the cat here?"

"Yes, as a matter of fact, it is."

"Very good."

"I'll bring it down." Eric turned to the stairs and returned with the cat in his hands. He couldn't tell whether it was the glint of gold reflected in the inky pupils of Singh's eyes or whether Singh was showing the first signs of life. Either way, for the first time, Eric saw a spark of vitality.

"Do you have a basement?" Singh asked, gazing at the cat.

A little startled by the question, Eric stammered, "Yes, of course. Why?"

"I have an instrument in this bag that must be used to examine the statuette in the dark."

"Okay." Eric shrugged. "Follow me." He turned and led Singh to the cellar door. Singh followed him down into the musty-smelling old basement and they stood under a single forty-watt bulb suspended from the low ceiling above. The height of the basement being inches less than his own, Eric stood stooped over.

Setting his briefcase on the bottom step of the stairway, Singh took the cat and crossed to a workbench covered with cobwebs and dust. He twisted the cat, inspecting it closely. Eric had no idea why he was doing it in the dim light of the basement, but then he wasn't the expert.

Motioning him over, Singh said, "Would you please bring my case?"

Eric turned right and left, spotted it, and carried to the bench.

Apparently fascinated by some aspect of the statuette, Singh held it close to his eyes and whispered, "Would you please open my case and bring me the device in the middle compartment?"

Eric nodded, flipped open the brass latch, and pulled the briefcase open. He peered inside but saw no instrument. Something, though, was wrapped in a pile in the bottom, and he assumed that that was what Singh meant. Reaching in, Eric suddenly froze. He sensed something . . . in the way prey feels the presence of a predator. It might have been the sound or he might have caught a glimpse. Frowning, he instinctively started to pull his hand away.

The krait tasted the air only once. Watching the big hand entering its lair, it coiled . . . then attacked. Shooting straight up out of the briefcase, it sank its pink fangs into the soft flesh of Eric's forearm.

Hot cold pain shot up his shoulder, forcing him to cry out.

Around Eric and already halfway up the stairs, Singh turned when he reached the top, then slammed and locked the door.

Wildly wringing his arm, Eric tried to rip the serpent away, but it hung on, caught in the fold of his shirt and tender flesh. Grabbing its tail, he tore it from his body and smashed it to death on the cold cement floor. But the lethal injection had been delivered. Poison began pumping through his veins.

Eric bolted for the stairs, banging his head on the low ceiling as he crossed the cellar. Climbing the steps in two leaps, he felt his arm start to numb. Then the door would not yield. Outraged, Eric began pounding on it with his fist.

Animal instinct dumped adrenaline into his system, and with his blood pressure rising, the poison moved quickly in his body. Eric backed away and threw himself against the door. The top hinge of the door creaked away from the doorjamb. Eric rammed it again and the wood beneath the hardware split further. Again and it yielded even more. He knew the forth or fifth battering would break through, but then a wave of dizziness and nausea washed over him.

Panting and trying desperately not to throw up, he dropped his head low and gasped for consciousness. He drew a deep breath and with all his might, threw himself full weight once more at the old oak door. It smashed open. Parat Singh stood on the other side. With one graceful kick to Eric's head, he sent the big man tumbling back down into the cold damp basement. Eric struggled to his feet and charged again up the creaky stairs. Singh slammed the door once more, and it smashed into the side of Eric's face, splitting open the speargun's gash. The stairway started to spin, his breathing became labored, and Eric tumbled back, first banging into the light and then cracking his head on the cold concrete floor.

When he heard only silence, Singh reopened the broken cellar door. Staring down at Eric splayed across the cement, he smiled slowly and stroked the golden cat cradled in his arms.

Then the hideous smile slowly disintegrated. Parat Singh saw a white belly curled like a rope, upside down under the swinging light, and realized he was staring at the limp corpse of Sheeli, his pet krait.

Thirty minutes later, a green Dodge Econoline panel truck pulled up to the front of the house and two men got out. Leaving the emergency lights flashing, they opened the back doors of the vehicle and unloaded a huge box.

From his vantage point across the road, Ed watched, clicking off shots as they worked. Armed with three new rolls of film, an olive-loaf sandwich, and a thermos of coffee, he had resumed surveillance an hour earlier.

Now one roll of film was used up, the sandwich was half gone, and the thermos untouched. Coffee in the morning gave Ed heartburn. He made a note of the make, model, and color of the truck. And with the aid of the telephoto lens, he could easily read the plate. The lettering on the side of the truck indicated that Eric Ivorsen was receiving a delivery of wholesale fish.

Ed frowned when he saw "GE Dishwasher" stamped in blue on the side of the box. Why would a fish truck with New York plates deliver a dishwasher? he asked himself. And that box handles too easily for a dishwasher, he thought, but that was what it said on the side, he was sure.

With almost no effort, the two strong young men wheeled it up the front steps, across the porch, and into the front door, opened by the skinny dark man who had gone in earlier. Several minutes later, they carried it back out, only this time it appeared heavier. Ed frowned again and took a few more pictures. They packed up the box, the skinny man climbed in behind it, and they all drove away. Activity then ceased at the Ivorsen house.

Ed waited an hour and then crossed the street. The time had come, he told himself, to take the bull by the horns and ask some direct questions. He knocked on the door. Prepared to explain himself as a retired scientist interested in buying a computer, he was disappointed when there was no answer.

Bruno Formidoni wheeled his Dodge truck into an underground parking garage on 82nd Street. Cruising to the farthest corner of the garage, he backed it into a space marked reserved, killed the engine, and then crawled in the back to help his brother Tony unload the box.

Singh walked around behind the truck to a steel door secured by two heavy-duty deadbolt locks. Unlocking both, he held the door open while Tony and Bruno struggled with the box, made cumbersome by Eric Ivorsen's body. The door led to a private basement directly below the New York shop of Objets d'Art Egyptien. It was through this secret room that some of the world's rarest treasures had passed. Duplicated by Singh and Smythe, the exact replicas were then substituted for the originals, which were smuggled to Paris for storage or sale.

The final substitutions in the collection of Queen Hareyet's temple gold was by far their most ambitious undertaking. Through the years, the process had always been the same. As one of the world's foremost Egyptologists, Sir Thatcher Smythe enjoyed open access to not only the Metropolitan, but also the Louvre and the London Museum. Smythe would take careful photographs of the object to be replaced. A copy was created in this basement and then carried to the museum. Left alone with the original, Smythe would compare the two pieces . . . sometimes returning to alter the copy a dozen times . . . until he was satisfied that there was no difference. Then he substituted the copy, authenticated it to museum officials, and it became a permanent part of the collections.

At first it had been difficult to afford the gold necessary for the duplications and as time wore on, Smythe had instructed Singh to sell off some of the earlier pieces to fund new acquisitions. In doing so, Parat Singh met Anil Fascione.

Instantly intrigued by the seemingly vast black market for Egyptian antiquities, Fascione had revealed that he would be willing to finance a larger operation . . . for a fifty percent cut of the take. After that, Smythe had had no need to sell off acquisitions to buy raw gold . . . Anil Fascione supplied all he could use. But along with the partnership came Sonny Pike . . . a business representative, Fascione had called him. An auditor at best, Smythe claimed privately to Singh, and a spy at worst.

Ultimately the stockpile grew, and any piece that went on tour was ripe for the picking. Thatcher Smythe stole from all three museums and laughed to himself when the Tut exhibit left New York. Lines of people waited to view artifacts, some of which he himself had created, while the originals were secreted in his warehouse in Paris. And now the collecting was almost over.

The wheels of the handtruck squeaked as Bruno pulled the cumbersome dishwasher box into the room.

Thatcher Smythe looked up from a workbench at the side near the door to the shop. "And?" he said in a voice full of hope and anticipation.

Parat Singh held up the golden cat but did not smile.

"This is wonderful," Smythe sighed, taking the statuette. Then he saw the distraught look in Singh's eyes and asked, "What is it? What's wrong?"

"It is Sheeli."

"Your pet?"

"Yes."

"What happened?"

"He killed her."

Smythe's face tensed. "So kill him."

"No. Let Sheeli's poison do it. It will be longer and more painful."

"I'm sorry, Parat," Smythe said, gently embracing Singh.

Singh took a deep breath and released it slowly.

Bruno dumped the dishwasher box over, and Eric's body tumbled out. Saliva, bubbling out of the corner of his mouth, ran down his chin. His breathing was irregular and labored, his eyes shut. Black and blue at the puncture, his arm was swollen red where the krait had struck. The gash on his face, just starting to heal, had opened and dripped blood.

"Whaddya want us to do with this clown?" Bruno asked.

"Place him in the coffin," Smythe said.

Bruno motioned Tony to a huge outer coffin. It was this box that had taken the longest to duplicate. Constructed of finely spliced cedar planking, it required the skills of a master sculptor to recreate the face, head, and folded hands that made this particular mummy box one of the most ornate ever discovered. Smythe had worked on it for nearly three years. The substitution was accomplished when he convinced the curators of the London Museum to allow the two coffins to go on a three-week tour to New York and Paris as part of a lecture series. With one short diversionary stop in the basement garage off 82nd Street, the tour went without hitch. Except that the coffins going back would be perfect counterfeits.

This outer coffin was six and a half feet long and bore the image of the face and hands of Queen Hareyet. The inner coffin, now in the cargo hold of the trawler *Whimbrel*, was different in only two ways—it was smaller and it was covered with gold. The duplicate now on display in the museum had been covered with plate.

Bruno grabbed Eric under the shoulders. Tony took his feet. Grunting, they hoisted him up and dropped him into the ancient box.

"He don't fit," Tony complained.

Smythe looked up and said, "What?"

"He's too long."

Like a surgeon overseeing an operation, Smythe gazed the length of the body and said finally, "Fold his legs up. It won't matter . . . he'll be dead in an hour anyway."

"What about the cat?" Singh asked.

"Now with our pipeline shut down, it is not so easy to move it," Smythe mused.

"This box will not be opened for inspection," Singh pointed out.

"Very well, we'll allow Mr. Ivorsen's corpse to see it safely across the ocean." Smythe set the cat at Eric's feet and motioned to Bruno and Tony, who placed the carved lid on the box. Smythe himself nailed it shut, using the same nails that had held it in place for twenty-five hundred years.

Nailed shut, the coffin was then lifted into a shipping crate marked with the museum's official stamps and stenciling. Locked and secured, it would first go to Customs, where Smythe would present his museum identification, an application for inspection waiver, and an affidavit attesting to the crate's content.

As always, the officer in charge, an agent who had come to know Smythe over the years, would automatically stamp the waiver and the unopened crate would be placed in the waiting plane. Smythe would repeat the process eight hours later in Brussels, Belgium.

"We must close down here," Smythe announced. "Bruno, you and Tony bring everything down from upstairs, pack it in those empty crates, and after you drop us at the airport, get rid of it."

"For good?" Bruno asked.

"A fire would be nice," Smythe answered.

"Right."

When Bruno and his brother reached the top of the stairs, Smythe turned to Singh and whispered, "Take care of them. Something slow so they have a chance to get rid of this mess after they drop us at Kennedy . . . but something permanent.''

Singh nodded.

"The shop in Brussels," Smythe asked. "It will not take long to empty?"

Singh shook his head.

With a twinkle in his eye, he concluded, "Then we will have brunch in Brussels and dinner in Paris."

CHAPTER 12

"Jesus, what've they got in here?" the ground crewman complained, as he tried to push the unusually large container to the side of the 747's cargo compartment.

Loaded on Sabena Airlines flight 548, the container and everything else on board was about to depart for Brussels, Belgium. Thatcher Smythe, reclining in a seat in the cabin above, waited patiently for the plane to leave the terminal. Parat Singh sat next to him, mourning the loss of Sheeli.

Inside the box, Eric Ivorsen's irregular breathing weakened, though the poison coursing through his body had not yet reached its full effect. Sweat poured from his forehead and bizarre hallucinations racked his mind. His legs, folded tight against his chest, throbbed and ached. Blood that had seeped into the healing gash on his face dried into a crusty brown splotch.

The airliner taxied onto the runway, received takeoff clearance, and began to roll. Thirty minutes later, it leveled out at thirty-three thousand feet. The temperature in the cockpit was a comfortable seventy degrees. Outside the aircraft, ten below zero. In the cargo hold, just above freezing. Inside the coffin, Eric's body temperature had

135

reached 105 when the cold started to penetrate the cramped little box.

The lowering temperature had two effects: It saved Eric Ivorsen from permanent brain damage and slowed his metabolism to a point where the poison became far less effective and the oxygen seeping through cracks in the ancient casket sustained him. It was the beginning of an eight-hour flight that Eric would spend drifting in and out of semiconsciousness ... wavering between shivering cold and blistering fever ... teetering on the edge of death.

"Where the hell are you?" Ben Chestle growled into the phone.

"Jersey."

"Aw, fer Chrissake! How much have you spent this time?"

"Well, I bought this fancy camera and ... none of your damn business! What I do with my retirement is up to me."

"The key word there, Pop, was retirement. You're no longer a cop. When you gonna accept that, for Chrissake?"

"Wait'll you see what I got ... then sass your old man," Ed Chestle said smugly.

That intrigued Ben. "Yeah, what?"

"You know what with all the summer people packin' up to go home, you just don't have time to investigate these things proper. That's why I have to give you a hand."

"Spare me the bullshit and tell me what you've got."

"I been runnin' a little background check on this Ivorsen character. Somethin' fishy goin' on."

"C'mon, Pop, I've got stuff to do here."

"See what I mean ... no time for good police work."

Ben heaved a deep sigh.

"I'm tellin' ya that somethin' ain't right here," Ed repeated.

"Like what?"

"Foreigners, for one thing. Lots of 'em. Comin' and goin' like there's no tomorrow. Carryin' stuff in ... carryin' stuff out."

"So what?"

"So I got plenty of pictures and a bunch of plates . . . thought we might run 'em through DMV."

"Awright," Ben Chestle sighed. "Give 'em to Halsey." Conceding that there was no use in trying to convince his father to give up the investigation, Chestle resigned himself to placating him instead.

Pete Halsey looked up at the mention of his name and asked, "What's going on?"

"Old Ed is playing Sherlock Holmes again. Doris and I made the mistake of havin' him over for his birthday the other night, and I musta mentioned the submarine thing. Next thing I know, he's gone. Been followin' that Ivorsen guy ever since. Now he's got a list of plates to run. Do me a favor and humor him."

"You got it." Halsey grinned and took the phone. After a few minutes he looked up at Ben and, wincing, whispered, "Your dad wants to know if we can request a search warrant for Princeton."

"Awww, Jesus . . . gimme that phone."

Halsey handed it over and grinned.

"Listen, you old fuckin' seagull, you pack your ass up and come home."

"Why should I?"

"You forgot your nitroglycerin pills, for one thing. You don't have a private detective's license, for another, and I'm not gonna bail your wrinkled butt out this time if you get arrested like you did in Falstaff!"

"I can buy more pills here," Ed snapped. "And they never would've arrested me in Arizona if you'd told 'em that I'm a chief of police."

"Don't argue with me, you cantankerous old bastard. I'm never going to mention an open case to you again."

"No way for a boy to talk to his father," Ed Chestle muttered and hung up.

"Christ!" Ben Chestle growled and did the same.

*　　*　　*

Ed Chestle drove out to Ivorsen's house for one last look around. Don't need any search warrant, he told himself, I'm just an old man poking around looking for a room to rent.

Several hard knocks at the front door brought no response. Walking around the back of the house, he found the kitchen door open and walked inside. Everything looked pretty normal inside except the broken hardware and split cellar door. Somethin' busted outta here, he decided, staring down into the basement. Then he saw the dead snake.

"I'll be a son of a pup," he muttered to himself.

"We've come a long way, Parat," Thatcher Smythe mused, his head back and his eyes closed. He should have looked relaxed. Instead his expression was that of bitterness. He was not a happy man.

Singh remained silent, staring out at the twinkling lights of the New England coast passing below. The steady drone of the plane's jet engines filled the cabin with a hypnotic hum.

On the verge of sleep, Smythe's mind drifted back forty-five years . . . to a time when he was strong and handsome . . . to a time when the future was bright with the promise of things to come. He had goals to conquer then, not scores to settle. He remembered the parties. Most of all, the parties . . . honoring him. They flashed before him, and the stern mask on his face relaxed for a moment. The scowl lines of bitterness etched into the corners of his mouth softened as he reminisced.

There were champagne toasts and violin music and dances with beautiful women. And they were captivated by his stories of the dig. They laughed at his jokes. They flirted openly, sometimes asking how a man could get by in the desert for all those months. And they always giggled when he answered that he made up for lost time with each visit to London. Their men were often jealous. Newspaper reporters came to call every week. Schoolchildren begged for autographs. Men of better education asked his opinions.

But then the war came along and ruined it all. The parties, the gaiety, the future. London ladies who used to gather around to hear his stories were instead suddenly interested in reports from the Continent. How were the boys doing? Was it true they had scored a victory in Calais? Could they really stop the Germans in Paris? No one cared anymore about Thatcher Smythe's victories in the deserts of Egypt . . . there was no archaeological exploration during the war.

The bitter scowl returned just as it had almost every night of his life. Before sleep, when most men dream of women, Thatcher Smythe fantasized revenge. An equitable return of property, was how he saw it.

He had conquered more than armies, he knew. By God, he had conquered time! They didn't care, though. They were more concerned with the blasted war. The fighting came and the parties ended. For five years, he was reduced to nothing more than a librarian in the Egyptology Department of the London Museum.

Then the war was over and the soldiers came home . . . what was left of them. And the self-righteous little blob of a nation began licking its wounds. No money for archaeologists, they said in officious tones, as if it were some sort of greedy request. Try the Americans, they said. And after he'd brought England millions in gold treasure. Why, the Queen Hareyet find alone was worth more than ten million pounds in 1937. God knew its worth today.

We'll find out, he thought, a wicked smile stretching across his face. I gave them millions in gold. And now I've taken it back.

"Would you like a cocktail?"

Snapping up, Smythe blinked opened his eyes and gazed at the stewardess next to him.

"A cocktail, sir?" she asked, pulling a cart of small bottles to the seat.

"Oh, uh, no thank you. I don't drink anymore."

"A magazine?" she offered, holding out several plastic-covered publications. Smythe took a *Time* and cradled it in his hands.

Parat Singh declined both libation and library, and the woman wheeled her cart away.

I used to drink, though, eh, Parat? he thought, gazing over at Singh. Poor pathetic Singh. A mere boy when he first saw him, Smythe recalled, standing knee-deep in the brown water of the Indus River. Holding up a four-foot cobra as if it were a prize possession. In a way it was, Smythe recalled learning later. To a Jogi youth, the snake represented manhood and position in the tribe. Singh owned three.

That day came floating back more vividly than ever. On a private archaeological exploration, financed before the wretched war broke out, he had gone to India to visit the Mosque of Jahan. And it was there that he first met Singh. Begging for baksheesh, the skinny little ten-year-old offered to carry his bags across the muddy water to the dry stone steps of Tatta.

Smythe accepted, and from that day on, Singh was with him. And in all the years that followed, they never once returned to Tatta.

Closing his eyes, Smythe could picture it all again. Thousands of shining white tombstones nestled against the rust-colored Makli Ridge. Like a beacon of beauty, the Great Mosque of Jahan rose from the midst of worshipers and life. Falling asleep, Smythe dropped the magazine in his hands to the floor. The sound woke him.

"Clumsy of me," he apologized. "I was remembering Tatta."

Parat Singh too remembered Tatta. His perception was a little different. He remembered it as it had been for him . . . a nightmare of crumbling brown stucco buildings teeming with people, beneath thousands of graves on the Makli Ridge. A river of tepid brown water carrying sewage, corpses, and stench to the sea. A dizzying daily kaleidoscope of filth, disease, hunger, pregnant women, Jogi tribesmen, and priests.

Singh closed his eyes as if the action would squeeze away the memory.

There in the middle stood the Great Mosque of Jahan, a mocking monument of opulence and wealth in the midst of a living nightmare of starvation and plague. Singh's arm jerked on the armrest.

"Wake up, Singh, you are dreaming," Smythe said, his hand gripping Singh's arm.

Singh responded slowly, "No . . . I am not."

"You must've been, my friend—you nearly tore off the armrest."

"Forgive me," Singh said softly.

Singh remembered that first meeting as an almost religious experience. He considered the opportunity to serve Thatcher Smythe an opportunity sent by God in return for good work he performed with the snakes. He had prayed for an escape from Tatta, and God had sent him Thatcher Smythe.

Now there was nothing he wouldn't do for his savior. Nothing.

In the cargo hold below, Eric Ivorsen was having dreams of his own . . . horrible painful nightmares of being crushed to death in a blazing-hot freezer. Sheeli's venom was seeping deeper into his brain. He felt a crushing weight on his chest, felt numb from the waist down. Through it all, he knew he was dying.

CHAPTER 13

"Miss McCabe, do you think you could spare a few minutes out of your busy little schedule to discuss the needs of this paper?" Carla Burke's tone was typically sarcastic and catty. She had purposely waited until they were in front of a group of Maggie's co-workers before asking the question.

Following her into an office in the *St. Petersburg Times* building, Maggie winced, realizing that her borrowed time had just gone into foreclosure.

She had never gotten along well with Carla and probably never would have worked for the *St. Petersburg Times Evening Independent* if Carla had not been away on a medical leave of absence when she applied for a job. Hired by the acting editor for the feature section of the paper, she began as an assistant but quickly advanced to her position as chief photographer even though Carla Burke thought it to be a premature promotion and said so.

For nearly five years, they had managed to maintain a working truce that produced award-winning feature writing and picture stories. The national recognition solidified Maggie's position and prevented Carla from denying her a

142

well-earned working vacation to Europe when Maggie split up with Carl Millbank.

Naturally, it was also Carla Burke who had been the most upset when Maggie ended up extending that vacation to include three extra weeks spent chasing around the world with Eric Ivorsen in search of the Viking Cipher papers. Still, the photographs of Salzburg, Vienna, and Zermatt were above average and the feature story that resulted worth the inconvenience of having the paper's best photographer away for all that time. Nothing was said to Maggie.

But then when she called and left word that she was taking yet another ten days off to do a story about a yacht trip to Newport, Carla Burke was furious. Not that the story was a bad idea—a picture tour of East Coast seaports hadn't been done in the paper, and everyone else in editorial liked the concept. Carla was furious because she hadn't thought of or authorized it. At the time, Maggie didn't really care—she just wanted to be with Eric. Now she was wondering if she shouldn't have given it all a little more thought.

Carla walked stiffly around her desk and sank into her swivel armchair with her lips pursed, annoyed. She stared at Maggie for a moment, then dropped her gaze to her desk, which was covered with galleys, proofs, and photos.

"I haven't seen the proofs yet for the photo layout on East Coast seaports," Carla said, searching through the various stacks of papers.

Maggie swallowed and answered, "There aren't any."

Carla looked up and blinked. "What?"

"All of my negatives and cameras were lost in a boating accident at the end of the trip."

"I am in no mood for jokes, McCabe." Carla liked to project an image of toughness. She dressed in masculine clothes, wore her hair in a severe little chop, and tended to use military jargon whenever the opportunity presented itself. Carla Burke had decided early on to become one of the boys.

"I'm afraid I am not joking. I wish I were," Maggie replied.

"Listen to me, young lady," Carla said through her teeth. "What are you trying to pull here?"

"Miss Burke, I'm truly sorry that I can't provide those photographs, but accidents are beyond my control."

Rocking back in her chair, Carla drummed her short colorless fingernails impatiently on her chair's armrests as if trying to calm herself. "How long have you been with us now, McCabe?" she asked.

"Four and a half years."

"And have you ever known me to be unreasonable?"

All the fucking time, Maggie thought, but answered, "No."

"Why, then, are you placing me in this position?"

No answer was required for that, Maggie knew. Carla was about to launch into one of her lectures.

"Now, I can understand how distressing it is to break up with a man you've been engaged to for seven years," Carla began, "and I believe we were more than generous in giving you time off to get over it. Nothing was said when those two weeks turned into five. Your photographs were good and the copy was acceptable. All in all, not bad."

"Thank you," Maggie said with her chin out. "But personally, I thought they were better than good. I thought they were terrific."

Carla snapped up, a little stunned by Maggie's confidence. "Yes, well. Now I'm in a quandary. I cannot have my little troops . . ."

Maggie bristled but held her tongue.

". . . just picking up and running off with their own ideas for stories. Personally, I've suggested, and believe, that you should be let go."

"What?" Maggie gasped.

"But," Carla continued, ignoring the cry of protest,

"apparently you've won the hearts of some others around here, and it has been agreed that you be given a chance to redeem yourself."

Maggie sat slightly openmouthed. She had never liked Carla Burke, and apparently Carla felt pretty much the same toward her.

"That's why you're going to work full-time for the next five Saturdays and Sundays. I want a picture story every Wednesday at oh nine hundred sharp. I'll give you your assignments on Friday mornings. You have them on my desk the following week. Understood?"

"Do I have a choice?" Maggie replied, trying not to explode.

"Sure you have a choice, McCabe." Carla grinned. "See that door over there?"

Maggie turned toward the newsroom's emergency exit.

"You can take your little cameras and cans of film and march right on through it if you like."

Turning back to her boss, Maggie said calmly, "You're a real bitch, you know that? I mean . . . have any of your little troops ever pointed that out before?"

"Two. One's a topless dancer in Fort Lauderdale and one's servicing sugar daddies in Palm Beach. I said you get one more chance. You just used up half of it."

Strung out in a long line of cars on the Montauk Highway, angry motorists cursed and swore at the driver of the white Nova. When he slowed to turn left into the police head-quarters parking lot, a young blond in a green Pinto pulled around on the road's shoulder and gave him the finger. With his myopic eyes riveted to the road immediately in front, Ed Chestle didn't notice.

He climbed slowly out of his car wearing the same rumpled plaid sports coat, brown pants, and orthopedic shoes that he'd had on for the last four days.

"Hi, chief," Pete Halsey said when he walked into the stationhouse.

"Hiya, Petey boy," Ed replied. Ed liked Halsey. Halsey still always called him chief.

"How's the case goin'?" Halsey asked with a grin.

"Got us some pictures of that Ivorsen character," Ed said proudly, patting his coat pocket. "Anything come back on those plates I asked you to check out?"

"All clean . . . in fact, two of those cars are registered to the feds. Interagency pool. I checked them out too. They're issued to some think tank down in Princeton. People all have top security clearances."

"Damn," Ed gummed. "Thought we mighta had somethin'."

"Sorry."

"Aw well, I had some fun bird-doggin' that sonofapup anyway," he sighed. "Gave me the slip, though." Ed Chestle didn't hear his son walk out into the big office.

"How's that?" Ben Chestle grumbled from behind.

Ed turned slowly around and stared into his son's face. "Nice to see you too, son," he said with a big smile.

"Yeah, yeah, welcome home. What did you just say?" Ben asked again.

"I said that Ivorsen guy gave me the slip."

"What are you talkin' about?"

"I was stakin' out his digs when all of a sudden he up and disappears. House was deserted."

"Maybe he just went to bed."

"Nah, I checked."

Ben didn't like the sound of that at all. "What do you mean, you checked?" he asked suspiciously.

"I went inside, okay? I knocked on the door, there wasn't any answer, so I went around back and walked inside. Only thing I found was a busted cellar door and a dead varmint."

"What kind of varmint?" Halsey asked.

"Snake."

"No kidding?" Halsey said.

"Never seen any like it around these parts. Banded sucker."

"Your plates turned out to be rentals and feds," Ben said, a note of pleasure in his voice.

"I know it. Petey told me. I got one more, though. Probably should run it. Petey don't mind, do ya?" he asked the young officer.

"Not at all."

Ed fumbled through his little red diary and read off the license-plate number of the Dodge Econoline truck.

"Get right on it," Halsey said and turned to the phone.

"Let's talk in my office," Ben said, leading the way.

Ed winked at Pete Halsey and followed Ben Chestle into an office that had been his own for nearly twenty years.

"Old place still feels like home," Ed said, looking around.

"Well, it ain't."

"You know," Ed said, squinting at his son, "I shoulda whipped you more when you was a boy. Woulda taught you more respect."

"Pop," Ben sighed, "I know you're tryin' to help, and believe me, I appreciate it . . ."

"Sure got a funny way of showin' it."

"These aren't the good old days . . . you can't just go walkin' into people's homes."

"Wouldn't have found nothin' out unless I did."

"So what did you find out? Eric Ivorsen wasn't home but a snake was. Big fuckin' deal."

"You got a foul mouth too. You never learned that from me."

"I give up," Ben said, throwing his big hands open.

"Simmer down, simmer down, son . . . and listen to what I got to say."

Ben looked across the desk into his father's eyes and sensed that the banter was over. The old man was serious, and Ben knew to listen.

"Somethin' is wrong down there. I took a bunch of pictures, and I think you better get 'em developed, because somethin' serious is going on. You take that snake I seen . . . that was no local garden-variety snake, that was a dangerous snake, and it died while killin' somethin' else. Its fangs were still out and drippin' venom."

"You sure?"

"Damn right I'm sure. And I'll tell you somethin' else. Ivorsen was home when this little foreign guy shows up. Few minutes later, that Dodge van drops off a dishwasher . . . exceptin' they don't drop it off, they take it with 'em, and what's more, it looked heavier goin' out than it did goin' in. And tell me why a wholesale fish truck is haulin' around dishwashers in the first place."

"So what are you tellin' me?"

"I think they grabbed Ivorsen and took him out in that box. He's a big sonofapup. Knockin' him out with a snake poison would be one way to handle him. No mess, no bother."

"You got pictures of all these people?"

Ed patted his coat pocket.

"Awright, let's run 'em."

Ed handed over the three rolls of film, stood, and walked to the door.

"Hey, Pop," Ben Chestle called out.

Ed turned slowly. "Yeah?"

"Thanks for the help."

"Anytime, son."

The trawler *Whimbrel* powered into the Le Havre docks shortly after dark. Casting lines to a dockhand, the crew secured the ship only for unloading and then assisted Sonny Pike in quickly transferring the small but precious cargo to shore. A light misty rain was falling, and the decks were slippery, the docks glistening wet.

Several people, passing along on the dock, stopped for a moment to marvel at the strange exploration craft that rested on the *Wimbrel*'s aft deck beneath huge powerful hoists. Out of the water, the ebony-black salvage submarine, with its long arms, looked a little less insectlike and a little more scientific. Still, with its heavily plated bow dented and some black paint scraped away, it generated a lot of interest.

Explaining to three curious young men in his broken French that the *Whimbrel* was an oceanographic research operation, Pike quickly dismissed the onlookers and went about the business of transporting the last of the shipment. The huge hoist lifted the blue plastic-coated crates and reinforced bogus lobster boxes onto a Mercedes truck that Thatcher Smythe had arranged to have waiting on the dock. Packed safely in its watertight crate, Queen Hareyet's gold inner coffin was the last item loaded.

Farther down the docks, about a hundred yards away, a burgundy Rolls-Royce with black windows sat with its lights off but its windshield wipers clearing the view in intermittent strokes. The man in the backseat watched with a keen eye as Pike supervised the unloading of the *Whimbrel*. When the operation was complete, Pike wandered over to the luxurious car. Its back door opened and he climbed inside. Several minutes later, he climbed out and the Rolls glided silently away.

As soon as the shipment was counted and receipted, Pike tipped the captain and crew with a stack of cash he had received in the Rolls. Anil Fascione rewarded his men handsomely for work well done.

Saluting a cold brief farewell to the three men he had worked with in the sub and on Digger Murdock's boat, Pike watched the *Whimbrel* pull out of port and steam out into the misty fog. Although he had worked with those men many times, and probably would again, he felt no comradery, no friendship. If he never laid eyes on them again, he would not care. He climbed up into the cab of the truck and began the drive to Paris.

At about the same time Pike left Le Havre, Thatcher Smythe and Parat Singh left Brussels Airport in a smaller truck that carried the sealed packing crate they'd picked up at Customs. They drove directly to the Place du Grand

Sablon and backed up to the Objets d'Art Egyptien front entrance.

Quickly and efficiently emptying the showroom and office of all treasures, furniture, and art, they completed the work Peake and McCorkle were supposed to have done, locked the front doors forever, and drove away.

They spoke very little on the small journey, and the only sounds in the truck were the rumble of engine, the slapping of windshield wiper, and the angry hiss of snakes. Packed in a wicker suitcase basket, the eight deadly cobras complained all the way to Paris.

By the time Pike reached the gray rain-soaked streets of the City of Light, his right hand was throbbing badly and it hurt whenever he turned. Promising himself a trip to a doctor as soon as he finished with Smythe and his auction, Pike tried to forget about the pain and remember the bonus that Fascione would pay him.

Turning off the Rue des Saints Pères in the heart of the antiquities district of Paris, he wheeled the Mercedes truck up to a warehouse door at the end of an alley courtyard on the Rue de Lille. He beeped the horn twice and the heavy brown metal doors parted.

Staring through the truck's windshield as its wipers rose and fell, Pike watched blurred sheets of water disappear. As falling raindrops spotted the glass once more, he watched Parat Singh pull open one door, and Thatcher Smythe pull open the other.

CHAPTER 14

The phone was ringing as Maggie came through the door. Expecting it to be Eric, she nearly tripped hurrying across the room to answer it.

"Miss McCabe?"

"Yes?"

"Ben Chestle."

"Oh, hi," she replied, disappointment in her voice.

"I've been trying to reach Eric Ivorsen and I'm having no luck. Is he with you, by any chance?"

"No, he's in Princeton."

Chestle paused before asking, "When was the last time you talked to him?"

"Monday. Two nights ago. Why?"

"I see." He sounded different than when they had met in the police station and later at the hotel. He sounded as if he cared.

"Why do you ask?" she inquired.

"I'm a little concerned, that's all."

"Why? What's happened?"

"Well, it's just that in the normal course of investigation into the loss of your yacht, we've asked the Princeton police to stop by his house. They report that he hasn't been home for the last two days. I needed to get some more information."

"He should've been. He didn't have any plans to be elsewhere."

"Well, I haven't been able to reach him day or night."

"Now you're getting me worried. Do you have reason to believe that something has happened?"

"Nothing concrete."

"Nothing concrete?!" Maggie blurted, becoming truly concerned. "Well, is there a chance that's something's happened to him?"

"I'm sure it's nothing," Chestle said, a little angry at himself for having alarmed her so. "If anything comes up, I'll give you a call."

"Wait a minute. What brought on all this sudden concern?" she demanded.

Chestle debated the wisdom of telling her about his father's snooping around, decided that she might in turn tell him something of use, and said, "One of my uh, most experienced investigators stopped by the house in Princeton. Something's come up on Digger Murdock, and—"

"What came up?"

Sharp little cookie, Chestle thought to himself before answering, "Well, Digger is now fishin' 'round the bend, if you know what I mean."

"I don't know what you mean," Maggie shot back.

Not all that sharp, Chestle realized. " 'Fishin' 'round the bend' means he's passed away. Another boating accident."

Maggie mistook his meaning. She said angrily, "You don't think Eric had anything . . ."

"No, no," he assured her. "It's just that I'm not so sure Digger's boating accident was any more an accident than the one you had."

"Was he the man in our room?"

Chestle pictured Murdock's corpse dangling in the wind. The hands—they were charred but complete. "No, Digger wasn't the man in your room."

"Who was it, then?"

"I don't know," Chestle admitted.

"You don't think he's done something to Eric?" Maggie asked in a tight voice. She was starting to become truly upset.

"I'm not jumping to that conclusion, and you shouldn't either," he said sternly.

"I'll try Eric and have him call you," she said, her mind racing to think where Eric might be other than his home. He's probably at the Institute, she told herself, and Chestle probably didn't think to call him there.

"Thanks, I'd appreciate that," he said.

"Just how long have you been trying to reach him?" she asked before hanging up.

"For the last two days."

Maggie bit her lip, admitting to herself that she too had expected to hear from Eric the day before. In fact, she was sure that he would call. When he had not, she'd told herself that he'd call tonight. Now she was afraid that he hadn't called because he couldn't.

Her voice softened and she asked in a whisper, "You don't really think Eric's been hurt, do you?"

Realizing that he'd managed to panic her for no real reason, Chestle took a deep breath and attempted to undo some of the damage he had already done. He answered confidently, "He's a big boy. I'm sure he's all right."

"He's dead."

Singh made the declaration while staring into the truck he'd driven from Brussels, at the packing crate that held the anthropoid coffin with Eric Ivorsen's remains. Sonny Pike's face lit up. Standing in the cavernous warehouse behind the Rue de Lille, they were in a building that had secretly held the stolen treasures of four of the world's greatest museums for almost twenty-five years.

Thatcher Smythe had purchased the place from the city of Paris in 1955, the year he first set his plan into motion. It took a year to build the Objets d'Art Egyptien shop on the street in front, three years to build the vault in the rear, and twenty-five years to build the collection it held. As of today, that collection was complete.

"The guy from the yacht?" Pike asked in disbelief, pointing his bandaged hand at the crate.

"He came to us with the cat," Smythe explained, walking from the cab of the truck Pike had driven in from Le Havre. Dripping rainwater puddled around its tires.

"And he's in that crate?" Pike grinned.

Singh nodded.

Pike sneered, "The sonofabitch was responsible for this!" He held up his bandaged right hand. A thumb protruded from the gauze on one side and a swollen pinky from the other. His left hand was bandaged as well, but at least he could use it.

"How did it happen?" Smythe asked with mild interest.

"When I was transferin' the lobster pot with the cat . . . his fuckin' yacht's prop ripped it outta my hands."

"He was a most annoying man," Smythe eulogized.

"I'll be damned, so you got him. I wish I had been there."

"He killed Sheeli," Singh sighed, staring at the ground.

Just as well, Pike thought, but did not show it. The snakes were the one part of working for Smythe and Singh that he didn't like. "What do you want me to do with him?" he asked.

Smythe looked at a schedule posted on the wall of the warehouse. It was the weekly cleaning schedule of the Paris sewer system. Smythe had been using it consistently for the past ten years to dispose of bothersome refuse, incriminating evidence, and the unpleasant by-products of being a murderous thief.

One of the most efficient waste-removal operations in the world, the Paris sewer system follows a closely regimented cleaning schedule. Engineered to permit passage of huge aluminum spheres for purgation, the arched tunnels that carry storm and household sewage away from the city parallel exactly the streets above. Every fourth day, sewer workers lower the ten-foot spheres into different sections of the system and then release floodwater to push them through the tunnels.

Ramming and smashing all solid waste and debris in the way, the rolling spheres wash along, propelled by thousands of tons of water. With their circumferences slightly smaller than the tunnel diameter, the huge aluminum globes permit jet sprays of pressurized water to escape from behind, blasting clean the paths ahead. Rodents and rubbish are crushed and washed along to the huge holding tanks for treatment.

Smythe used this process to his advantage. Dropped into the manhole in the warehouse floor at precisely the proper time, all discarded items simply fell into the Alma South evacuation tunnel, were crushed beyond recognition, and disappeared into the bowels of the earth, never to be seen again.

"According to this," Smythe said, looking from his watch to the schedule, "you can drop him in anytime today. After that we have to wait until next Monday. And I believe he'd stink by then, and our esteemed guests wouldn't appreciate that. Get rid of him now."

Snipping open the wires that secured the crate and held the U.S. Customs seal, Smythe opened the container. The face of Queen Hareyet smiled up at the three men. Hinged, the container wall fell open, permitting Pike to slide the outer coffin out onto the warehouse floor.

"Careful," Smythe cautioned. "Let me open it."

Carefully removing the nails, he freed the lid. Lifting it away, they stared down at Eric Ivorsen. Ghostly white, he looked lifeless. His lips were a sickly blue, his eyes were closed, and his legs were stuck to his chest. The gash on his face was brown with dried blood. Pike was about to grab him by the hair when a noise in the front shop startled all three men. The possibility of being caught with Eric's dead body dictated immediate action and ended closer inspection of the corpse.

"What's that?" Pike snapped in a desperate whisper.

"It could be one of the salespeople from the shop next door . . . they're always snooping," Smythe said. "Quick, get rid of the body."

"Rigor mortis hasn't set in yet," Pike said, folding down Eric's long legs.

"He must've lasted longer than we thought," Smythe said, hurrying to open the manhole cover. Singh pried it open with a crowbar used to open the wooden packing crates. Pike grabbed Eric under the arms and dragged him backward to the open pit. He didn't feel the weak pulse that was keeping Eric barely alive. He dropped Eric headfirst into the hole and then kicked him in the rest of the way.

Splashing down into a steady little stream of floating scum, Eric hit the tunnel floor with a sickening thud, and lay on his side crumpled over face down. Above, Pike replaced the manhole cover, and the scraping hollow sound of iron sliding on concrete filled the dripping dark tunnel. The only light was from a utility lamp a hundred feet down the passage.

Bubbling in a puddle of gray water, Eric breathed out. The sensation of cool against his face reached his brain and kicked it into semiconsciousness. Weakly, Eric groaned and then, helplessly sliding on the slimy tunnel floor, tumbled over on his back. He drew breath, but remained unconscious. With his legs straight for the first time in twenty-four hours, his circulatory system began slowly functioning somewhat normally, but he did not move a muscle for almost another hour.

Workmen in the Alma sewer station, two miles up the system, unhooked the cables that held the huge aluminum globe. Settling into place in the far end of the evacuation tunnel, the ball floated in a pool of rancid water.

Flipping a switch over the overflow hydraulic valve, a

worker released a flood of clean rainwater being held in the Rapp flush reservoir. Water gushed into the tunnel and the globe began to move.

The dank air in the subterranean passage began to move. A sudden foul wind coursed through the entire length of the Alma evacuation tunnel.

Turning his head, Eric moaned. Oily scum, matted in his hair, dripped across his forehead. His eyes opened slightly, and for the first time in twenty-four hours he was aware of light. But with no firm grip on reality, he could not comprehend his location or circumstance. He smiled.

Hallucinating from the poison and high fever, he decided that he was on his basement floor staring up at the forty-watt bulb. Then he realized that the bulb was too far away and recessed and covered with metal caging. It made no sense. He must be dreaming again. But the smell was so rank. You don't smell things in dreams, he remembered. Then a chill shook him. Impossible. You don't feel temperature and you don't smell things.

Swirling in delirium, his mind strained for logic.

The yacht, he decided. That's where he must be. It was suddenly clear. Water all around. Bilge water—cold, dank, odorous. The yacht.

After a moment, he took another deep breath. In a little while, he told himself he would get up and go topside.

Pushed by tons of water, the huge ball smashed along, purging the tunnels.

A pack of sewer rats, fleeing from rainwater flowing down from the streets above, skittered out into the tunnel through a storm-sewer inlet below the Pont de la Concorde, seconds before the raging onslaught turned the curve beneath the Quai d'Orsay.

Terrified by the hissing tumult, the rats began scrambling up the tunnel walls. But it was no use, the globe passed over them, crushing their bodies into jelly that was itself washed away by the water behind.

Lolling back and forth, Eric's head dripped stagnant

water. He tried and found that he could in fact lift it now. Struggling to sit up, he gasped for breath and shook with chills. He dropped his head in his shaking right hand and rubbed his eyes. The wind was increasing. Turning on his side, he rolled into a crawling position and started to move toward the wall and then toward the light over the ladder. He knew if he could get to the hatch, he could climb up on deck and the sun would warm him. Climbing up the slick moss-covered bricks, he managed to get to his feet.

Stumbling along the tunnel, he became frustrated. The yacht is not this big, he told himself. Where's that hatch ladder?

Then he saw it . . . down the tunnel . . . recessed into the hull. Only its rungs were iron, not oak. Strange. he thought, he had installed it himself. And he had used oak. Maybe Uncle Charles had replaced it and hadn't told him.

Funny sound. Engine needs work. Bad valve maybe. He'd tell Uncle Charles.

The sewer purge had reached Pont Solferino and the sound of gushing water and metal banging brick echoed through the tunnels ahead. Moving faster and faster as more and more water built up behind, the huge globe crashed ahead, smashing headlong into a thick beam of lumber that had fallen into the tunnel from a construction hole on the Rue de Bellechasse near the reconstruction of the Gare d'Orsay. A loud grinding scream filled the tunnel as the aluminum sphere jammed.

Vibrating from the pent-up pressure behind, it began to shudder and grind, water shooting from everywhere.

With an ear-splitting snap, the eight-inch timber bowed and broke. Instantly reduced to sticks and splinters, it was sucked into the whirlpool as the globe exploded by . . . a thousand yards upstream from Eric Ivorsen on his knees in the swill.

Limping badly, Eric fell two more times before reaching the iron rungs recessed in the slippery brick wall. Licking his lips, he stared through half-closed eyes at the ladder and tried to make his legs climb. His right would, but his left would not.

Grunting a high-pitched cry, he reached into a recess of iron bars and with superhuman effort, managed to get his foot up on the first rung. Then his left leg wouldn't move. A trickle of water fell on his head from a grip hole in the manhole cover above.

Pulling himself up, he managed to raise his right foot to the second rung. His left leg dangled uselessly in the air. An oily current of putrid water washed by on the tunnel floor, carrying discarded candy wrappers, litter, and floating waste.

Five hundred feet down the tunnel, the aluminum globe turned the curve and thundered ahead, a foaming wave of rat corpses, toilet paper, and scum preceding it in a spraying boil.

Eric climbed, rung by rung, one excruciatingly slow step at a time.

He was still half in the tunnel and half in the chimney to the dripping manhole in the street above when he heard the sounds of gushing water and clanging metal.

He realized immediately what was happening . . . Uncle Charles had finally turned on the bilge pumps. He considered going back down to make sure they were working but decided that his legs couldn't take it and he'd be better on deck.

Crying out, he strained up two more steps.

The globe bounced off the walls, water spraying from above and below.

Eric felt something grab his dangling left foot. It had terrific grip. Almost pulling him down. He gazed down into the white spray, and watched his foot washing back and forth. Carelessly, he lifted it out. Suddenly the tunnel below was a lightning blast of silver. Then just as suddenly, a black and hissing river. The cold wind made him shiver even more. He stared at the torrent for a little while and then up at the dripping manhole above. He saw the under-side of the *Lady Barbara*'s hatchcover and pulled himself until he could climb no more.

Oblivious to the ocean of sewage rocketing by beneath him, Eric precariously hung to the top rung of the ladder with his left arm and pushed on the impossibly heavy manhole cover with his right.

Hatchcover jammed, he told himself. Should've fixed it in Bermuda.

The edge of the iron plate separated from the oily tarmac of the rain-soaked street. It rose an inch and fell. Then he managed to lift it enough to get his hand out. It fell again, crushing his fingers. The pain made him reel. Squeezing his fingers into a bloody fist, he managed to raise the cover enough to push his arm out. Then his shoulder, and with one final heave, the iron cover fell off balance and pivoted, gouging into his back. Eric grunted from the blow. Pushing back with all his strength, he slid it out of the way and dragged himself out into a rain-washed alley of the Rue de Beaune.

Ice on deck, he realized with his cheek scraping pebbles. Got to be careful when we stand. Slippery. He crawled toward the mast and, pulling himself up, managed to stand. He gazed up to see how she was trimmed. The Rue de Beaune street sign came into focus, and Eric mouthed the words.

The fact that it was in French did not dispel the delusion, merely altered it. He was still burning with fever and poisoned by venom, and his perception of reality was a twisted shivering nightmare that was taking place in a whirling confusion of past, present, and pain. Dizzy with fever and weak from no food, Eric began to wander the streets of Paris.

The familiar names suddenly triggered a memory so powerful it began to control his actions—the delusion of the yacht faded into a dream of salvation. Slurring over and over the same unintelligible sound as he staggered along, he wandered to the Seine and stared at the choppy surface being slashed by wind-driven rain.

Dripping with sweat and rainwater, Eric staggered across the Pont du Carrousel bridge. He knew where to go but it seemed so far away. Now he finally understood what he was supposed to do. Falling against a café awning support, he reached down and tore up a handful of flowers that filled a planter near the street. With his jaw slack and his mouth hanging open, Eric Ivorsen stumbled on. He had to bring a bouquet. That's what you do, his twisting mind told him.

He roamed the almost deserted streets of Paris for almost two hours, sometimes shivering uncontrollably, sometimes burning with fever. The purpose kept him going, and while he made several wrong turns, he was headed in the right direction for what he had to do.

Crossing the Boulevard Montmartre, he became aware of a throbbing in his arm. Staring down through half-closed dull eyes, he saw the krait working its fangs into his flesh. Screaming for it to get off, he smashed at the delusion with his fist full of flowers until he no longer imagined it was there.

Two lovers, huddled under an umbrella, gave the swaggering derelict wide berth. He was obviously drunk or crazy, and too big to risk trouble with. The showers did little to wash away the stench he carried, and the young girl almost became ill when she got a whiff as he approached. Eric stumbled by, the now blossomless flowers dripping mud and petals from his fist.

Rain began falling in sheets. Puddles turned into tiny rivers that washed over his already waterlogged shoes. Sloshing forward, he crossed the Place Pigalle and climbed the neon-lit glistening back streets of Montmartre. Breathing hard and fighting for consciousness, he finally reached his destination and walked through the open iron gates.

Splashing through puddles of mud, he felt the world start

to spin. Staggering, he plodded on, but fell twice. Wet dirt stuck to his chin and hair.

Eric picked himself up and, with tears of mud dribbling in rain-washed streaks on his face, managed to walk ten more yards. Finally, he was unable to go on, but it didn't matter . . . he had reached her. A smile came slowly to his shivering lips.

Falling to his knees on a muddy mound covered by overgrown grass, he set down his fist full of flower stems, closed his eyes, and collapsed at the base of a white granite stone. The simple inscription was in French and read:

BRIGETTE MOREL IVORSEN
LOVING WIFE OF ERIC
BORN MARCH 21, 1953
DIED AUGUST 4, 1975.
GOD NEEDED HER BEAUTY IN HEAVEN

CHAPTER 15

"No," Maggie cried into the phone. "I haven't been able to reach him either."

Several of her co-workers looked up and then just as quickly looked away when Maggie returned their curious stares. Carla Burke walked into the newsroom, and everybody immediately tried to look busier than he really was.

Maggie lowered her voice and asked again, "When did you say your investigator last saw him?"

"Tuesday," Ben Chestle answered.

"And what exactly did he see?"

"A guy came to the door, went inside, and a little while later left with the guys who delivered a dishwasher. Or were supposed to."

"I don't understand," Maggie whispered. She looked up and saw that Carla Burke was headed for her desk. The last thing Maggie needed was her interference. Thankfully, one of the copy editors stopped Carla halfway across the room and held her attention long enough for Maggie to finish the conversation with Ben Chestle.

"I don't understand it either . . . that's why I'm going to check out the license plate and the guys who made the delivery. Or didn't make the delivery," Chestle was saying.

"I still don't understand," Maggie replied, her attention once again directed to the gravel-voiced policeman.

"There was no new dishwasher inside the house, and the old one looked like it had been there for years," he explained.

"Maybe they delivered something else."

"Probably did, but I won't know for sure until I check 'em out."

"Call me the minute you know something."

"I promise," Chestle said and hung up.

Carla Burke stepped up behind Maggie and cleared her throat, making Maggie jump. Then she asked in a sing-songy voice, "Personal call?"

Before Maggie could answer, Carla glided into her office and closed the door.

Maggie didn't know what to do. All of her calls to Eric's house had gone unanswered. The Institute was as interested in knowing his whereabouts as she was, and Ben Chestle hadn't located him either. Slim though it was, the hope of his tracking down Eric through the license plate was the only one she had.

There was one more thing she could do.

Maggie picked up the phone and asked for directory assistance in Newport, Rhode Island. Four minutes later, Lady Barbara Falcounbridge was on the other end of the line.

"Hello." Her voice and accent were unmistakable.

"This is Maggie McCabe. I need your help." Maggie's tone said more than her words.

"Of course," Lady Barbara replied without hesitation. "What is it?"

"I'm afraid Eric is . . . gone."

Lady Barbara considered this for a moment and then asked, "Have you had words?"

"No, nothing like that," Maggie blurted, and then told the story Ben Chestle told.

Lady Barbara knew serious trouble when she heard it. "We should meet at once."

"Where?" Maggie asked.

Lady Barbara thought for a moment and then answered, "Perhaps Princeton would be best. Claude and I will meet you at Eric's house at three."

"I'll try to get a flight . . . but with all the low fares, most of the airlines are booked," Maggie said, frustration creeping into her voice. "I may not be able to make it until tomorrow."

"Maggie," Lady Barbara interrupted, "when I said we should meet at once, I meant at once."

"But I just explained—"

"Claude will arrange transportation for you," Lady Barbara announced and then disappeared from the phone for a minute. When she returned she said, "Claude said that you are to go to the general aviation terminal at St. Petersburg Clearwater Airport."

"You mean Tampa Airport," Maggie corrected her.

"No, specifically not Tampa Airport. St. Petersburg Clearwater Airport. Are you familiar with it?"

"Yes, of course, but almost no scheduled airlines fly to Newark or New York," Maggie protested.

"Maggie, over the years, I've found it most wise to trust Claude's judgment in just about everything. I suggest you do the same."

"Okay," Maggie said, skepticism in her tone. "I'll be at the St. Pete Clearwater Airport in an hour and a half."

"Pack some extra clothes. I've also learned over the years that adventures with the Ivorsens somehow always take longer than you'd expect."

"I've noticed that too."

"See you this afternoon."

"I'm on my way."

Maggie had just about reached the newsroom door when she felt a claw grab her elbow. She spun around to see Carla Burke grinning back.

"On your way to get this weekend's assignment, no doubt," Carla said sweetly.

Maggie said nothing.

"The Annual Car Show at Bayfront Center. I want a centerfold of color shots. Got it?"

Maggie knew the best thing to do was simply to yes her. "Got it."

"Tomorrow's Saturday, remember? See you bright and early," Carla whispered.

"I'll work on it at home," Maggie muttered but did not stop.

"You'll work on it here," Carla commanded.

"Sure I will," Maggie said as she ran from the room, "when pigs fly."

"What did you say?" Carla snapped. "Come back here, young lady!"

Maggie ignored the order and ran to her car.

Carla Burke whirled around and marched directly in the door marked Managing Editor. Arthur Kearns looked up from his desk and saw that she was fuming mad.

"What is it this time, Carla?" he asked.

"McCabe again . . . and this time I want that little bitch fired!"

An hour and a half later, almost to the minute, Maggie parked her car in the general aviation terminal parking lot at Clearwater Airport. Carrying a hastily packed suitcase, she walked into the building and suddenly realized that she had no idea what to do next.

"Maggie McCabe, please pick up a red courtesy phone. . . . Maggie McCabe, please pick up the nearest red courtesy phone." The echo of the loudspeaker bounced through the building.

Maggie did as she was told.

"Miss McCabe?" The confident voice was that of a young man.

"Yes?"

"Your charter is ready. Please come to gate number twelve. We're all set."

Maggie carried her suitcase through the glass doors of gate twelve out into the bright midday sun. Spotting a young man wearing dark-blue slacks, a white short-sleeved shirt, and aviator sunglasses, she walked toward him. He was standing in front of a blue-and-white Cessna 310 being tanked up by a fuel truck behind. The left engine cowl was open and an airport worker was checking something inside.

"Here, let me get that for you, Miss McCabe," the young man said, taking the suitcase from her hand. He started off toward the Cessna.

"Anyone going to be joining you?" he asked.

"No," Maggie said.

"Very good," he said with a broad smile.

Maggie was about to climb into the Cessna when he continued past it, looked back, and said, "Excuse me, Miss McCabe, but we'll be flying in this."

He nodded across the tarmac at a sparkling sleek Learjet 25D with its cabin door open and its engines humming a low idling whine. The pilot was in the cockpit busy flipping switches on the instrument panel above his head.

Maggie's mouth fell slightly open as she gazed at the private jet. Solid white with "Ronson Aviation" lettered in red across the tail, the sleek plane looked as if it were out of one of the fantasy perfume ads that filled her paper's magazine section's Christmas issue. The handsome young pilot inside smiled and waved. The copilot placed Maggie's bag in the cargo compartment and waited for her to climb aboard.

"Make yourself at home," he said.

Maggie climbed into the plane and fell back into one of only six deep cushioned armchairs that filled the cabin. The copilot secured the cabin door, then eased into the right cockpit seat.

Adjusting their headsets, the two young men began talking on the radio, and in a few seconds the engine whine increased. The plane started to roll.

When they reached the end of the taxiway, Maggie watched the pilot switch a knob on the radio. After going through a checklist with the man to his right, he advised the tower that they were ready to take off.

Receiving clearance, the sleek aircraft rolled out onto the runway, straightened, and then began to rocket along. Twenty seconds later, the pilot eased back on the yoke, the runway vibrations ceased, and the plane shot into the sky.

The copilot turned around and said, "There's a bar there behind you if you'd like a drink."

"Oh, no thank you," Maggie said, still awed.

"I'll make coffee when we reach altitude," he said.

Maggie nodded. Glancing around at the posh interior and the two telephones next to her seat, she leaned forward and said, "Excuse me, but what does this flight cost?"

"About thirteen hundred, I'd say. It's a prepaid open-ended charter out of our Mercer County facility . . . so we're at your disposal for as long as you like."

Maggie's eyes widened. "One thousand, three hundred dollars to fly from Clearwater to Mercer County?"

"No, ma'am." He laughed. "Thirteen hundred an hour."

Maggie fell back in her seat, did a quick multiplication, and mumbled to herself, "Holy shit."

Ben Chestle didn't like driving around New York City. Other drivers were inconsiderate, and he was out of his jurisdiction, which meant that even if he wanted to pull some bastard over to teach him road etiquette, he couldn't do it. Cruising down 6th Street in Brooklyn, he also couldn't find a place to park.

Pulling the unmarked Chrysler in front of a fire hydrant, he climbed the steps of a brownstone and squinted at the names on the mail slots in the old building's entrance vestibule. The New York Department of Motor Vehicles computers showed this particular address to be the home of Bruno Formidoni, the owner of the Dodge Econoline that Ed had taken a picture of. Chestle pushed a black button next to the name Formidoni. When, after five minutes, no one answered the bell, he knocked on the door.

"Whaddya want?" a voice of indeterminable gender rasped from inside.

"I want to talk to Bruno Formidoni," Chestle announced.

"He didn't say nothin' to me about visitors."

"Police," Chestle called out.

The door opened a crack. A little old lady with her hair in curlers looked up at him. "What's he done this time?"

"What'd he do last time?" Chestle asked with raised eyebrows.

"You're the cop," she pointed out.

"I just want to ask him some questions."

"That's what you guys always say. The next thing I know, I'm readin' in the paper that some punk down the street killed his own mother."

"You think Bruno Formidoni is capable of killing his own mother?"

"No," she answered smugly. "She's been dead for ten years."

Ben stared at her, and she opened the door for him to enter. Her hair was messy, her right fingers stained yellow from too many cigarettes, and her skin drawn and gray. Wrapping herself a little tighter in a well-worn housecoat, she stepped out of the way and nodded up the stairs.

"Bruno and Tony are in their room on the third floor. Been up there for two days watchin' TV."

"Thanks."

Chestle climbed the stairs, and the little old landlady peered up the stairwell behind him, straining to hear what was going on. She heard him knock, but didn't hear any answer.

After listening to him try several more times, she grabbed her pocketbook and climbed up to the third floor too.

"Want me to open it for you?"

"You have a key?" Chestle asked.

"It's my house, ain't it?"

She fished in her bag and produced a set of keys. Picking through, she isolated the one that fit the apartment door and opened it. A horrid stench drove her back into the hall. Chestled winced too but walked into the room. He had to step back into the hall to take a deep breath of fresh air. Holding it, he walked back into the apartment.

The television was blaring a game show, the lights were on even though it was the middle of the day, and the Formidoni brothers were both dead and rotting on the floor. A pizza covered with flies sat half-eaten on a table in the middle of the room.

Whispering prayers in Italian, the landlady hurried back down the stairs and slammed herself in her apartment. Chestle used his handkerchief to pick up the Formidoni's phone and call the New York police.

An hour later, Ben Chestle walked out of the building with an NYPD officer from the 60th Precinct and agreed that there had been no struggle. The gas jets were all turned off, so it didn't look like accidental gas suffocation.

The New York cop said they'd have to wait for an autopsy.

Ben Chestle answered, "Don't be surprised if cause of death turns out to be snake poisoning."

"Snakebite? You been out in the sticks too long, chief," the cop suggested with a smile.

"A tenspot says I'm right," Chestle said, looking sideways at the younger cop.

"You're on. I'll up my money next weekend. Me and a couple of the boys rented a place in Hampton Bays for the weekend."

"Or you can drop mine off." Chestle grinned.

"One way or another, I'll see you next weekend," he said as Chestle climbed into the Chrysler.

"Oh, and if you guys plan to be raising hell . . . leave your off-duty pieces home," Chestle warned.

The young cop blinked at Chestle, stepped back from the car, and said, "Next time you're in New York, don't park in front of a hydrant."

By the time he drove all the way back out to the eastern end of Long Island, Chestle was tired, stiff, and not looking forward to an end-of-the-summer Friday night in the Hamptons.

He parked the Chrysler and frowned as he got out. Walking over to a long charcoal-gray Cadillac limousine, he peered into the black glass, saw only the driver, and walked around.

"Hey, Pete," he called, walking through the Municipal Building's back door, "who belongs to the hearse?"

Pete winced, and holding a finger to his lips, pointed to Chestle's office.

Lady Barbara Falcounbridge, Claude Bocuse, and Maggie, having met in Princeton and having learned almost nothing about Eric's whereabouts, had decided that the best thing to do was talk directly to Chestle and so had taken the Learjet to Westhampton Beach. Claude called ahead during the short flight and arranged to have ground transportation waiting when they arrived. In accordance with Lady Barbara's wishes, it was a limo.

Introductions were made quickly, and Maggie got right to the point. "We cannot find Eric. He was supposed to call me and didn't. He hasn't contacted Lady Barbara, and the Institute for Advanced Study doesn't have any idea of his whereabouts either." She was on the verge of tears.

"Awright, look" Chestle said. "NYPD is runnin' a check on the Formidoni brothers. I'll give them a call and see if I can't speed them up."

"Is there nothing else that can be done?" Lady Barbara asked.

"Yeah, maybe," he said and pulled open a drawer at the side of his desk. Extracting the file folder that Ed had put together, he pulled out a thick stack of 8×10 photographs. "Recognize any of these people?" he asked.

One by one the photos were passed around. It wasn't until the last four that Maggie saw a face she recognized other than Eric's. Standing on the porch, with black brief-case in hand, was the sinister skinny Parat Singh.

"This one!" she gasped, jutting her finger at the photo.

The last three photos showed Singh holding the door for Bruno and Tony Formidoni. Chestle looked down and sighed.

"What is it, Officer Chestle?" Lady Barbara asked.

"I just left those guys . . . in body bags. Not the guy holding the door . . . the other two."

"They are dead?" Claude asked.

"Afraid so."

Pointing at Singh, Claude asked Maggie, "How do you know this man?"

"He was with Thatcher Smythe. The man from the museum."

Lady Barbara glanced at Claude, who turned to Chestle and asked, "May I use your telephone?"

Explaining that an emergency existed, Claude persuaded the museum to have Jean Paul LeBrun return the call immediately. Contacted at home, he did so and it was quickly determined that he knew nothing of Parat Singh. All he had to offer was that Smythe had returned to Europe and would not be back until the Egyptian exhibit opened a month later.

"Singh mentioned a shop," Maggie remembered, "with offices in Brussels and in New York."

"What was the name?" Chestle asked.

Pounding her fist lightly against her forehead, Maggie

tried to recall the name. "Something French, like, Egyptian Antiques and Objects or Antique Egyptian Objects and Art. God, I can't remember!"

"It'll come," Lady Barbara said calmly. "Officer Chestle, do you have coffee?"

"Huh? Oh yeah, sure," Chestle replied and then called out, "Hey Pete, you wanna make some coffee?"

Claude flipped through the Manhattan Yellow Pages until he reached the antiques and fine arts section. Then he looked up and inquired, "Objets d'Art Egyptien?"

"That's it!" Maggie cried.

"Offices in New York, Brussels, and Paris," he said, "but only the New York and Brussels addresses are listed. Only two phones as well."

Lady Barbara turned to him and said, "Contact the airport, arrange for a crew to fly us to Europe. With the Learjet we'll undoubtedly be stopping to refuel in Gander . . . we'll dine there. Maggie and I will go to Brussels and Paris. Officer Chestle, can you assist Claude in looking into this New York office?"

Pete Halsey carried in a tray that held four different-size mugs filled with oily instant coffee, a box of sugar cubes, and a jar of cream substitute. Staring down his nose at the conglomeration of ingredients, Claude looked up at Halsey as if in disbelief.

Listening to the ravishing Lady Barbara tick off commands and questions, Chestle leaned around Halsey to answer, "Gosh, no. I can't get away until Monday. This is a big weekend out here, and I just won't have the time. Well, maybe I could shoot in Sunday night."

Halsey set the tray on Chestle's cluttered desk, looked up at his hard-boiled boss, and smiled at his mild language and polite responses. This Lady Barbara's got the old man's blood pressure up, he concluded.

"I fear that time is of the essence and think it imperative that we move rapidly. Still, if you do not have the time . . ." she began.

"I just won't have the time tonight or tomorrow," Chestle said again.

"I do," his father piped up, suddenly appearing in the office doorway. "Got nothin' but," Ed said defiantly.

CHAPTER 16

Cold midnight winds swept Newfoundland's Gander airport. Except for the man behind the counter in the coffee shop and the young attendant at the general aviation terminal, the place was deserted. At one time one of the world's most heavily utilized airfields, Gander, like a roadside diner bypassed by a new highway, was a victim of the extended range of modern jetliners. Now used for small business jets, military aircraft, and jetliner emergency, the facilities had shrunk but remained comfortable.

"Chief Chestle hasn't heard from his father or Claude," Lady Barbara announced as she stepped from the phone booth. "And it's too early in the morning for me to call Brussels."

"Who do you plan to call?" Maggie asked.

"On the off chance that Eric is in Brussels or Paris, I am counting on his contacting one of several people."

"Who?" Maggie wanted to know.

"In Brussels, an old friend of his uncle's. In Paris, either the front desk at the Ritz, because we've always traded messages there, or the Morels."

"We're ready," the young Learjet pilot called out.

Walking a half-step behind Lady Barbara as they approached the refueled Learjet, Maggie cleared her throat and asked, "Do you know how much all of this is costing?"

"It doesn't matter," Lady Barbara answered and climbed up into the plane.

Three hours later, the sleek jet banked left, dropped gracefully from the gray morning sky over Shannon, Ireland, and landed to refuel one more time.

"I'm scared," Maggie admitted while she and Lady Barbara were alone in the plane.

Lady Barbara took her hand and said, "I am frightened too, but all we can do is move forward."

"What if we don't find him?" Maggie asked, her chin quivering slightly. Fatigue and jet lag were starting to drag her down.

"Maggie, believe it or not, I have been in this situation before . . . when Charles took Eric off to look for some ridiculous primate farm on the Amazon."

Maggie's face brightened. "Eric's told me about that . . . a monkey farm Uncle Charles won in a poker game."

Lady Barbara smiled slowly. "They were lost for a month, and I thought I'd die of worry."

"But they made it."

Lady Barbara nodded, and Maggie felt better. The pilots climbed back aboard, and within fifteen minutes, they were airborne again and headed for Brussels, Belgium.

Arranged for by radio while en route, a limousine was waiting at Brussels International when Lady Barbara and Maggie exited Customs. Following the exact route that Parat Singh had three days earlier, it took them directly to the Place du Grand Sablon and stopped in front of the shop Objets d'Art Egyptien.

Maggie hurried out of the car and tried the shop's front door, but she found it locked. A small sign, suspended on a string, hung at an angle on the inside of the glass. She guessed correctly that, translated, it meant "closed." Peering inside, she could see that the shop's shelves and display cases had been emptied. The front showcase was bare. No treasures. No art. And although Maggie did not realize it, something else had disappeared. There were no snakes.

Cupping her hands on the window glass around her eyes, she squinted to look deeper into the darkened office. The walls had been stripped clean of all decoration, there was no desk or table on which to work, and rugs that had protected the shop's wood floors from pedestrian traffic had been removed as well. A large ring of wear surrounded a rectangle of polished floor in the middle of the evacuated room. Objets d'Art Egyptien, Brussels, was clearly out of business.

Lady Barbara walked into the small bookshop next door and spoke to the proprietor in flawless French. But all she was able to learn was that Parat Singh's shop had become vacant sometime during the early morning hours two days earlier. The bookstore owner had no idea why, when, or where Singh had moved. He was simply glad that he had.

Desperate, tired from the journey, and afraid, Maggie turned to Lady Barbara with tears in her eyes and cried, "What do we do now?!"

"We call Officer Chestle again to see if Claude has learned any more," she replied in a cool confident tone. "And then we proceed to Paris."

"So you're a frog, eh?" Ed Chestle said as he drove the white Nova into the Queens Midtown Tunnel.

"I am French, *oui*," Claude replied, finding it difficult not to be outraged by the crude epithet.

"I liked France . . . was there for the big one . . . W.W. II."

"It is a beautiful country," Claude replied, attempting civility.

"Saw a girlie show at that windmill joint in Pig Alley that I remember to this day."

Claude prayed that he would be spared a detailed account. His prayers went unanswered.

Chuckling, Ed said, "These little Frenchies came out kicking their skirts up so high, we could see what they had for lunch."

Claude winced.

With a nostalgic smile stretched across his face, Ed remembered a dozen pairs of creamy white thighs swaying back and forth in frilly folds of black lace. He shook his head and sighed, his smile growing into a grin.

"It is a beautiful country," Claude repeated, thinking back to his childhood in the village of Beaune. He pictured Burgundy's misty rolling hills, winding rivers, and lush green vineyards. For a brief moment, he was there again. Walking through the medieval streets, past the Hotel-Dieu with Petra's grandmother when she was just a little older than Petra. He could see her face. Her innocent smiles.

Remembering all their unrealized plans, dashed hopes, and unfulfilled dreams, Claude stared into the exhaust-clogged tunnel of traffic ahead.

"Bagged me a coupla Krauts in France," Ed recalled, oblivious to Claude's lack of interest.

Claude turned his eyes and looked over at the chattering old man who was roughly the same age as himself.

". . . farmhouse outside Rambouillet. They chopped down a friend of mine from Riverhead . . . Stoshew Pulaski. Used to pitch against his brother in high school. Anyway, I chucked a grenade into this Kraut foxhole and blew the two guys that killed Stosh right outta the ground. Tried a little spin on 'er like I used to use on my curveball. Worked good."

Smiling sadly, Claude turned and said softly, *"Merci."*

"Anytime." Ed grinned. "Anytime.

When they reached the Madison Avenue shop of Objets d'Art Egyptien, they found a charred storefront with plywood sheets in place of plate-glass windows. Orange-and-white New York City Fire Department "No Trespassing" stickers stood out against a background of gray weathered wood, blackened cracked glass, and soot-scorched stone.

The front door, smashed in by firefighters responding to the Formidoni brothers' final felony, was chained shut. The stink of burned wood still hung in the air. Dried rivulets of ash stained the sidewalk to the gutter.

"Jewish lightnin'," Ed commented.

Claude checked himself.

Ed marched into the dress shop next door, discovered that the fire marshals suspected the fire began in the basement, and led Claude around the block to the underground parking garage.

They found the basement door chained as well, but with no one around to witness a break-in, Ed smashed away the small padlock that held it. Inside they wandered through what was left of Thatcher Smythe's workshop. Bruno and Tony had done as they were told. All flammable material had been stacked and torched.

Picking through the debris for almost an hour, Ed and Claude found nothing useful.

"This ain't doin' us diddly," Ed muttered.

Then Claude turned over a charred slat from the front of a packing crate. Singed at the corners and scorched in the middle, the hand-lettered mailing label was nevertheless still legible. They had discovered the Paris address of Objets d'Art Egyptien.

Ed Chestle picked up the phone and called his son, Ben.

"They're gone. Torched the place as they went."

"Anything to go on?" Ben asked.

"Bunch of packing-crate stuff in the basement. Looks like a bomb went off, but Claude here found some address for another shop in Paris, France." Ed read the mailing label, and Ben wrote it down.

"Nose around some more. See if this LeBrun guy is any help. And call me if you get anything. Lady Barbara has been calling every hour, and the other line's ringing now . . . it's probably her."

* * *

Setting the mauve phone on its cradle in the Learjet's cabin, Lady Barbara turned to Maggie and said, "They've abandoned the New York shop as well . . . but Claude and Mr. Chestle have discovered an address for the shop in Paris."

"What do we do?"

Holding up a finger, Lady Barbara replied, "If Eric is in Paris, and he is able, he will either leave a message at the Ritz or go to the Morels."

"Who are the Morels?" Maggie asked innocently.

Lady Barbara looked up and hung up the phone. "Eric has not mentioned the Morels?"

"No."

Lady Barbara thought for a moment and then said, "First let me see if the hotel's front desk is holding any messages." After a brief wait, the connection was made, but the expression on Lady Barbara's face indicated that no messages waited. She picked up the phone again and placed a second call.

The rather long conversation was in French, which Maggie did not understand. But then a sudden relief in Lady Barbara's tone made Maggie reach over and touch her arm. When she saw Lady Barbara smile, her face lit up and she knew Eric was all right.

Lady Barbara thanked whomever she had spoken to and hung up the phone.

"He is in the Hôpital Beaujon in Clichy."

"Thank God," Maggie whispered. "What happened?"

"Gendarmes found Eric collapsed and unconscious. They contacted the Morels and asked if they could identify him."

"Oh, thank God," Maggie repeated, and with confusion wrinkling her brow, asked, "How did the gendarmes know to go to the Morels?"

Biting her lip, Lady Barbara took a deep breath and answered, "Because the gendarmes found Eric at their daughter's grave."

Maggie's frown deepened. "I don't understand. Why would Eric go to a graveyard? Who are the Morels?"

Lady Barbara looked directly in Maggie's green eyes and said, "They are Eric's in-laws."

Maggie considered this for a moment, trying to place the relationship. Then, as she comprehended what Lady Barbara was saying, her mouth fell slightly open.

"Eric is a widower," Lady Barbara said softly.

"But I . . . he never said . . ."

"Do not feel betrayed," Lady Barbara warned. "He did not tell us until many years after Brigette passed away."

"Eric was married?" Maggie whispered, staring past Lady Barbara, her gaze unfocused.

"For two weeks. Then Brigette died of leukemia."

Maggie blinked, and her gaze returned to Lady Barbara.

"They met when Brigette was nineteen. Eric was twenty-five, spending the summer in Paris. She fell in love with Eric at their first meeting and apparently worshiped him from that moment on. After her funeral, he burned almost five hundred letters that she'd written to him over a two-year period. When I asked Eric why he had decided to destroy them, he explained that they were meant for no one else's eyes and that he had their message locked in his heart . . . he needed not to reread even one."

Maggie took a deep breath and released it slowly. Lady Barbara continued, "Brigette's mother wrote to Eric in Princeton and revealed that her daughter was dying. He was at Brigette's side the next morning. Even though weak, she was still up and around at that point and still quite beautiful, but terribly sad."

Maggie swallowed.

"When Eric asked what he could do to make her happy, Brigette confessed that her only dream was to be married to him and have his children. They were married that afternoon, and she died two weeks later. Still close to her parents, he visits whenever he's in Paris. We accompanied him on one such visit, and that is how we came to learn the story. Brigette's father told Charles what a good son-in-law Eric had been over the years. Charles nodded as if he understood completely, although neither of us had any idea what he meant. Later in the car, Eric explained everything."

"Did Eric love her as much as she loved him?" Maggie asked softly.

"That is a question only he can answer. If you decide that you really must know, then you should ask Eric. I think it would be best, though, to give it some thought."

Maggie hesitated before asking, "I don't look like her or anything like that, do I?"

Lady Barbara smiled and replied, "Of course, I've only seen pictures, but you may rest assured that your beauty is completely different."

Slightly embarrassed at having asked the question, Maggie stammered, "It's just that I, uh, don't like the idea of competing with a memory."

"Maggie, you're not competing with anyone."

Maggie, anxious to move away from that topic, said, "What happens now?"

"When we reach Paris, we will visit Eric."

"What about the antique shop?"

"After we visit Eric, we'll have a look around."

At Objets d'Art Egyptien on the Rue de Lille, Paris, Thatcher Smythe, Parat Singh, and Sonny Pike completed the last-minute plans for that afternoon's auction. The gloomy warehouse had been hastily but effectively converted into a rather eclectic auction house. The huge vault, built into the back of the warehouse, had been emptied of all its treasures, and they were now on display in a circle in the middle of the warehouse. Illuminated only by the greenish light from lamps suspended from the warehouse's high ceilings, the incredible wealth looked somehow cheap . . . each piece gaudy. Even the Cat of Bastet did not measure up to its counterfeit counterpart on display in New York. The dim light barely glinted in its rich emerald eyes.

Barred shut with a huge steel crossbar, the warehouse garage doors were sealed and would not open again until after the auction was over and payments made.

The shop's front entrance, guarded by Pike, and the sealed garage doors were only two of the three ways in or out of the building. The other was the route Eric had taken—through the manhole into the Paris sewer system. And Queen Hareyet's outer coffin, once again holding the queen's mummified remains inside the golden inner coffin, sat blocking that.

Singh crossed the vast room, carrying his black school-bag briefcase in one hand and a wicker suitcase in the other. Hissing inside the wicker case were his eight cobras from the Brussels shop as well as most of his precious snaking paraphernalia.

The cobras would not replace Sheeli, he knew, but they would help take his mind off his loss and would provide nourishment when he did eventually replace the precious krait. Coiled in uncomfortable tight little piles in the basket, each of the lethal young cobras was angry. Instinct for self-preservation, however, kept them from striking at each other. Spitting mad and hissing, they complained loudly but kept their deadly fangs sheathed.

Distracted by the loud hissing, Thatcher Smythe turned to his companion and said, "Parat, it might be best if you put your little friends in the vault. They have a disquieting affect on Mr. Pike, and we wouldn't want them to upset any of this afternoon's guests."

Singh nodded without comment, walked to the vault, and inserted a heavy steel key into the massive deadbolt lock. Unlocking the door, he pulled it open and set the wicker basket on the cold cement floor inside. Pushing the vault's thick steel door shut, he closed it but left the key protruding from the mechanism. Then he returned to assist Smythe.

For Thatcher Smythe, this day marked a dream come true. He gazed around the vast warehouse and smiled.

Today, he knew, would be the ultimate reward. Thirty years of plotting and twenty-five years of work meant that today he would become a rich man. A man who would return to London society. Of course, he told himself, he would carry on as usual, but he would slowly join the right clubs. He could afford that now. He would entertain the ladies once more. After several months, he decided, he would gracefully retire from his work and then travel for pleasure.

Sonny Pike considered this day to be nothing more than the end of an assignment. His boss had told him to cooperate and keep an eye on the money, and that's just what he planned to do. As soon as the auction ended, he would help Smythe count the cash, split it in two, and take half to Fascione.

A man uncomfortably used to double-dealing and treachery, Sonny Pike was cursed with a suspicious nature that ran close to paranoia. He thought constantly about what could go wrong. Smythe was too old to give him any trouble, but Singh could be dangerous, especially with those goddam snakes.

The bidders themselves wouldn't be a problem, but they would be bringing some heavy cash, and that meant muscle to protect it. The terms of the auction mandated that they themselves were to enter the building alone, but still, the Rue de Lille would be lined with black limos and well armed hoods. A big problem, Pike decided, if somebody decided to change the rules.

Reaching into his seabag, he extracted a silver-gray Browning Challenger III automatic pistol. Inspecting the clip to make sure it was full, he rammed his bandaged right hand against the magazine and it clicked tight inside the gun's walnut handle. Then he stuffed the weapon in his waistband and pulled his sweater down to conceal it.

"Please give me a hand," Smythe called out, his voice bouncing in the vast room. He sounded far away, small.

Pike looked up to see the old Egyptologist bending over Queen Hareyet's huge lifelike wooden casket.

"We must stand it up," Smythe groaned.

Singh helped, and with Pike's help they managed to stand the heavy burial box on its end.

"Who the hell would want this thing?" Pike grunted as he pushed it.

"Mr. Carlton Beaumont of Dallas, Texas," Smythe answered. "It is our one sure sale!"

"It better not be," Pike warned, glaring at the smiling Smythe.

"Do not worry, Mr. Pike . . . the real money will be bid on all that you see spread around us. But Mr. Beaumont has been persistent over the years, and it is his one-million-dollar standing offer that persuaded your Mr. Fascione to finance the rest of this auction."

Smythe carefully opened the outer casket, revealing the golden coffin inside. Arms crossed, ebony eyes gazing up at the dim lights, Queen Hareyet's likeness, sculpted in gold, was identical to the outer casket's face. While the two sculptures retained their beauty for thousands of years, the same could not be said of the queen herself. Inside, wrapped in tattered linen soaked in tar, Queen Hareyet had long ago shriveled into a leathery brown skeletal carcass.

Dragging a mahogany lectern to the center of the room, Smythe pointed at a carpet roll near the sealed garage doors. "Please bring that here," he commanded.

Singh took one end and Pike the other. Setting its edge at the lectern's base, they kicked at the carpet and watched an oriental rug roll out across the grease-stained floor. Unfurled, the exquisite masterpiece transformed that part of the warehouse into something quite extraordinary. And it was an eerie metamorphosis. Now the center of this grim gray building was a pool of beauty surrounded by irreplaceable treasure. Smythe stepped back and drank in the scene. Pike didn't notice; he kept glancing toward the doors even though the bidders would not arrive for hours.

Singh carried canvas folding chairs to Smythe, who placed them in a row that faced the lectern. The echo of his footsteps ceased as he stepped onto the carpet with the last two chairs.

"There now," Smythe declared, brushing his hands after positioning the chairs. "That should do nicely."

Flipping open the auction manifest, he peered down through the glasses on the tip of his nose, read each item aloud, and then looked up over the rims to see Singh confirm its presence. Circling the room in order of its appearance on the list, each object was in correct position for bidding. The golden Cat of Bastet was last. Smaller than many of the other objects, less ornate than some, it was still this particular piece that would generate the most interest.

Singh believed it to be cursed or possessed of a spirit. Smythe considered it to be simply an infatuation of popularity. Even when he had first uncovered it in 1937, it had been this piece that was photographed and wired to news services all over the world. Like King Tut's golden mask, it was the treasure that symbolized the entire find. Smythe felt no attachment to it other than for the money it would bring.

Sonny Pike glared at the cat as if it were his own personal nemesis. It was. It had already cost him three fingers from his right hand, a good slab of flesh from his left, and two loosened teeth as a result of Eric Ivorsen's first punch. Walking from the warehouse into the showroom of Objets d'Art Egyptien, he took up a position at the shop's front entrance and waited for the first guest to arrive.

CHAPTER 17

"He is resting."

Standing in the long hospital corridor just outside Eric's room, Maggie, Lady Barbara, and the doctor spoke in hushed voices. And since the conversation was in French, Maggie had to wait for Lady Barbara to translate everything that was said. It was annoying, because she was anxious to see Eric, and the doctor seemed to be hesitant about allowing the visit.

"May we go in?" Lady Barbara asked again.

The doctor looked from Lady Barbara to Maggie and finally agreed. "Yes, yes, but if he is asleep, please do not disturb him. Whatever ordeal he has been through has been exhausting and taken its toll on his strength. His blood count is normal now, and the fever has broken, but he has been left very weak. It would be best if he could spend at least three more days recuperating. And please do not be alarmed by his appearance. . . ."

As Lady Barbara relayed the doctor's warnings and advice to Maggie, he opened the door to the room. Lady Barbara walked into the small white room first, and was greeted by the pungent scent of antiseptic spray and fresh flowers. She looked down at Eric, blinked in disbelief, and, biting her lip, stepped out of Maggie's way.

Even though forewarned, Maggie gasped when she saw Eric lying on the bed. Sound asleep and ghostly white, he looked very ill and terribly weak. Her tanned, robust, and powerful Eric barely resembled the man lying before her now. Once again bandaged over, the gash on his face looked sore, infected. His right arm, lifeless, with his hand lying open, was stained brown with a splotch of dried iodine that surrounded two purplish holes just below his elbow. An intravenous bottle dripped nourishment into his left arm. His thick dark hair was gone, replaced by bluish stubble and white bandages.

"What happened to him?" Maggie whispered, tears in her eyes.

Lady Barbara turned to the doctor and repeated the question in French.

The doctor shrugged. "He has been unconscious until this morning. He has not been awake long enough to tell us what put him in the condition in which he was found."

"And just what was that?"

"Ahhgh," the doctor said. "It was disgusting. We had to disinfect his entire body. He was covered with stench . . . as if he had crawled through a sewer."

"He looks so terribly pale," she whispered.

"He had a dangerous fever and probably had not eaten for days. We have no idea how long he lay in the graveyard. Much longer and he could have simply stayed there."

"What happened to his head?"

"Nasty abrasions on his scalp made it necessary to shave away the hair," the doctor answered, and then added with a smile, "But tell the young lady that it will grow back."

"You have no idea what affliction caused this?" Lady Barbara asked.

"If you look closely at the right arm, you will notice two puncture wounds. It is a venomous bite. Probably snake."

"He is recovering?" Lady Barbara asked with doubt in her voice.

"Oh yes, he looks a hundred percent better than when

he was brought in. He will be fine in a matter of days," he replied confidently. "I will leave you now. Please do not wake him. He needs sleep more than visitors." Winking once, he turned and walked from the room.

Gently patting Eric's forehead, Maggie stared down at his arm. A moment later she looked up at Lady Barbara with pleading eyes and worry wrinkled across her brow.

"The doctor assures me that he will be fine within days. The crisis has passed. It might be best if we just let him rest."

"I don't want to leave him," Maggie insisted.

"He must rest . . . and so must we."

"But someone he knows should be here when he wakes up!"

"We can stay a little while if you like, until Jean Morel arrives."

An hour later, Eric had still not awakened. Jean Morel arrived with fresh flowers and Eric's clothes, which had been boiled clean and pressed. A short man with a bald spot surrounded by graying curly brown hair, Morel smiled warmly when he saw Lady Barbara, his blue eyes twinkling.

Introductions were made, and he seemed genuinely happy to meet Maggie. But she was still too concerned about Eric to notice or care. And since Lady Barbara and Jean Morel spoke in French, she had nothing to offer the conversation and so turned to hold Eric's hand.

Lady Barbara explained briefly the events of the past week to Morel. He was not surprised to learn that Eric had gotten involved with another adventure—he had become used to that through the years. He was, however, distressed to see Eric's condition. This sort of thing had never happened before. Eric and his uncle had always managed to escape their escapades unscathed. This was different, and Jean Morel said so to Lady Barbara.

"I know," she replied with a sigh.

"But how did he get to Paris?" Morel asked.

"We don't know."

"Who did these things to him?" he demanded angrily. Sounding like a father bent on revenge, he said, "This is an outrage."

Lady Barbara nodded. Maggie glanced up at the angry words and waited for a translation. Lady Barbara explained, then Maggie nodded too.

After a few moments, Morel's smile returned, and he shrugged. "At least he is now well and among loved ones."

Glancing down at Maggie stroking Eric's hand, Lady Barbara smiled. *"Oui."*

"Where are you staying?" Morel said. "We have room at the house."

"Thank you, but I've already arranged accommodations at the Ritz," Lady Barbara explained. "Maggie and I have been up all night, and we can both use a little rest."

"If Eric wakes, I should tell him you are there?"

"Yes, but first we must stop by an antiquities shop on the Rue de Lille . . . do you know the street?" she asked.

"Yes, the Left Bank," Morel said. "Seventh arrondissement."

"We are looking for an establishment called Objets d'Art Egyptien."

"You are playing detective?" he asked with suspicion.

Lady Barbara smiled. "Just a little."

"Well then, you must be careful. If you are dealing with the people who did this to Eric, you are dealing with murderers," he warned, waving a finger.

"We're just stopping by to see if they are open for trade."

"And then you go right to the hotel?" he insisted.

"Directly," she promised.

"Good. We will call you there and you will join us for dinner and afterward we come again to visit Eric."

"That sounds fine."

The first splinter of purple cloud streaked the late-afternoon sky above the Paris skyline. Four limousines and one small truck were parked on the narrow Rue de Lille, and two more limos were parked around the corner on the Rue de Beaune. Behind the wheel of each was a chauffeur for each of the five men and two women inside the warehouse busily trying to outbid each other on the goods which surrounded them. Several of the bidders carried smart-looking briefcases, filled with stacks of cash, into the shop. But the more experienced left their money with the armed bodyguards who drove their cars.

When yet another limo turned into the street, Sonny Pike, sitting in the front shop, didn't notice. He hadn't actually counted each guest and he assumed that these were just the last arrivals running a little late.

"This is odd," Lady Barbara said, leaning forward in the backseat of the long Mercedes limousine. Passing the other elegant automobiles, she and Maggie peered at the solemn drivers waiting.

"What's going on?" Maggie asked.

"I can't imagine," Lady Barbara answered. "Let's have a look."

Stepping from the Mercedes, they walked to the shop's entrance and glanced inside. The showcases were empty, but there was movement behind the glass. Then suddenly the front door was opened for them.

It was not until they had reached the front of the shop that Sonny Pike recognized Maggie. While he had seen her only in the mirror in the bedroom, he was sure it was her.

"Come in," he said in a low voice.

"No, that's quite all right," Lady Barbara replied, suddenly sensing danger. "We were just browsing. Perhaps another time." She glanced down at his heavily bandaged right hand and started to back away.

"Perhaps now," he snarled, ripping his pistol from his waistband and pointing it between her breasts.

Maggie gasped. Lady Barbara remained silent but stepped reluctantly into the shop, and Maggie followed.

"Coincidence seeing you again," Pike said to Maggie.

"Have we met?" she asked, frightened and bewildered.

"Not the way I'd like," he sneered, closing the door with his right hand and jabbing Maggie's bottom with the barrel of the gun in his left.

She shot a terrified glance at Lady Barbara.

"Walk through there," he said, waving the gun's barrel toward the backroom door. "And don't say a word."

They obeyed. Stepping out of the relatively well-lit shop into the dark shadows of the vast warehouse, they were greeted by the eerie sight of seven collectors of stolen art, Sir Thatcher Smythe, and Parat Singh gathered on a priceless oriental rug surrounded by a fortune in Egyptian gold.

Illuminated in the haze of grim green light glowing down in the center of the enormous dark hall, the group looked zombie-like, their unsmiling faces dark. From their varied dress it was obvious that they were either of distinctly different nationalities or in costume. In the bizarre setting, costume would have made more sense.

Seated in a semicircle before a lectern, the group of seven appeared to be composed of two well-dressed Europeans; one American, a Texan, judging by the Western-cut suit and cowboy boots; a sheik draped in a flowing white robe; a heavyset black man wearing a lime-green suit and a broad-brimmed hat; an olive-skinned woman Lady Barbara guessed to be Polynesian; and another woman who wore wraparound sunglasses even in the dark. Lady Barbara blinked. Maggie shuddered.

"And now, ladies and gentle—"

In the middle of introducing the next piece to be bid, Thatcher Smythe looked up, saw Maggie, and fell silent in midsentence. His jaw went slack, and he looked down at his audience. Then, stammering, he quickly recovered, and then said to the group before him, "Excuse me, ladies and gentlemen. My assistants have arrived and I must see to their needs."

Locking a smile on his face, he stepped away from the

lectern and, carefully controlling himself, crossed the room at a casual gait.

Singh remained expressionless. The anxious bidders busied themselves taking notes and conversing among themselves. No one took much notice of the recent arrivals.

Reaching Pike at the front shop's door, Smythe seethed, "What is she doing here?"

"Browsing," Pike shot back sarcastically.

"Lock them in the vault," Smyth ordered. "Parat will take care of them."

"I want to have a little fun with this one first," Pike said, lifting a thick strand of Maggie's chestnut hair with the Browning's barrel. His cold cruel eyes surveyed her from top to bottom, pausing to admire her full blouse.

"Later," Smythe snapped. "Lock the front. We must finish this now. They may have been followed." He spun around to make sure none of his bidders had heard him.

Parat Singh, standing in the shadows, stared out of the gloom at Smythe smiling to the crowd. Waiting for his command, Singh knew that if Smythe beckoned, the women were to die.

Pike watched with his gun swaying back and forth from Maggie to Lady Barbara as Smythe turned away from the small crowd masked with a tense smile. It disintegrated into a vicious sneer as he leaned to Lady Barbara and said, "Make no sounds. These people care not what your troubles are. If you cooperate, you will be set free. If you do not, you will die."

Then, leading Maggie and Lady Barbara across the warehouse, Smythe once again locked a smile on his lips and walked them to the entrance of the huge vault. Pulling open the thick steel door, he ushered them inside, pushed the door almost all the way closed, and motioned for Singh.

Walking past him, Singh said softly, "I will be right out."

"No sounds if possible," Smythe whispered. "It might make our guests uncomfortable."

Maggie, like Lady Barbara, walked halfway into the dimly lit concrete room, realized they were trapped, and turned to face the door.

Stepping into the vault behind them, Singh crossed to his wicker basket and pulled away the latch rod that held it closed. He rapped at the sides with the rod to infuriate the snakes, and then pulled the lid open.

Stepping quickly away, he straightened, grinned a hideous toothy smile, and walked back out into the warehouse, locking the door behind. He would come back and gather his little friends after the auction. After they had served him as they always had.

Thatcher Smythe was back at the lectern, his face illuminated from below by a small light at the top of the stand. The seven guests waited patiently for the resumption of the auction.

Glancing once more at the manifest, Smythe then looked up and cleared his throat and continued, "I direct your attention to item ten—the gilded wood, gold, silver, and natural crystal figure of an ibis. Forty-one centimeters in length, it is from the Ptolemaic Period—three hundred B.C. . . ."

Imprisoned in the gray concrete vault lit only by a single dim yellow bulb suspended from the low ceiling above, Lady Barbara Falcounbridge and Maggie McCabe watched the first deadly cobra slide up over the rim of the wicker suitcase, drop to the chamber's floor, and slither out across the room.

Like a stream of living rope, the hissing serpents flowed over the basket edge—wriggling, writhing, and squirming over one another until the basket was empty.

Heads flattened and swayed. Slippery black tongues licked the air. Silently and relentlessly, the slithering snakes advanced.

*   *   *

At approximately the same time Maggie and Lady Barbara disappeared into Thatcher Smythe's vault, Eric opened his eyes. Focusing, he saw Jean Morel and smiled. For the first time in two days he could think clearly and could remember some of what had happened. Although it seemed like an impossible nightmare, he recalled vividly Parat Singh and the krait. Beyond that, his memory was a haze of freezing hot claustrophobia, rivers of rancid water, and a muddy field of graves. He took a deep breath and mumbled hello.

Jean Morel smiled, walked close to the bed, and took his hand.

"How long have I been here?" Eric asked, not fully aware of who was next to him.

"Almost two days."

Still weak, Eric closed his eyes and swallowed. After a moment's rest he looked over at the man holding his hand and said, "I could eat a horse."

"Careful, you are in France," Morel laughed.

"By God I am," Eric replied, astonished. He looked quickly around the room and then directly at Morel. "Jean Morel?" he asked, brightening.

"I brought you this." Morel grinned, producing a small paper sack that contained a small cheese, a split of red wine, a piece of fresh bread, and an apple. "I did not ask the doctor's permission," he said in a conspiratorial whisper.

"Just as well," Eric replied, pulling open the bag. "He would probably say no and I'd still be hungry." The small meal was gone within minutes. Eric let out a long sigh, and wiping his mouth with his good arm, said, "You don't know how good that tasted."

"Of course I do," Morel joked. "It is from my kitchen."

Looking again at the strange surroundings, Eric asked, "How did I get here?"

"Paris?"

"No, the hospital. I have no idea how I got to Paris either, but I think it must have to do with a strange little man named Parat Singh," Eric replied, and then quickly recounted the episode with Singh in his basement.

Jean Morel listened to the story, shaking his head and trying to understand. Then he explained to Eric how the gendarmes had found a giant derelict at Brigette's grave. Calling the Morels on the off chance that they could help identify the drunkard, the efficient police were hard pressed to accept the fact that they had in custody one of the world's leading scientists.

"Why?" Eric asked.

"Perhaps you should look in the mirror!" Morel chuckled.

Eric propped himself up in the bed and looked at his reflection in a small mirror on the wall across the room. For a moment, he couldn't believe his eyes. He reached up and brushed his shaved head, wincing when he touched the spot on which he had landed in the sewer.

Falling back on the crisp white bed, he started to laugh and then remembered, "You must wire a friend of mine in the United States . . . Maggie McCabe. She'll be worried."

"But she is here . . . with Mademoiselle Falcounbridge!" Eric frowned, and Morel explained.

"How long have I been in this hospital?"

"Two days," Morel replied.

With his face relaxing into a smile, Eric said, "Well, if Maggie's with Lady Barbara, they'll be staying at the Ritz."

"*Oui*, and they said you should call them there as soon as they return from the antiquities shop."

Eric's smile disappeared instantly. "What antiquities shop?"

"Objets d'Art Egyptien," Morel remembered. "On the Rue de Lille."

The name rang a bell. Then it rang several. A moment later, the whole alarm system went off. Objets d'Art Egyptien was the shop owned by Parat Singh in New York. And Brussels.

Tearing the intravenous needle from his arm, Eric was off the bed, across the room, and pulling his clothes on. He fell once as he stepped into his slacks. Then again as he tied his shoes.

"You must rest!" Morel pleaded.

"Call the police," Eric demanded, ignoring the plea. "Have them meet me at that shop right away." He stumbled once against the wall in the hospital corridor as he ran from the room to the building's entrance.

Dashing in front of a cab, he ignored the driver's heated admonitions and demanded to be taken to the Rue de Lille. Gasping for breath, he sank back in the seat and watched in frustration as late-afternoon Paris traffic slowed into a crawling blockade.

CHAPTER 18

"You afraid of snakes?" Maggie whispered as she watched them moving across the room. Her voice was tight. She seemed either on the verge of total panic or amazingly in control.

"Deathly," Lady Barbara gasped, moving back against the wall away from a snake licking the air. "Are you?"

"No," Maggie admitted in a businesslike tone. "I grew up with them. My father never had the son he hoped for, and so I became the replacement. We used to catch them all the time whenever he took me camping."

"What do we do?" Lady Barbara whispered desperately.

"Well, first of all, we have to be careful. These are cobras. Poisonous." Maggie jumped sideways toward the empty wicker case.

"You have my oath that I shall touch not one," Lady Barbara managed to squeak out, glaring in horror at two slithering forms moving closer.

"Are you wearing pantyhose?" Maggie asked, moving around behind two of the snakes to the open wicker case. Secured by tiny clips on the walls inside, Singh's small leather noose and milking equipment were just what Maggie had hoped to find.

"What?" Lady Barbara gasped, frozen by the sight of a slithering cobra slowly winding its way closer.

"Are you wearing pantyhose?" Maggie repeated.

"Yes. Why do you ask?" Lady Barbara's unblinking stare remained riveted to the swaying cobra that had now coiled less than four feet away.

"I'm not, and I'll need yours to bag these guys."

"You want my hosiery?"

"As soon as possible."

"Keep them away, please," Lady Barbara begged as she reluctantly complied with Maggie's request.

Maggie bent to the cobra nearest Lady Barbara, and with one lightning-quick jerk she grabbed its tail and sent it sliding back across the floor. Coiling into an angry little pile in the corner of the vault, the surprised snake paused to determine what had happened.

Hiking her skirt up over her waist, Lady Barbara wriggled out of her pantyhose and tossed it across to Maggie.

Maggie spread the waist open, holding it like a sack, and picked up Parat Singh's little leather noose. Then, circling around the room, she quickly snared every snake, dropping each one into the bulging nylon. When she was finished, she emptied the whole hissing pile back into Singh's wicker case and slammed it shut. Holding down the top with her foot, she looked up and grinned.

Lady Barbara let out a long sigh of relief. "Thank you," she whispered, staring at Maggie with a new sense of admiration.

Maggie nodded. "At least we're out of the pot for a while."

"But into the embers," Lady Barbara added.

"Maybe we can douse them too," Maggie said and leaned down to the wicker case. Holding the lid on tight, she shook it back and forth on the cement floor, listened to the hissing and spitting inside, and knew the snakes would now be uncontrollably furious.

"That might work," she declared and carried the case carefully to the vault's locked door.

"What am I bid for item number thirty-one? This is a solid gold Shawabti figurine of the scribe Amenemhet. It is twenty-four centimeters in height and it is from the time of King Thutmose, approximately 1400 B.C." Thatcher Smythe's enthusiasm grew with each object offered.

"Ninety thousand dollars," the man from Abu Dhabi said in a thick Arabian accent.

"One hundred," the slender woman with the sunglasses countered.

"One ten," one of the two Europeans bid.

"Come, come," Smythe said with glee. "This piece is worth more than two times as much. . . ."

Sonny Pike watched the laborious bidding for a few minutes, thought about Maggie bending over in front of that mirror back in Westhampton, and decided to slip away to reward himself for all the hard work he'd done.

Unaware that Singh had released the snakes, he decided that the vault was as good a place as any for a quick piece of ass—thick enough to be soundproof, so even if they screamed a little bit, so much the better; he liked it that way. No one was paying any attention to him, he told himself, and Singh would kill the two broads anyway, so what was the harm in working off a little tension? Circling around the room, he made his way to the vault door, waited until the bidding reached a particularly heated volley, and then quietly released the door's thick deadbolt lock.

Rock-hard in anticipation, he stepped sideways into the vault and eased the door closed behind him.

Parat Singh turned in time to see the thick door close. A smile came to his lips.

When she heard the mechanism click, Maggie snatched up the wicker case, shook it violently, and then balanced it precariously on her right arm. She gripped the top with her left hand and aimed for the opening door. With her fist poised to rip the case open and thrust its contents forward, she held her breath.

Sonny Pike slipped in sideways, and at the same time leaned back to close the vault door. Then, turning toward Maggie, he frowned at the hissing case in her arms. Bewildered and annoyed, he demanded, "Whaddya think you're doin'?"

Maggie ripped open the lid, tossed the serpents forward, and jumped back. Four enraged snakes shot out as if launched by springs. Two others fell to the floor. The other two somehow managed to stay in the case as it fell.

Sonny Pike didn't even have a chance to think about pulling his gun. One cobra buried its fangs in his right cheek, another its fangs in his upper lip, another in his neck, and the last sank its deadly venom in Pike's arm as he tried to cover his face. A guttural cry of terror escaped from his throat, building to a high-pitched shrieking wail. Combined with the hissing of the snakes, Pike's bloodcurdling screams filled the cold concrete vault with the primal sound of animal death.

Maggie, with her hands clamped over her ears, backed across the room to Lady Barbara and watched in horror as the two coiled snakes on the floor struck as well. One hit Pike's left leg and the other his right foot.

In a pathetically futile attempt to halt the relentless onslaught, he flailed wildly at the serpents with his bandaged hands. Squirming through the air, one flew off Pike's arm, over Maggie's head, and smacked against the concrete wall. The snakes at his feet struck again.

With milky white venom dripping from the holes in his face and arms, Sonny Pike crumpled to his knees on the gray cement floor, stopped screaming, and then fell forward, face first. Bouncing once, he was dead. Blood leaked from his mouth and nose.

When the horrible sounds had ceased, Maggie was breathing hard. Fumbling for the leather noose, she counted only seven snakes. Spinning left and right, she quickly located and snared the one that Pike had managed to throw off. She dropped it into the makeshift pantyhose sack and began moving on the others.

Lady Barbara, opening her eyes for the first time since Maggie had pulled open the case, took one look at Sonny Pike and breathed, "Dear God have mercy."

Parat Singh had caught Pike's surreptitious entry into the vault out of the corner of his eye. Following behind, he listened, and when he heard the muffled screams from inside, he relocked the door and returned to the auction.

A convenient turn of events, he told himself. He knew that they would still have to pay Anil Fascione a portion of the take, but now Smythe's silent partner had no representative to account for the correct sum. Smiling, Singh watched Smythe point to the last object to be offered—the golden cat.

Maggie felt sick to her stomach, but held it down as she began to ensnare the snakes slithering over and away from Pike. Bagging the enraged serpents proved difficult. As they fell squirming into the stretched legs of the pantyhose, they tried to climb and the result was an eerie limblike movement in the nylon. Maggie had to constantly shake the rising reptiles to the bottom of the bag. Several tried to strike, but Maggie managed last-second jolts that sent them spitting back down to the others.

Plucking the last two out of the wicker case, she snapped the lethal nylon sack into the case, dropped the whole hissing pile inside, and slammed down the cover. She knew the trapped snakes would quickly find their way out of the pantyhose. Perched sitting on the disgusting case of snakes, Maggie glanced over at the swollen face of Sonny Pike's corpse and felt sour gorge rise from her gut.

"Quick," she gasped. "Put your foot on this."

Lady Barbara took a deep breath and put one foot on

the wicker top. Maggie lost her battle to keep her last meal down.

Unable to move from the case, Lady Barbara watched helplessly as Maggie got sick. Coughing and gasping for breath, Maggie finally straightened up and threw her head back for a deep gulp of air.

"Are you going to be all right?"

"Yes," Maggie gasped.

Lady Barbara turned to Pike's body, rolled him on his back, and located the Browning automatic in his waistband. Extracting the small pistol, she released the magazine, inspected it, and then snapped it expertly back into the grip.

Pulling back the slide, she pumped a round into the chamber and said in her most proper English accent, "Let this be a lesson to them. . . . One simply does not fuck with Falcounbridge and McCabe."

Stunned, Maggie looked up and replied, "Well put."

"I draw your attention to our last item, the Sacred Cat of Bastet. Solid gold with emerald eyes, it is thirty-one centimeters high. Discovered in Saqqara, it is from the Late Period, 400 B.C. I am opening the bidding on this piece at five hundred thousand dollars."

The sheik nodded.

"I have five hundred, do I hear six?"

"Six," one of the Europeans said.

"Seven," the elegantly dressed Tahitian woman countered.

"Eight," the sheik said.

Only the man from Texas did not join in the bidding. He had purchased Queen Hareyet's coffin and was interested in nothing more. Because of its size, he had been the only bidder, as Smythe had predicted. One million dollars was the opening, closing, and only bid. Confident that he would make the acquisition, the Texan was the only one in the group whose chauffeur bodyguard was waiting outside in a truck rather than a limousine.

"One million five," the woman in the sunglasses called out.

Silence followed.

"One million five?" Smythe asked.

"The woman nodded.

"One million six," the sheik grunted.

"Two million," the woman responded without missing a beat.

Again there was silence.

When it became clear that she would top any offer, the bidding stopped, the gavel fell, and Thatcher Smythe was a rich man.

One by one the purchasers filed out the front door of the shop. Singh unbarred the warehouse garage door, and one by one the successful bidders reappeared in the alleyway courtyard outside. Six limousines and Beaumont's truck pulled into the courtyard and parked in a circle. The purchaser of the Sacred Cat of Bastet was first in line. Although she had placed bids on several pieces, they had been unsuccessful and it was only the Cat that she would leave with.

She stepped up to Smythe, counted out forty stacks of crisp new thousand-dollar bills, and placed them on the lectern. After carefully scrutinizing a random bill from each stack of fifty, he nodded, and Parat Singh handed her the prize. Accompanied by her chauffeur, she climbed in the back of her long white Lincoln Continental and drove away.

The remaining transfer of money for possessions did not take long. Only the outer and inner gold coffins posed a problem, and that was because of their cumbersome size. Beaumont paid his million and watched without comment as his chauffeur assisted Parat Singh in the loading of his mummy queen.

Queen Harayet, still reposing in her golden inner casket,

was once again closed up inside the larger coffin and loaded into the back of the truck.

Although he wondered what the Texan was going to do with her, Thatcher Smythe never asked.

The stacks of brand-new thousand-dollar bills were packed neatly into Parat Singh's black schoolbag briefcase. Bulging, it grew heavier and fatter as each artifact disappeared into the hands of buyers.

When Parat Singh closed the garage door and replaced the steel bar that sealed it, the bag contained just over five million dollars.

The cab carrying Eric finally broke free of a traffic jam on the Champs Élysées. Speeding around the Obelisk in the Place de la Concorde, the small Peugeot crossed the Seine and shot across the oncoming traffic on the Quai d'Orsay. Veering right on the Boulevard St. Germain and then quickly left, the driver expertly took the responsive car through a tight little S-turn that put them on the long narrow Rue de Lille.

Ahead, a black limousine, just pulling out of the alley, swerved onto the sidewalk to avoid smashing into an arriving police car. With its blue light flashing, the police car screeched to a sideways stop, blocking the narrow street. Then Beaumont's truck bounced out of the alley into the street. Turning left, the driver swerved his truck away from the police car, directly toward the cab, and stepped on the gas.

Bouncing up on the sidewalk, the cab almost managed to get out of the truck's path. But the truck snagged the cab's left rear bumper, spinning the little Peugeot back out into the street. The truck lost control, hit the curb, and bounced into the air. Balanced precariously on two wheels, it rolled along, teetered for a moment, then fell over on its side. An earsplitting screech of metal twisting on pavement echoed down the street. Eric snapped around to see the truck's rear doors pop open and Queen Hareyet's coffin spill out onto the Rue de Lille.

Leaping from the taxi with the cabbie yelling for him to come back, Eric ran for the two stunned gendarmes who'd jumped out of the police car. The sight of the towering bandaged bald American made the two Frenchman back away, truly frightened. Jabbering quickly in French, Eric convinced the two men that they would need assistance and that he was on their side. One policeman raced back to his car to radio for assistance. The other policeman sprinted for the alley. Eric ripped at the antique shop's front door, but it would not budge.

With one blasting kick, the door splintered open and Eric was inside. Running through the back office, he found the warehouse door. About to grab the doorknob, he saw that it was turning by itself.

Frozen, Eric waited for the door to open. Creaking slightly, the door yawned open. Laughing to Singh behind, Smythe stepped halfway into the room, looked up at Eric, and blinked. It was impossible. As if he'd seen a ghost, his face went white, his eyes widened, and he began breathing fast. At the same time, Parat Singh peered over his shoulder, saw Eric, and pulled Smythe back into the warehouse, slamming the heavy door. Before Eric could rip it back open, Singh had locked it.

Running across the room to the garage door, Smythe and Singh heard the police outside trying to pry it open. Singh spun and bolted for the manhole. Thatcher Smythe froze. His right hand went to his chest and a grimace contorted his face. Turning red, he let out a short cry and fell to one knee on the warehouse floor. Still gripping the black bag full of money in his left hand, he crumpled to the floor.

"Parat!" he gasped in a tight whisper.

Pulling at the heavy manhole cover that would give them one last chance to escape, Singh looked up and saw

his stricken employer. Dropping the iron plate, he raced to
him.

"What is it?" he asked desperately.

"My heart . . . pain . . ."

Unsure of what to do, Singh reached out his bony hand
to touch the man he loved. But it was too late . . . Sir
Thatcher Smythe had joined the pharaohs.

The sound of hammer blows echoed through the vast
warehouse. Dimples of dented metal appeared on the inside of the garage doors as the police tried to batter their
way in. Behind him, the thud of smashing kicks echoed
from the shop. Eric Ivorsen was coming through.

Like a rat snatching food and running to consume it,
Parat Singh ripped the black briefcase from Smythe's
deathgrip, dashed across the room, and scrambled down
into the sewers of Paris.

Inside the vault, Maggie and Lady Barbara heard the
muffled commotion coming from the warehouse outside.
Bracing herself with feet spread, Lady Barbara cradled the
automatic in her left hand, aimed it at the door, and
waited. Beyond her and to one side, Maggie stood ready to
once again launch the snakes.

They agreed that a surprise attack was their only hope of
survival.

"You toss those hideous little creatures and I'll open
fire," Lady Barbara said.

Maggie heard movement outside and nodded.

Even with the French policeman helping, it took a full
five minutes to kick open the reinforced door to the
warehouse.

The room was now bare except for the rug, chairs, and
abandoned lectern. Eric saw the vault across the room and
wondered if it could possibly have an escape door. Then
he saw the key and slowly turned it. The mechanism clicked
and Eric pulled the thick steel door.

Maggie and Lady Barbara attacked.

Glancing up in the nick of time, Eric saw the gaping wicker case swing toward him. He jumped back as the air filled with a tangle of squirming snakes. A blast from the chamber plastered him flat against the wall.

"Eric!" Maggie cried out when she recognized him.

"Maggie?" he asked, peering slowly into the vault.

"You're all right!"

Still breathing hard, he replied, "Funny way to celebrate it."

Lady Barbara gasped when she realized how close she had come to taking off his head. "Oh, Eric . . . if you had not ducked, that shot would have killed you."

"If I hadn't ducked, it wouldn't have mattered."

Slithering across the warehouse, Singh's cobra's were escaping themselves.

Eric circled the warehouse as the policeman ran to the crumpled body near the garage doors.

Kneeling next to Thatcher Smythe's corpse, the policeman said in French, "I'll call an ambulance," and ran quickly for the front shop.

When Eric reached the open manhole, he knew what had happened. Peering down into the cold dank cavern below, he took a deep breath and looked up at Maggie and Lady Barbara.

"You're not going in there?" Maggie asked.

Whispering, Eric instructed them, "When the police come back, tell them what I've done, then go back to the hotel and wait."

"But . . ." Maggie protested.

Lady Barbara touched her arm and Maggie looked into her eyes. Eric climbed down the rusted iron rungs and disappeared.

Dropping into the sewer, Eric shuddered, his subconscious screaming at him to get out. Echoing in the darkness to the right, footsteps faded. Moving quickly and purposefully, but not running.

Eric began moving toward the sound, and, jogging, he gained ground quickly. Because the tunnels twisted in relation to the streets above, he had no clear view down the arched passages. He had to rely on his hearing.

Suddenly there was a perceptible change in the tunnel. The still, dank air began to move. A breeze of stench began moving past him from behind. Conditioned animal instinct told Eric that this was not a good sign. Glancing over his shoulder, he saw nothing alarming, but a voice within him screamed again for him to get out.

Running harder and gulping the rancid damp air, he curved around to a long straightaway below the Quai d'Orsay and saw in the fading distance the rapier-thin silhouette of Parat Singh.

Singh, about to climb a manhole ladder to the street, looked up and realized that Eric would catch him if he tried. Dropping back down and turning, he ran farther down the tunnel, deeper into the darkness.

Normally, Eric superior physical condition would have allowed him to overtake the fleeing Singh easily, but in his weakened state, he could barely gain ground.

Sloshing through swill and stagnant water, the underground chase went on for almost ten minutes before Singh's stamina began to fail him. The briefcase full of money slowed his escape. Growing heavier and heavier as he tired, the case became an incredible handicap.

By the time Eric caught up to the winded Singh, the putrid breeze in the tunnel was a wind. Running up behind Singh, Eric was about to clock him on the back of the head, but a strangely familiar sound made him turn instead.

Gushing and spraying water, a huge aluminum sphere was being propelled through the tunnels from behind. Eric saw the ball flash under a light, growing bigger, coming closer. Spinning around, he saw that the next manhole ladder was too far away, but he ran for it anyway. Stark animal fear gave him the strength to sprint. Passing the tired Singh, Eric pumped hard trying to escape the aluminum ball.

There was no time even to look back. He ran with all his might from the clanging, watery projectile boiling only a hundred feet behind. Then he heard it . . . a horrible grinding crunch and an earsplitting scream.

Spinning, Eric saw the huge aluminum sphere jammed against the tunnel wall by Singh's body. The black briefcase, caught in the wash, was being pushed down the tunnel by water gushing from around the circumference of the ball.

Hesitating for a moment, Eric dashed back to grab it, praying that Singh's body would hold the deadly sphere.

Vibrating as pressure built, the dented globe slowly rolled, inch by inch, crushing bone. With his black eyes wide, Singh watched Eric race down the tunnel, trying desperately to beat the clock. Like the victim of a boa constrictor, Singh had no air with which to scream. Crushed from his lungs by the relentless ball, his screams were just final gasps. The only sound from Parat Singh was the sound of popping organs and crunching bone.

Then the sphere broke through. A thunderous pop echoed down the tunnel and the ball shot on, propelled by thousands of tons of water.

Standing at the entrance to the Achères sewage treatment station, Maggie and Lady Barbara waited for the French policemen to emerge. Inside, workmen and police watched as debris, sludge, and water washed into the huge treatment pools. By the time the human remains reached the spillover, they were nothing more than a flow of broken bones, bloated chunks of flesh and organ, and pieces of bloody skull, stripped clean of skin and hair. Because the crushed remains arrived in so many parts, it was impossible to determine whether if reassembled they would make one body or two. A policeman walked out and so informed Lady Barbara.

Translating for Maggie, she cautioned her not to become upset. "We will return to the hotel, as Eric asked us to do."

But Maggie was upset. The ride back to the Ritz was a silent one.

Checking at the front desk, Lady Barbara was told that there had been no messages from Eric, and that made Maggie sick with worry. By the time they reached the room, she was shaking. But when they walked into the room, they found a bouquet of roses on the writing desk near the courtyard windows. Maggie looked for a card but found none. Lady Barbara picked up the phone and asked to be connected with the hotel florist.

"Those are from Eric," she announced while waiting for her connection.

"How do you know?" Maggie demanded.

"Count them."

As Maggie picked her way through the blossoms, Lady Barbara spoke in French to the hotel florist. The conversation was brief. She hung up and said to Maggie, "They were ordered by phone and delivered only a few minutes ago."

"Eric?" Maggie asked hopefully.

"The florist advises me that the order was placed anonymously . . . I'm sure it was Eric. How many roses?"

"Ten," Maggie answered, obviously confused.

Lady Barbara smiled. "You and I make the even dozen. Terribly corny but impossible to resist."

Relieved, Maggie broke into a wide relaxed grin and asked, "But where is Eric?"

"Putting things in order," Lady Barbara said in a knowing voice. "No doubt."

CHAPTER 19

"They want you in there."

Maggie blinked at the receptionist and then looked up at the conference room she was pointing to. The *St. Petersburg Times* executive staff usually used the room only for high-level meetings. Whenever one of the staff was called in, it usually meant bad things were about to happen. Maggie swallowed and tapped on the door.

"Go on in and wait," the receptionist said. "They'll join you in a few minutes."

Stepping into the sunny room, Maggie found it deserted. A huge oval table surrounded by comfortable chairs filled the center of the room, and file cabinets lined one wall. She chose a chair, sat down, and sighed, thinking about all that had happened in the past two weeks. She was finding it hard to follow Lady Barbara's advice to be patient.

Returning to Newport with Lady Barbara, Maggie had discovered that she, Claude, and Petra were planning a quick trip to Brazil to attend a wedding. They had the Learjet drop Maggie off in Tampa en route. Now it all seemed like a dream, and not a terribly pleasant one at that.

A first-class ticket back to Europe was waiting in her

mailbox when she got home. The enclosed note from Eric turned out to be an invitation for her to join him in St. Tropez. Exhausted, still a little frightened, and worried about her job, Maggie waited for his call, hoping he would understand why she would not accept.

"The sun is shining," he said when she picked up the phone, "the Mediterranean is still warm, and le beaujolais nouveau est arrivé."

"The sun is shining here as well," she replied, "the Gulf is like a bathtub, and the pina coladas runneth over."

"I have business to finish here."

"I have a career to try to hold onto here."

Eric sighed. "Playing hard to get, eh?"

"I don't want you to think I'm easy," she teased.

"I'll be home for the first official meeting of the Viking Cipher group next month. Can I visit as soon as I've taken care of that?"

"I'll pencil you in," she giggled.

Thinking back over that conversation, Maggie smiled. Then she remembered that she was about to face the music for running out on Carla Burke. Her smile disappeared.

Shaking her head and trying to sort it all out in her mind, Maggie knew she was about to be fired. Carla hadn't been in her office when Maggie came in, and that meant she was probably in with Kearns.

"Miss McCabe?"

Maggie snapped up to see the newspaper's publisher, Samuel Poole, enter the room. He was followed by Carla Burke's immediate boss, managing editor Arthur Kearns. Expecting Carla to be right behind him, Maggie was surprised when Art turned and closed the door.

"Hello, Mr. Poole," she said.

He nodded hello but was obviously going to let Kearns do the dirty work.

"You've been away for a few days?" Art asked.

"Yes, I can explain—"

"Don't bother," he cut her off. "Sam and I are running

a little late for a meeting across town. Let me come right to the point of this meeting, Maggie. You took a trip earlier this year to Salzburg and Vienna. We liked the work you did on that. Then you took off for Switzerland. That was pretty good too, and we agreed to a sailing story you were supposed to deliver two weeks ago—"

"Listen, I'm sorry about all the time I've taken."

"Please don't interrupt," he said. "I understand from Carla Burke that that story didn't work out."

"No. What happened was that the boat we were sailing—"

"I don't care about the boat. It's the feature we care about."

"I know, I'm sorry," Maggie blurted, shaking her head.

"We were counting on that story as a complement to a piece we're doing about the America's Cup competition."

Why don't they just get it over with? Maggie thought to herself. She didn't need to hear all the reasons for her being fired.

"The point is, we need that story now."

Maggie stared down at the table and sighed.

"How soon can you shoot those seacoast towns again?"

Snapping up, Maggie asked, "Again?"

"Yes, and we want good careful copy . . . like what you did on that Zermatt story."

"But I thought you wanted me to leave!"

"Leave?" Pool said. "We want you to be feature editor."

"Me?" she said, her eyes suddenly wide.

"Sorry to just toss this at you, Maggie," Art explained, "but things are a bit hectic, as always."

"Feature editor?" Maggie asked in a disbelieving tone. "What about Miss Burke?"

"Carla is no longer with the paper." Art chuckled, as if she should have known. "Where have you been?"

"Paris," Maggie answered before thinking.

There was a moment of silence before Sam Poole asked Kearns, "Art, just how much are we paying this girl?"

"You've been in Paris?" Art asked, smiling and trying to understand.

"Oh, just for the weekend," Maggie blurted.

"Un huh," he nodded with eyebrows raised. "Of course, . . . Paris for the weekend."

"Heh, heh." Maggie tried to make it sound as if she had been joking.

Glancing at his watch, Poole reminded Kearns, "We're late, Art."

"Right," Art said and turned to Maggie. "So what do you say—you want the job?"

"Sure!" Maggie said.

"Congratulations," he shot back. Reaching across the table, he shook her hand. Samuel Poole did the same, and then the two men left for their meeting.

Dazed, Maggie wandered out to the receptionist and asked, "What happened to Carla?"

"Fired her last Friday night."

"Why?"

"I think she just pissed off Kearns one time too many."

"I always liked those guys," Maggie mused as she walked to a desk that was no longer hers. Packing the contents of the drawers into an already overtaxed cardboard carton, she emptied the steel desk that had been her home away from home for nearly five years.

Wandering past the desks of co-workers, Maggie was treated to a spontaneous chorus of congratulations, good-natured insults, and more than one or two suggestions on how to run the show.

Crossing to Carla Burke's glass-walled cubicle, Maggie walked to her new desk, tore off a piece of masking tape, and plastered her name over Carla Burke's metal name-plate outside.

CHAPTER 20

Eric, walking along Marseille's Canabière, glanced at his reflection in the window glass of a small boutique. Wearing a brand-new wardrobe, a light-blue silk sports jacket over a cool white cotton shirt and slacks, he appeared healthy and strong. His hair had grown back to a crewcut length, and except for the thin scar on the right cheek of his sunburned face, he looked more like a tastefully dressed tourist on vacation than a man about to negotiate a delicate business deal with a kingpin of the criminal world.

He had spent the first week after escaping the tunnel recuperating in St. Tropez. The morning runs along the beach gave him strength and appetite. The afternoon swims and sun cleared up the cuts and infections on his skin. And a steady diet of gourmet food made it all the more pleasant.

The people invited to be part of the Viking Cipher were contacted individually, and all except Wyndham agreed to participate. Explaining that there would be just a short delay in setting up the schedule, Eric asked everyone to reconvene a month later.

The rest of the time had been spent trying to locate the man who had bankrolled Thatcher Smythe's auction, and it was a process that proved to be extremely difficult.

Jean Morel visited the police almost every day. It took a while, but finally identification of Sonny Pike's body provided the one and only clue.

Morel was able to learn that Pike lived in Marseille, had most recently been associated with a salvage operation, and was considered by Interpol to be a flunky for the head of the French Mafia. Morel passed all of this along to Eric. After that, it was only a matter of spending one or two of Smythe's thousand-dollar bills to learn the name Anil Fascione, drug-smuggling kingpin of Marseille. And that information brought Eric to this small café.

Wandering in, Eric took a seat near the street and ordered the house specialty. The young waitress flirted openly when she took his order, and whenever Eric glanced in her direction, she winked.

Whistling and making kissing sounds as they passed, several American sailors acknowledged her charms as she brought Eric's lunch. Setting down a glass of crystal-clear white wine, she turned to Eric and said in French, "American men . . . talk talk talk."

Eric chuckled and disagreed.

Alone at a small table for two, Eric took his time devouring the midday meal and then sat back to wait, relaxing over a cup of strong coffee. Several minutes later, the burgundy Rolls-Royce pulled to the curb and an expensively dressed man stepped from the back seat. Silver-haired and wearing black sunglasses, he was tan and looked as if he'd just come off a vacation at one of the nearby Riviera resorts. He had. His driver and another man remained in the car, stonefaced.

Although almost every table at the sidewalk café was empty, the man purposely sat at the very next table. After dispatching the waitress with an order for a cup of coffee, he turned to Eric and waited.

Eric spoke first. "You would be Anil Fascione . . . you got my message."

Fascione remained silent.

"I understand that you are in the salvage business, among other things."

"I have many businesses," Fascione acknowledged in a tone that did not reveal his mood. It was neither friendly nor ominous.

"I've recently lost a motor sailer yacht . . ."

"I've heard," Fascione replied.

"I want her raised and restored."

"You do, eh?" Fascione laughed a deep throaty chuckle.

"I am willing to pay."

The laughter disappeared into a long sigh, and then Fascione said, "This could cost millions of dollars."

"As it happens, I have millions of dollars," Eric replied. He reached into his coat pocket, extracted a safe-deposit key, and dropped it in front of Fascione's right hand. "Five million, one hundred and eighty thousand, to be exact."

"And where did a man your age get this money?"

"My broker sold off some art. Objets d'Art Egyptien . . . you've heard of them?"

Fascione nodded and smiled. "The firm you mention owes me a great deal of money. Half of the sum you mentioned, to be exact. Apparently they've paid it you."

"No question," Eric shot back. "That key before you opens the safe-deposit box in which it is all neatly stacked."

"And you tell me what bank the box is in after your boat is returned?"

"Precisely."

Fascione considered the proposal and asked, "Why should I trust you to give me the name of the bank. You may have another key and you may decide to move the money after we restore this boat."

"Mr. Fascione," Eric said sincerely, "your reputation extends far and wide, as does, no doubt, the reach of your associates in America. I have a life to live. I wish to do so in peace. My proposal is a business proposition. Smythe's half of this money is more than enough to cover the expense of raising and restoring the yacht *Lady Barbara*.

As an extra added bonus, you get any overage as well as the money that already belongs to you."

Picking up the key and twisting it in the sunlight, Fascione smiled and said, "I will see what I can do."

"I am told that you are a man who does whatever he pleases."

Fascione nodded and stood. "I like this deal. And I will trust you, Mr. Ivorsen." He dropped the key in his coat pocket.

As soon as he stood, a square block of a man stepped from the front of the Rolls and opened the back door for Fascione to enter.

Walking from the café, Fascione left behind an untouched cup of coffee and the equivalent of a ten-dollar tip. When he reached his car, he climbed into the backseat and the door was closed. The bodyguard returned to the front.

Then the black back window slid down and Fascione spoke one last time to Eric. "By the way, Mr. Ivorsen, when your yacht is ready, should I contact you at your home in Princeton or will I find you at the home of your lovely girlfriend, Miss McCabe? Tampa, Florida, is it not?"

Eric looked directly into Fascione's sunglasses, smiled slowly, and replied, "It is reassuring to know that you are such a thorough man. The china destroyed when the yacht sank was Dresden, and the silver, Tiffany."

Laughing, Fascione's face disappeared behind a rising line of black glass and the Rolls pulled away from the curb.

EPILOGUE

The first meeting of the Viking Project group had gone pretty much as Eric had expected. Brandt asked more questions than were necessary. Ling Chu reserved her comments until the meeting came to a close. Lowndes and Goldman each expressed deep-seated concerns about government interference. And nobody mentioned Wyndham.

The end result of the four-hour debate was a decision to begin recreation of the research program that had been the cornerstone of the original work done by Eric's father, Albert Einstein, and Hans Schmidhuber.

Using equipment secured by Eric, Ariel Goldman would establish a communication network that would allow any member to contact any other, or all of the others, by simply activating home-based terminals. Lowndes agreed to assist Eric in canvassing colleagues to develop a competent and reliable staff of researchers. Brandt reluctantly agreed to be responsible for introducing the project to scientists in Europe. Ling Chu would handle Asia.

Work began immediately. Within three weeks, the group managed to establish realistic goals for phase one. Slowly, a blueprint to link the greatest minds in the world began to emerge from the chaos. And the Viking Cipher came back to life.

Eric found it impossible to get away for the visit he had promised Maggie. As it turned out, a trip to Tampa was not necessary . . . Maggie came to New York.

Crossing Sackler Hall in the Metropolitan Museum of Art, Eric carried her camera equipment, balancing a tripod in one hand and a light screen in the other. They followed a gaggle of reporters and photographers, all of whom had been invited to the opening of the new Egyptian exhibit.

When they reached the entrance to the new hall, Jean Paul LeBrun greeted them with a secret smile and a brief raising of the eyebrows.

This grand opening, postponed for almost eight weeks because all the pieces confiscated in Paris had to be authenticated and returned, was never fully explained to the press. The museum issued a statement stating simply that several new acquisitions had been located in a warehouse in Paris and that they were so important that they would be added immediately to the exhibit . . . even if it meant rescheduling the opening.

It was ironic, LeBrun thought . . . the one reporter not demanding to know what had caused the delay was one of the two people responsible for it. The other person was juggling her equipment.

"Miss McCabe and Monsieur Ivorsen," LeBrun whispered, "as you can see, the show has gone on. How can I thank you?"

"No need," Eric said. "Glad to have helped."

Glancing around the room with all the articles confiscated finally set in their proper places, Eric nodded. Staring at Queen Hareyet's spotlighted coffin, he thought back to how undignified it had looked cracked open on the Rue de Lille.

"There were some very unhappy collectors, I am told," LeBrun said. "Their money disappeared into the Seine, it is said."

"So I understand," Eric replied.

"Thank God, the police arrived in time to recover most of the pieces."

Eric nodded.

"Monsieur Smythe is perhaps lucky that he did not recover from his heart attack," LeBrun said sadly.

"I hope he rests in peace," Maggie said.

Glancing around the room once more, Eric added, "First he'll have to answer to the original owners of everything surrounding us."

LeBrun nodded. "Some say it is the curse of the Cat of Bastet . . . bad luck befalls whoever claims ownership. Even for a short time."

"True enough. We lost a yacht."

Walking up behind the thick glass case with the glittering golden statuette, Eric admired it again. A small crowd of reporters stood pointing and whispering. When they moved away from the front of the case, Eric leaned to LeBrun and whispered, "It seems to be your problem now."

LeBrun shook his head and smiled. Eric frowned and LeBrun led him around to the front of the case. A small white card with black lettering hastily placed inside the exhibit revealed the truth. It bore only one word: REPLICA.

"It was the one piece the Paris police did not retrieve," LeBrun explained. "Whoever purchased her got away."

"The police have no idea?"

"No, none of the—shall we call them collectors?—would reveal the identities of the others. Articles were returned voluntarily in exchange for dropping charges. No arrests, no ugly publicity, and we got our treasures back. Unjust perhaps, but practical."

"But someone got away with the cat?" Maggie asked.

"*Oui.*"

"Well," she philosophized, "while it was quite beautiful, I'm happy never to see it again."

The Golden Cat of Bastet, secreted in a well-concealed closet, stared again into the darkness just as she had for two thousand, five hundred years . . . with a knowing smile on her lips.

ABOUT THE AUTHOR

Rick Spencer's interests include the acquisition and restoration of historic buildings. He and his wife Betsy live in a restored Victorian house in the heart of the Cranbury National Historic District outside Princeton, New Jersey. ALL THAT GLITTERS is the second novel in this exciting new series, The Viking Cipher.